The
Honorable Miss.
L. T. Meade

THE HONORABLE MISS

A Story of an Old-Fashioned Town

BY

L. T. MEADE

AUTHOR OF "THE YOUNG MUTINEER, " "WORLD OF GIRLS, "
"A VERY NAUGHTY GIRL, " "SWEET GIRL GRADUATE, " ETC.

NEW YORK
HURST & COMPANY
PUBLISHERS

The Honorable Miss: A Story of an Old-Fashioned Town

L. T. Meade

Illustrated by F. Earl Christy

CHAPTER I.

BEATRICE WILL FIT.

"So, " continued Mrs. Meadowsweet, settling herself in a lazy, fat sort of a way in her easy chair, and looking full at her visitor with a complacent smile, "so I called her Beatrice. I thought under the circumstances it was the best name I could give—it seemed to fit all round, you know, and as *he* had no objection, being very easy-going, poor man, I gave her the name. "

"Yes? " interrogated Mrs. Bertram, in a softly surprised, and but slightly interested voice; "you called your daughter Beatrice? I don't quite understand your remark about the name fitting all round. "

Mrs. Meadowsweet raised one dimpled hand slowly and laid it on top of the other. Her smile grew broader.

"A name is a solemn thing, Mrs. Bertram, " she continued. "A name is, so to speak, to fit the person to whom it is given, for life. Will you tell me how any mother, even the shrewdest, is to prophecy how an infant of a few weeks old is to turn out? I thought over that point a good deal when I gave the name, and said I to myself however matters turn 'Beatrice' will fit. If she grows up cozy and soft and petting and small, why she's Bee, and if she's sharp and saucy, and a bit too independent, as many lasses are in these days, what can suit her better than Trixie? And again if she's inclined to be stately, and to hold herself erect, and to think a little more of herself than her mother ever did—only not more than she deserves—bless her—why then she's Beatrice in full. Oh! and there you are, Beatrice! Mrs. Bertram has been good enough to call to see me. Mrs. Bertram, this is my daughter Beatrice. "

A very tall girl came quietly into the room, bowed an acknowledgment of her mother's introduction, and sat down on the edge of the sofa. She was a dignified girl from the crown of her head to her finger-tips, and Mrs. Bertram, who had been listening languidly to the mother, favored the newcomer with a bright, quick, inquisitive stare, then rose to her feet.

"I am afraid I must say good-bye, Mrs. Meadowsweet. I am glad to have made your daughter's acquaintance, and another day I hope I shall see more of her. I have of course heard of you from Catherine, my dear, " she added, holding out her hand frankly to the young girl.

"Yes. Is Catherine well? " asked Beatrice, in a sweet high-bred voice.

"She is well, my dear. Good-bye, Mrs. Meadowsweet. I quite understand the all-roundness and suitability of your choice in the matter of names. "

Then the great lady sailed out of the room, and Beatrice flew to the window, placed herself behind the curtain and watched her down the street.

"What were you saying about me, mother? " she asked, when Mrs. Bertram had turned the corner.

"I was only telling about your name, my dearie girl. *He* always gave me my way, poor man, so I fixed on Beatrice. I said it would fit all round, and it did. Shut that window, will you, Bee? —the wind is very sharp for the time of year. You don't mind my calling you Bee now and then—even if it doesn't seem quite to fit? " continued Mrs. Meadowsweet.

"No, mother, of course not. Call me anything in the world you fancy. What's in a name? "

"Don't say that, Trixie, there's a great deal in a name. "

"Well, I get confused with mine now and then. Mother, I just came in to kiss you and run away again. Alice Bell and I are going to the lecture at the Town Hall. It begins at five, and it's half-past four now. Good-bye, I shall be home to supper. "

"One moment, Bee, I am really pleased that your fine friend's mother has chosen to call at last. "

Beatrice frowned.

"Catherine is not my fine friend, " she said.

"Well, your *friend*, then, dearie. I am glad your friend's mother has called. "

"I am not—that is, I am absolutely indifferent. Now, I really must run away. Good-bye until you see me again. "

She tripped out of the room as lightly and carelessly as she had entered it, and Mrs. Meadowsweet sat on by the window which looked into the garden.

Mrs. Meadowsweet had the smoothest and most tranquil of faces. She had taken as her favorite motto in life, that somehow, if you only allowed them, things did fit all round. Each event in her own career, to use her special phraseology "fitted. " As her husband had to die, he passed away from this life at the most fitting moment. As Providence had blessed her with only one child, a daughter was surely the most fitting companion for a widowed mother. The house Mrs. Meadowsweet lived in fitted her requirements to perfection. In short, she was fat and comfortable, both in mind and body; she never fretted, she never worried; she was not rasping and disagreeable; she was not fault-finding. If her nature lacked depth, it certainly did not lack affection, generosity, and a true spirit of kindliness. If she were a little too well pleased with herself, she was also well pleased with her neighbors. She was not especially appreciated, for she was considered prosy and commonplace. Prosy she undoubtedly was, but not commonplace, for invariable contentment and unbounded good-nature are more and more difficult to find in this censorious world.

Mrs. Meadowsweet now smiled gently to herself.

"However Beatrice may take it, I *am* glad Mrs. Bertram called, " she murmured. "*He'd* have liked it, poor man! he never put himself out, and he never interfered with me, no, never, poor dear. But he liked people to show due respect—it's a respect to Beatrice for Mrs. Bertram to call. It shows that she appreciates Beatrice as her daughter's friend. Mrs. Bertram, notwithstanding her pride, is likely to be very much respected in Northbury, and no wonder. She's a little above most of us, but we like her all the better for that. We are going to be proud of her. It's nice to have some one to be proud of. And she has no airs when you come to know her, no, she hasn't airs; she's as pleasant as possible, and seems interested too, that is, as interested as people like us can expect from people like her. She didn't even condescend to Beatrice. I wonder how my little girl would have taken it, if she had condescended to her. Yes, Jane, do you want me? "

3

An elderly servant opened the drawing-room door.

"If you please, ma'am, Mrs. Morris has called, and she wants to know if it would disturb you very much to see her? "

"Disturb me? She knows it won't disturb me. Show her in at once. And Jane, you can get tea ready half-an-hour earlier than usual. I daresay, as Mrs. Morris has called she'd like a cup. How do you do, Mrs. Morris? I'm right glad to see you, right glad. Sit here, in this chair—or perhaps you'd rather sit in this one; this isn't too near the window. And you'll like a screen, I know; —not that there's any draught—for these windows fit as tight as tight when shut. "

Mrs. Morris was a thin, tall woman. She always spoke in a whisper, for she was possessed of the belief that she had lost her voice in bronchitis. She had not, for when she scolded any one she found it again. She was not scolding now, however, and her tones were very low and smothered.

"I saw her coming in, my dear; I was standing at the back of the wire blind, and I saw her going up your steps, so I thought I'd come across quickly and hear the news. You'll tell me the news as soon as possible, won't you? Mrs. Butler and Miss Peters are coming to call in a few minutes. I met them and they told me so. They saw her, too. You'll tell me the news quickly, Lucy, for I'd like to be first, and it seems as if I had a right to that much consideration, being an old friend. "

"So you have, Jessie. "

Mrs. Meadowsweet looked immensely flattered.

"I suppose you allude to Mrs. Bertram having favored me with a call, " she continued, in a would-be-humble tone, which, in spite of all her efforts, could not help swelling a little.

"Yes, dear, that's what I allude to; I saw her from behind the wire screen blind. We were having steak and onions for dinner, and the doctor didn't like me jumping up just when I had a hot bit on my plate. But I said, it's Mrs. Bertram, Sam, and she's standing on Mrs. Meadowsweet's steps! There wasn't a remonstrance out of him after that, and the only other remark he made was, 'You'll call round presently, Jessie, and inquire after Mrs. Meadowsweet's cold. ' So here I am, my dear. And how *is* your cold, by the way? "

"It's getting on nicely, Jessie. Wasn't that a ring I heard at the door bell? "

"Well, I never! " Mrs. Morris suddenly found her voice. "If it isn't that tiresome Mrs. Butler and Miss Peters. And now I won't be first with the news after all! "

Mrs. Meadowsweet smiled again.

"There really isn't so much to tell, Jessie. Mrs. Bertram was just affable like every one else. Ah, and how are you, Mrs. Butler? Now, I do call this kind and neighborly. Miss Peters, I trust your cough is better? "

"I'm glad to see you, Mrs. Meadowsweet, " said Mrs. Butler, in a slightly out-of-breath tone.

"My cough is no better, " snapped Miss Peters. "Although it's summer, the wind is due east; east wind always catches me in the throat. "

Miss Peters was very small and slim. She wore little iron-gray, corkscrew curls, and had bright, beady black eyes. Miss Peters was Mrs. Butler's sister. She was a snappy little body, but rather afraid of Mrs. Butler, who was more snappy. This fear gave her an unpleasant habit of rolling her eyes in the direction of Mrs. Butler whenever she spoke. She rolled them now as she described the way the east wind had treated her throat.

Mrs. Butler seated herself in an aggressive manner on the edge of the sofa, and Miss Peters took a chair as close as possible to Mrs. Morris, who pushed hers away from her.

Each lady was anxious to engross the whole attention of Mrs. Meadowsweet, and it was scarcely possible for the good-natured woman not to feel flattered.

"Now, you'll all have a cup of tea with me, " she said. "I know Jane's getting it, but I'll ring the bell to hasten her. Ah, thank you, Miss Peters. "

Miss Peters had sprung to her feet, seized the bell-rope before any one could hinder her, and sounded a vigorous peal. Then she rolled her eyes at Mrs. Butler and sat down.

Mrs. Morris said that when Miss Peters rolled her eyes she invariably shivered. She shivered now in such a marked and open way that poor Mrs. Meadowsweet feared her friend had taken cold.

"Dear, dear—I only wish I had a fire lighted, " she said. "Your bronchitis will be getting worse, if you aren't careful, Jessie. Miss Peters, a cup of tea will do your throat good. It always does mine when I get nipped. "

"Don't encourage Maria in her fancies, " snapped Mrs. Butler. "There's nothing ails her throat, only she will wrap herself in so much wool that she makes herself quite delicate. I tell her she fancies she is a hothouse plant. "

"Oh, nothing of the kind, " whispered Mrs. Morris.

"That's what I say, " nodded back Mrs. Butler. "More of the nature of the hardy broom. But now we haven't come to discuss Maria and her fads. You have had a visitor to-day, Mrs. Meadowsweet. "

"Ah, here comes the tea, " exclaimed Mrs. Meadowsweet. "Bring the table over here, Jane. Now this is what I call cozy. Jane, you might ask cook to send up some buttered toast, and a little more cream. Yes, Mrs. Butler, I beg your pardon. "

"I was remarking that you had a visitor, " repeated Mrs. Butler.

"Ah, so I had. Mrs. Bertram called on me. "

"And why shouldn't she call on you, dear? " suddenly whispered Mrs. Morris. "Aren't you quite as good as she is when all's said and done? Yes, dear, I'll have some of your delicious tea. Such a treat! Some more cream? Thank you, yes; I'll help myself. Why shouldn't Mrs. Bertram call on Mrs. Meadowsweet? That's what I say, ladies, " continued Mrs. Morris, looking over the top of her cup of tea in a decidedly fight-me-if-you-dare manner.

"Nobody said she shouldn't call, " answered Mrs. Butler. "Maria, you'll oblige me by going into the hall and fetching my wrap.

There's rather a chill from this window—and the weather is very inclement for the time of year. No, thank you, Mrs. Morris, I wouldn't take your seat for the world. As you justly remark, why shouldn't Mrs Bertram call on our good friend here? And, for that matter, why shouldn't she cross the road, and leave her card on *you*, Mrs. Morris? "

Mrs. Morris was here taken with such a fit of bronchial coughing and choking that she could make no response. Miss Peters rolled her eyes at her sister in a manner which plainly said, "You had her there, Martha, " and poor Mrs. Meadowsweet began nervously to wish that she had not been the honored recipient of Mrs. Bertram's favors.

"She came to see me on account of Beatrice, " remarked the hostess. "At least I think that was why she came. I beg your pardon, did you say anything, ladies? "

"Oh! fie, fie! Mrs. Meadowsweet, " said Miss Peters, "you are too modest. In my sister's name and my own, I say you are too modest. "

"And in my name too, " interrupted Mrs. Morris. "You are too humble, my dear friend. She called to see you for *your own dear sake* and for no other. "

"And now let us all be friendly, " continued Miss Peters, "and learn the news. I think we are all of one mind in wishing to learn the news. "

Mrs. Meadowsweet smoothed down the front of her black satin dress. She knew, and her friends knew, that she would have much preferred the honor of Mrs. Bertram's call to be due to Beatrice's charms than her own. She smiled, however, with her usual gentleness, and plunged into the conversation which the three other ladies were so eager to commence.

Before they departed they had literally taken Mrs. Bertram to pieces. They had fallen upon her tooth and nail, and dissected her morally, and socially, and with the closest scrutiny of all, from a religious point of view.

Mrs. Meadowsweet, who never spoke against any one, was amazed at the ingenuity with which the character of her friend (she felt she must call Mrs. Bertram her friend) was blackened. Before the ladies left Mrs. Meadowsweet's house they had proved, in the ablest and most thorough manner, that Mrs. Bertram was worldly and vain, that she lived beyond her means, that she trained her daughters to think of themselves far more highly than they ought to think, that in all probability she was not what she pretended to be, and, finally, that poor Mrs. Meadowsweet, dear Mrs. Meadowsweet, was in great danger on account of her friendship.

"I don't agree with you, ladies, " said the good woman, as they were leaving the house, but they neither heeded nor heard her remark.

The explanation of their conduct was simple enough. They were devoured with jealousy. Had Mrs. Bertram called on any one of them, she would have been in that person's estimation the most fascinating woman in Northbury.

CHAPTER II.

MRS. BERTRAM'S WILL.

And Mrs. Bertram did not care in the least what anybody thought of her. She was in no sense of the word a sham. She was well-born, well-educated, respectably married, and fairly well-off. The people in Northbury considered her rich. She always spoke of herself as poor. In reality she was neither rich nor poor. She had an income of something like twelve hundred a year, and on that she lived comfortably, educated her children well, and certainly managed to present a nice appearance wherever she went.

There never was a woman more full of common sense than Mrs. Bertram. She had quite an appalling amount of this virtue; no one ever heard her say a silly thing; each step she took in life was a wise one, carefully considered, carefully planned out. She had been a widow now for sis years. Her husband had nearly come into the family estate, but not quite. He was the second son, and his eldest brother had died when his heir was a month old. This heir had cut out Mrs. Bertram's husband from the family place, with its riches and honors. He himself had died soon after, and had left his widow with three children and twelve hundred a year.

The children were a son and two daughters. The son's name was Loftus, the girls were called Catherine and Mabel. Loftus was handsome in person, and very every-day in mind. He was good-natured, but not remarkable for any peculiar strength of character. His mother had managed to send him to Rugby and Sandhurst, and he had passed into the army with tolerable credit. He was very fond of his mother, devotedly fond of her, but since he entered the army he certainly contrived to cost her a good deal.

She spoke to him on the subject, believed as much as she chose of his earnest promises to amend, took her own counsel and no one else's, gave up her neat little house in Kensington, and came to live at Northbury.

Catherine and Mabel did not like this change, but as their mother never dreamt of consulting them, they had to keep their grumbles to themselves.

Mrs. Bertram considered she had taken a wise step, and she told the girls so frankly. Their house in Kensington was small and expensive. In the country they had secured a delightful old Manor—Rosendale Manor was its pretty name—for a small rent.

Mrs. Bertram found herself comparatively rich in the country, and she cheered the girls by telling them that if they would study economical habits, and try to do with very little dress for the present, she would save some money year by year, so that by the time Catherine was twenty they might have the advantage of a couple of seasons in town.

"Catherine will look very young at twenty, " remarked the mother. "By that time I shall have saved quite a fair sum out of my income. Catherine looked younger at twenty than Mabel at eighteen. They can both come out together, and have their chances like other girls. "

Catherine did not want to wait for the dear delights of society until she had reached so mature an age. But there was no murmuring against her mother's decree, and as she was a healthy-minded, handsome, good-humored girl, she soon accommodated herself to the ways and manners of country folk, and was happy enough.

"I shall live on five hundred a year at Rosen dale Manor, " determined Mrs. Bertram. "And I have made up my mind that Loftie shall not cost me more than three. Thus I shall save four hundred a year. Catherine is only seventeen now. By the time she is twenty I shall have a trifle over and above my income to fall back upon. Twelve hundred pounds is a bagatelle with most people, but I feel I shall effect wonders with it. Catherine and Mabel will be out of the common, very out of the common. Unique people have an advantage over those who resemble the herd. Catherine and Mabel are to be strongly individual. In any room they are to be noticeable. Little hermits, now, some day they shall shine. They are both clever, just clever enough for my purpose. Catherine might with advantage be a shade less beautiful, but Mabel will, I am convinced, fulfil all my expectations. Then, if only Loftie, " but here Mrs. Bertram sighed. She was returning from her visit to Mrs. Meadowsweet, walking slowly down the long avenue which led to the Manor. This avenue was kept in no order; its edges were not neatly cut, and weeds appeared here and there through its scantily gravelled roadway. The grass parterre round the house, however, was smooth as velvet, and interspersed with gay flower-beds. It looked like a little agreeable oasis in the middle of a woodland, for the avenue was shaded by forest trees, and the house itself had a background of two or three acres of an old wood.

Mrs. Bertram was tired, and walked slowly. She did not consider herself a proud woman, but in this she was mistaken. Every line of her upright figure, each glance of her full, dark eyes, each word that dropped from her lips spoke of pride both of birth and position. She often said to herself, "I am thankful that I don't belong to the common folk; it would grate on my nerves to witness their vulgarities, —their bad taste would torture me; their want of refinement would act upon my nature like a blister. But I am not proud, I uphold my dignity, I respect myself and my family, but with sinful, unholy pride I have no part. "

This was by no means the opinion held of her, however, by the Northbury folk. They had hailed her advent with delight; they had witnessed her arrival with the keenest, most absorbing interest, and, to the horror of the good lady herself, had one and all called on her. She was petrified when this very natural event happened. She had bargained for a life of retirement for herself and her girls. She had never imagined that society of a distinctly lower strata than that into which she had been born would be forced on her. Forced! Whoever yet had forced Mrs. Bertram into any path she did not care to walk in?

She was taken unawares by the first visitors, and they absolutely had the privilege of sitting on her sofas, and responding to a few icy remarks which dropped from her lips.

But the next day she was armed for the combat. The little parlor-maid, in her neat black dress, clean muslin apron, large frilled, picturesque collar, and high mob-cap, was instructed to say "Not at home" to all comers. She was a country girl, not from Northbury, but from some still more rusticated spot, and she thought she was telling a frightful lie, and blushed and trembled while she uttered it. So apparent was her confusion that Miss Peters, when she and her sister, Mrs. Butler, appeared on the scene, rolled her eyes at the taller lady and asked her in a pronounced manner if it would not be well to drop a tract on the heinousness of lying in the avenue.

This speech was repeated by Clara to the cook, who told it again to the young ladies' maid, who told it to the young ladies, who narrated it to their mother.

Mrs. Bertram smiled grimly.

"Don't repeat gossip, my dears, " she said, Then after a pause she remarked aloud: "The difficulty will be about returning the calls. "

Mabel, the youngest and most subservient of the girls, ventured to ask her mother what she intended to do, but Mrs. Bertram was too wise to disclose her plans, that is, if she had made any.

The Rector of Northbury was one of the first to visit the new inhabitants of the Manor. To him Mrs. Bertram opened her doors gladly. He was old, unmarried, and of good family. She was glad there was at least one gentleman in the place with whom she might occasionally exchange a word.

About a fortnight after his visit the Rector inclosed some tickets for a bazaar to Mrs. Bertram. The tickets were accompanied by a note, in which he said that it would gratify the good Northbury folk very much if Mrs. Bertram and the young ladies would honor the bazaar with their presence.

"Every soul in the place will be there, " said Mr. Ingram. "This bazaar is a great event to us, and its object is, I think, a worthy one. We badly want a new organ for our church. "

"Eureka! " exclaimed Mrs. Bertram when she had read this note.

"What is the matter, mother? " exclaimed Mabel.

"Only that I have found a way out of my grand difficulty, " responded their mother, tossing Mr. Ingram's note and the tickets for the bazaar into Catherine's lap.

"Are you so delighted to go to this country bazaar, mother? " asked the eldest daughter.

"Delighted! No, it will be a bore. "

"Then why did you say Eureka! and look so pleased? "

"Because on that day I shall leave cards on the Northbury folk—not one of them will be at home. "

"Shabby, " muttered Catherine. Her dark cheek flushed, she turned away.

Mabel put out her little foot and pressed it against her sister's. The pressure signified warning.

"Then you are not going to the bazaar, mother? " she questioned.

"I don't know. I may drop in for a moment or two, quite at the close. It would not do to offend Mr. Ingram. "

"No, " replied Mabel. "He is a dear, *gentlemanly* old man. "

"Don't use that expression, my love. It is my object in life that *all* your acquaintances in the world of men should be gentlemen. It is unnecessary therefore to specify any one by a term which must apply to all. "

Mrs. Bertram then asked Mabel to reply to Mr. Ingram's note. The reply was a warm acceptance, and Mr. Ingram cheered those of his parishioners who pined for the acquaintance of the great lady, with the information that they would certainly meet her at the bazaar.

Accordingly when the fateful day arrived the town was empty, and the Fisherman's Hall (Northbury was a seaport), in which the bazaar was held was packed to overflowing. Accordingly Mrs. Bertram in a neat little brougham, which she had hired for the occasion, dropped her cards from house to house in peace; accordingly, too, she caught the maids-of-all-work in their undress toilets, and the humble homes looking their least pretentious.

The bazaar was nearly at an end, when at last, accompanied by her two plainly-dressed, but dainty looking girls, she appeared on the scene.

The Northbury folk had all been watching for her. Those who had been fortunate enough to enter the sacred precincts of the Manor watched with interest, mingled with approval. (Her icy style was quite *comme-il-faut*, they said.) Those who had been met by the frightened handmaid's "not at home" watched with interest, mixed with disapproval, but all, all waited for Mrs. Bertram with interest.

"How late these fashionable people are, " quote Miss Peters. "It's absolutely five o'clock. My dear Martha, do sit down and rest yourself. You look fit to drop. I'll keep an eye on the door and tell you the very moment Mrs. Bertram comes in. Mrs. Gorman Stanley has promised to introduce us. Mrs. Gorman Stanley was fortunate enough to find Mrs. Bertram in. It was she who told us about the drawing-room at the Manor. Fancy! Mrs. Bertram has only a felt carpet on her drawing-room. Not even a red felt, which looks warm and wears. But a sickly green! Mrs. Gorman Stanley told me *as a fact* that the carpet was quite a worn-out shade between a green and a brown; and the curtains—she said the *drawing room* curtains were only cretonne. You needn't stare at me, Martha. Mrs. Gorman Stanley never makes mistakes. All the same, though she couldn't tell why, she owned that the room had a *distingué* effect. *En règle*, that was it; she said the room was *en règle*. "

"Maria, if you could stop talking for a moment and fetch me an ice, I'd be obliged, " answered Mrs. Butler. "Oh! " standing up, "there's Mrs. Gorman Stanley. How do you do, Mrs. Gorman Stanley? Our great lady hasn't chosen to put in her appearance yet. For my part I don't suppose she's any better than the rest of us, and so I say to Maria. Well, Maria, what's the matter now? "

"Here's your ice, " said Miss Peters; "take it. Don't forget that you promised to introduce us to Mrs. Bertram, Mrs. Gorman Stanley. "

Mrs. Gorman Stanley was the wealthy widow of a retired fish-buyer. She liked to condescend; also to show off her wealth. It pleased her to assume an acquaintance with Mrs. Bertram, although she thoroughly despised that good lady's style of furnishing a house.

"I'll introduce you with pleasure, my dear, " she said to Mrs. Butler. "Yes, I like Mrs. Bertram very much. Did you say she was out when you called? Oh! she was in to me. Yes, I saw the house. I don't think she had finished furnishing it. The drawing-room looked quite bare. A made-up sort of look, you understand. Lots of flowers on the tables, and that nasty, cold, cheap felt under your feet. Not that *I* mind how a house is furnished. " (She did very much. Her one and only object in life seemed to be to lade her own mansion with ugly and expensive upholstery.) "Now, what's the matter, Miss Peters? Why, you are all on wires. Where *are* you off to now? "

"I see the Rector, " responded Miss Peters. "I'll run and ask him when he expects Mrs. Bertram. I'll be back presently with the news. "

The little lady tripped away, forcing her slim form through the ever-increasing crowd. The rector was walking about with a very favorite small parishioner seated on his shoulder.

"Mr. Ingram, " piped Miss Peters. "Don't you think Mrs. Bertram might favor us with her presence by now? We have all been looking for her. It's past five o'clock, and —"

There was a hush, a pause. At that moment Mrs. Bertram was sailing into the room. Miss Peters' exalted tones reached her ears. She shuddered, turned pale, and also turned her back on the eager little spinster.

Nobody quite knew how it was managed, but Mrs. Bertram was introduced to very few of the Northbury folk. They all wanted to know her; they talked about her, and came in her way, and stared at her whenever they could. There was an expectant hush when she and the Rector were seen approaching any special group.

"I do declare it's the Grays she's going to patronize, " one jealous matron said.

But the Grays were passed over just as sedulously as the Joneses and the Smiths. Excitement, again and again on the tenter-hooks, invariably came to nothing. Even Mrs. Gorman Stanley, who had sat on Mrs. Bertram's sofa, and condemned her felt carpet was only acknowledged by the most passing and stately recognition. Little chance had the poor lady of effecting other introductions; she realized for the first time that she was only a quarter introduced to the great woman herself.

The fact was this: There was not a soul in Northbury, at least there was not an acknowledged soul who could combat Mrs. Bertram's will. She had made up her mind to talk to no one but Mr. Ingram at the bazaar. She carried out her resolve, and that though the Rector had formed such pleasant visions of making every one cheerful and happy all round, for he knew the simple weaknesses and desires of his flock, and saw not the smallest harm in gratifying them. Why should not the Manor and the town be friendly?

Mrs. Bertram saw a very good reason why they should not. Therefore the Rector's dreams came apparently to nothing.

CHAPTER III.

A GENTLEMAN, MADAM.

Only apparently. Every one knows how small the little rift within the lute is. So are most beginnings.

Mrs. Bertram felt, that in her way, she had effected quite a victory. She stepped into her brougham to return to Rosendale Manor with a pleasing sense of triumph.

"I am thankful to say that ordeal is over, " she remarked. "And I think, " she continued, with a smile, "that when the Northbury people see my cards, awaiting them on their humble hall-tables, they will have learnt their lesson. "

Neither of the girls made any response to this speech. Mabel was leaning back in the carriage looking bored and cross, but Catherine's expression was unusually bright.

"Mother, " she exclaimed suddenly, "I met such a nice girl at the bazaar. "

"You made an acquaintance at the bazaar, my dear Catherine, " answered Mrs. Bertram with alacrity. "You made an acquaintance? The acquaintance of a girl? Who? "

"Her name is Beatrice Meadowsweet. She is a dear, delightful, fresh girl, and exactly my own age. "

Catherine's dark face was all aglow. Her handsome brown eyes shone with interest and pleasure.

"Catherine, how often, how very often have I told you that expressions of rapture such as you have just given way to are underbred. "

"Why are they underbred, mother? " Catherine's tone was aggressive, and Mabel again kicked her sister's foot.

The kick was returned with vigor, and Catherine said in an earnest though deliberate voice:

17

The Honorable Miss: A Story of an Old-Fashioned Town

"Why are expressions of rapture underbred? Can enthusiasm, that fire of the gods, be vulgar? "

"Kate, you are cavilling. Expressions of rapture generally show a lack of breeding because as a rule they are exaggerated, therefore untrue. In this case they are manifestly untrue, for how is it possible for you to tell that the girl you have just been speaking to is dear, delightful, and fresh? "

"Her face is fresh, her manners are fresh, her expression is delightful. There is no use, mother, you can't crush me. I am in love with Beatrice Meadowsweet. "

Mrs. Bertram's brow became clouded. It was one of the bitter defeats which she had ever and anon to acknowledge to herself that, in the midst of her otherwise victorious career, she could never get the better of her eldest daughter Catherine.

"Who introduced you to this girl? " she asked, after a pause.

"The Rector. He saw me standing by one of the stalls, looking what I felt—awfully bored. He came up in his kind way and took my hand, and said: 'My dear, you don't know any one, I am afraid. You would like to make some acquaintances, would you not? ' I replied: 'I am most anxious to know some of the nice people all around me. '"

"My dear Catherine! The *nice* people! And when you knew my express wishes! "

"Yes, mother, but they weren't mine. And I had to be truthful, at any cost. Beatrice was standing not far off, and when I said this my eye met hers, and we both smiled. Then the rector introduced me to her, and we mutually voted the bazaar close and hot, and went out to watch the tennis players in the garden. We had a jolly time. I have not laughed so much since I came to this slow, poky corner of the world. "

"And what were you doing, Mabel? " questioned her mother. "Did you, too, pick up an undesirable acquaintance and march away into the gardens with her? Was your new friend also fresh, delightful and dear? "

"I wish she had been, mother, " answered Mabel, her tone still very petulant. "But I hadn't Kate's luck. I was introduced to no one, although lots of people stared at me, and whispered about me as I passed. "

"And you saw this paragon of Catherine's? "

"Yes, I saw her. "

"What did you think of her, May? I like to get your opinion, my love. You have a good deal of penetration. Tell me frankly what you thought of this low-born miss, whom Catherine degraded herself by talking to. "

Mabel looked at her sister. Catherine's eyes flashed. Mabel replied demurely:

"I thought Miss Meadowsweet quiet-looking and graceful. "

Catherine took Mabel's hand unnoticed by their mother and squeezed it, and Mrs. Bertram, who was not wholly devoid of tact, thought it wisest to let the conversation drop.

The next day the Rector called, and Mrs. Bertram asked him, in an incidental way what kind of people the Meadowsweets were.

"Excellent people, " he replied, rubbing his hands softly together. "Excellent, worthy, honorable. I have few parishioners whom I think more highly of than Beatrice and her mother. "

Mrs. Bertram's brow began to clear.

"A mother and daughter, " she remarked. "Only a mother and a daughter, Mr. Ingram? "

"Only a mother and a daughter, my dear madam. Poor Meadowsweet left us six years ago. He was one of my churchwardens, a capital fellow, so thoroughgoing and reliable. A sound churchman, too. In short, everything that one could desire. He died rather suddenly, and I was afraid Mrs. Meadowsweet would leave Northbury, but Bee did not wish it. Bee has a will of her own, and I fancy she's attached to us all. "

"I am very glad that you can give us such a pleasant account of these parishioners of yours, dear Mr. Ingram, " responded Mrs. Bertram. "The fact is, I am in a difficult position here. No, the girls won't overhear us; they are busy at their embroidery in that distant corner. Well, perhaps, to make sure. Kate, " Mrs. Bertram raised her voice, "I know the Rector is going to give us the pleasure of his company to tea. Mr. Ingram, I shall not allow you to say no. Kate, will you and Mabel go into the garden, and bring in a leaf of fresh strawberries. Now, Mr. Ingram I want you to see our strawberries, and to taste them. The gardener tells us that the Manor strawberries are celebrated. Run, dears, don't be long. "

The girls stepped out through the open French window, interlaced their arms round one another and disappeared.

"They are good girls, " said the mother, "but Kate has a will of her own. Mr. Ingram, you will allow me to take you into my confidence. I am often puzzled to know how to act towards Catherine. She is a good girl, but I can't lead her. She is only seventeen, only just seventeen. Surely that is too young an age to walk quite without leading strings. "

Mr. Ingram was an old bachelor, but he was one of those mellow, gentle, affectionate men who make the most delightful companions, whose sympathy is always ready, and tact always to the fore. Mr. Ingram was full of both sympathy and tact, but he had also a little gentle vanity to be tickled, and when a handsome woman, still young, appealed to him with pathos in her eyes and voice, he laid himself, metaphorically, at her feet.

"My dear madam, " he responded, "it is most gratifying to me to feel that I can be of the least use to you. Command me at all times, I beg. As to Miss Catherine, who can guide her better than her excellent mother? I don't know much about you, Mrs. Bertram, but I feel— forgive me, I am a man of intuition—I feel that you are one to look up to. Miss Catherine is a fortunate girl. You are right. She is far too young to walk alone. Seventeen, did you say—pooh—a mere child, a baby. An immature creature, ignorant, innocent, fresh, but undeveloped; just the age, Mrs. Bertram, when she needs the aid and counsel of a mother like you. "

Mrs. Bertram's dark eyes glowed with pleasure.

"I am glad you agree with me, " she said. "The fact is, Mr. Ingram, we have come to the Manor to retrench a little, to economize, to live in retirement. By-and-bye, I shall take Catherine and Mabel to London. As a mother, I have duties to perform to them. These, when the time comes, shall not be neglected. Mr. Ingram, I must be very frank, I *don't* want to know the good folk of Northbury. "

Mr. Ingram started at this very plain speaking. He had lived for thirty years with the Northbury people. They had not vulgarized him; their troubles and their pleasures alike were his. His heart and soul, his life and strength were given up to them. He did not feel himself any the less a gentleman because those whom he served were, many of them, lowly born. He started, therefore, both inwardly and outwardly at Mrs. Bertram's plain speech, and instantly, for he was a man of very nice penetration, saw that the arrival of this lady, this brilliant sun of society, in the little world of Northbury, would not add to the smoothness of his lot.

Before he could get in a word, however, Mrs. Bertram quickly continued:

"And Catherine is determined to make a friend of Beatrice Meadowsweet. "

"She is quite right, Mrs. Bertram. I introduced Miss Catherine to Beatrice yesterday. They will make delightful companions; they are about the same age—I can vouch for the life and spirit possessed by my friend Bee, and if I mistake not Miss Catherine will be her worthy companion. "

Mrs. Bertram laughed.

"I wish I could tell you what an imp of mischief Kate is, " she said. "She is the most daring creature that ever drew the breath of life. Dear Mr. Ingram, forgive me for even doubting you for a moment. I might have known that you would only introduce my daughter to a lady. "

The Rector drew himself up a very little.

"Certainly, Beatrice Meadowsweet is a lady, " he replied. "If a noble heart, and frank and fearless ways, and an educated mind, and a refined nature can make a lady, then she is one—no better in the land. "

"I am charmed, *charmed* to hear it. It is such a relief. For, really Mr. Ingram, some people from Northbury came and sat on that very sofa which you are occupying, who were quite too—oh, well, they were absolutely dreadful. I wonder if Mrs. Meadowsweet has called. I don't remember the name, but I suppose she has. I must look amongst the cards which have absolutely been showered on us and see. I must certainly return her visit and at once. Poor Mr. Meadowsweet—he was in the army perhaps! I am quite glad to know there are people of our position here. Did you say the army? Or perhaps a retired gentleman, —ah, I see Catherine and Mabel coming back. Which was Mr. Meadowsweet's regiment? "

Poor Mr. Ingram's face grew absolutely pink.

"At some time in his life poor Meadowsweet may have served in the local volunteers, " he replied. "He was however, a—ah, Miss Catherine, what tempting strawberries! "

The rector approached the open French window. Mrs. Bertram followed him quickly.

"A—what? " she repeated. "The girls needn't know whom we are talking about. A gentleman who lived on his private means? "

"A gentleman, madam, yes, a *gentleman*, —and he lived on his means, —and he was wealthy. He kept a shop, a draper's shop, in the High Street. Now, young ladies, young ladies—I call this wrong. *Such* strawberries! Strawberries are my special weakness. Oh, it is cruel of you to tempt me. I ought to be two miles from here now. "

"You ought not, " said Catherine in a gay voice. "You must sit with us on the lawn, and drink our tea, and eat our strawberries. "

Catherine had given a quick, lightning glance at her mother's face. She saw a cloud there, she guessed the cause. She felt certain that her mother would consult Mr. Ingram on the subject of Beatrice. Mr. Ingram's report was not satisfactory. Delightful! She felt the imp of mischief taking possession of her. She was a girl of many moods and tenses. At times she could even be sombre. But when she chose to be gay and fascinating she was irresistible. She was only seventeen, and in several ways she was unconventional, even unworldly. In others, however, she was a perfect woman of the world, and a match for her mother.

CHAPTER IV.

TWO LETTERS.

Northbury was so completely out of the world that it only had a postal delivery twice a day. The early post was delivered at eight o'clock, so that the good people of the place could discuss their little items of outside news over their breakfast-tables. The postman went round with his evening delivery at seven. He was not overwhelmed by the aristocracy of Rosendale Manor, and, notwithstanding Mrs. Bertram's open annoyance, insisted on calling there last. He said it suited him best to do so, and what suited Sammy Benjafield he was just as determined to do, as Mrs. Bertram was to carry out her own schemes.

Consequently, the evening letters never reached the Manor until between eight and half-past. Mrs. Bertram and her daughters dined at seven. They were the only people in Northbury who ate their dinner at that aristocratic hour; tea between four and five, and hot, substantial and unwholesome suppers were the order of the day with the Northbury folk. *Very* substantial these suppers were, and even the Rector was not proof against the hot lobster and rich decoctions of crab with which his flock favored him at these hours.

For the very reason, however, that heavy suppers were in vogue at Northbury, Mrs. Bertram determined to adhere to the refinement of a seven-o'clock dinner. Very refined and very simple this dinner generally was. The fare often consisting of soup made out of vegetables from the garden, with a very slight suspicion of what housekeepers call stock to start it; fish, which meant as often as not three simple but fresh herrings; a morsel of meat curried or hashed would generally follow; and dessert and sweets would in the summer be blended into one; strawberries, raspberries or gooseberries from the garden forming the necessary materials. Cream did not accompany the strawberries, and the rich wine in the beautiful and curiously-cut decanters was placed on the table for show, not for use.

But then the dinners at the Manor were so exquisitely served. Such napery, such china, such sparkling and elegant glass, and such highly-polished plate. Poor little Clara, the serving-maid, who had not yet acquired the knack of telling a lie with *sang froid* absolutely

24

trembled, as she spread out her snowy table-cloths, and laid her delicate china and glass and silver on the board.

"It don't seem worth while, " she often remarked to the cook. "For what's an' erring? It seems wicked to eat an' erring off sech plates as them. "

"It's a way the quality have, " retorted Mrs. Masters, who had come from London with the Bertrams and did not mean to stay. "They heats nothing, and they lives on *sham*. Call *this* soup! There, Clara, you'll be a sham yourself before you has done with them. "

Clara thought this highly probable, but she was still young and romantic, and could do a great deal of living on make-beliefs, like many other girls all the world over.

As the Bertrams were eating their strawberries off delicate Sevres plates on the evening of the day when Mr. Ingram had disclosed the parentage of poor Beatrice Meadowsweet, the postman was seen passing the window.

Benjafield had a very slow and aggravating gait. The more impatient people were for their letters, the more tedious was he in his delivery. Benjafield had been a fisherman in his day, and had a very sharp, withered old face. He had a blind eye, too, and walked by the aid of a crutch but it was his boast that, notwithstanding his one eye and his lameness, no one had ever yet got the better of him.

"There's Benjafield! " exclaimed Mabel. "Shall I run and fetch the letters, mother? "

Mrs. Bertram rose slowly from her seat at the head of the board.

"The post is later than ever, " she remarked; "it is past the half-hour. I shall go myself and speak to Benjafield. "

She walked slowly out through the open window. She wore an evening dress of rusty black velvet with a long train. It gave her a very imposing appearance, and the effect of her evening dress and her handsome face and imperious manners were so overpowering that the old postman, as he hobbled toward her, had to mutter under his breath:

"Don't forget your game leg, Benjafield, nor your wall eye, and don't you be tooken down nor beholden to nobody. "

"Why is the post so late? " inquired Mrs. Bertram. "It is more than half-past eight. "

"Eh! " exclaimed Benjafleld.

"I asked why the post was so late. "

"Eh? I'm hard of hearing, your ladyship. "

He came a little nearer, and leered up in the most familiar way into the aristocratic face of Mrs. Bertram.

"Intolerable old man, " she muttered, aloud: "Take the letters from him, Catherine, and bring them here. "

Then raising her voice to a thin scream, she continued:

"I shall write to the general post-office on this subject; it is quite intolerable that in any part of England Her Majesty's Post should be entrusted to incapable hands. "

Old Benjafield, fumbling in his bag, produced two letters which he presented to Catherine. He did so with a dubious, inquiring glance at her mother, again informed the company generally that he was hard of hearing, and hobbled away.

One of the letters, addressed in a manly and dashing hand, was for Catherine. The other, also in manly but decidedly cramped writing, was addressed to Mrs. Bertram.

She started when she saw the handwriting, instantly forgot old Benjafield, and disappeared into the house.

When she was gone Mabel danced up to her sister's side, and looked over her shoulder at the thick envelope addressed in the manly hand.

"Kate, it's from Loftie! " she exclaimed.

"Yes, it's from Loftie, " responded Catherine. "Let us come and sit under the elm-tree and read what he says, May. "

The girls seated themselves together on a rustic bench, tore open the thick letter, and acquainted themselves with its contents.

"Dearest, —I'm coming home to-morrow night. *Must* see the mater. Have got into a fresh scrape. Don't tell anyone but May—I mean about the scrape.

"Your devoted brother,

"LOFTUS. "

Catherine read this letter twice, once to herself, then aloud for Mabel's benefit.

"Now, what's up? " exclaimed Mabel. "It must be very bad. He never calls you 'dearest;' unless it's awfully bad. Does he, Kitty? "

"No, " said Catherine. "Poor mother, " she added then, and she gave a profound and most ungirlish sigh.

"Why, Catherine, you have been grumbling at mother all day! You have been feeling so cross about her. "

"You never will understand, Mabel! I grumble at mother for her frettiness, but I love her, I pity her for her sorrows. "

Mabel looked full into her sister's face.

"I confess I don't understand you, " she said. "I can't love one side of a person, and hate the other side; I don't know that I love or hate anybody very much. It's more comfortable not to do things very much, isn't it, Kitty? "

"I suppose so, " replied Catherine, "but I can't say. That isn't my fashion. I do everything very much. I love, I hate, I joy or sorrow, all in extremes. Perhaps it isn't a good way, but it's the only way I've got. Now let us talk about Loftus. I wonder if he is going to stay long, and if he will make himself pleasant. "

"No fear of that, " responded Mabel. "He'll be as selfish and exacting as ever he can be. He'll keep mother in a state of fret, and you in a state of excitement, and he'll insist on smoking a cigarette close to the new cretonne curtains in the drawing-room, and he'll make me go out in the hot part of the day to gather fresh strawberries for him. Oh, I do think brothers are worries! I wish he wasn't coming. We are very peaceful and snug here. And mother's face doesn't looked harassed as it often did when we were in town. I do wish Loftus wasn't coming to upset everything. It was he turned us away from our nice, sprightly, jolly London, and now, surely he need not follow us into the country. Yes, Catherine, what words of wisdom or reproof are going to drop from your lips? "

"Not any, " replied Catherine. "I can't make blind people see, and I can't bring love when there is no love to bring. Of course, it is different for me. "

"How is it different for you? "

"I love Loftus. He gives me pain, but that can be borne, for I love him. "

At this moment Mrs. Bertram's tall figure was seen standing on the steps of the house. It was getting dark; a heavy dew was falling, and the air was slightly, pleasantly chill after the intense heat of the day. Mrs. Bertram had wrapped a white fleecy cloud over her head. She descended the steps, stood on the broad gravel sweep, and looked around her.

"We are here, mother, " said May, jumping up. "Do you want us? "

"I want Catherine. Don't you come, Mabel. I want Catherine alone. "

"Keep Loftus's letter, " said Catherine, tossing it into her sister's lap. "I know by mother's tone she is troubled. Don't let us show her the letter to-night. Put it in your pocket, May. "

Aloud she said, —

"Yes, mother, I'm coming. I'll be with you directly. " She ran across the grass, looking slim and pale in her white muslin dress, her face full of intense feeling, her manner so hurried and eager that her mother felt irritated by it.

"You need not dash at me as if you meant to knock me down, Kate, " she said.

"You said you wanted me, mother. "

"So I did, Catherine. I do want you. Come into the house with me. "

Mrs. Bertram turned and walked up the steps. She entered the wide hall which was lit by a ghostly, and not too carefully-trimmed, paraffin lamp. Catherine followed her. They went into the drawing-room. Here also a paraffin lamp gave an uncertain light; very feeble, yellow, and uncertain it was, but even by it Catherine could catch a glimpse of her mother's face. It was drawn and white, it was not only changed from the prosperous, handsome face which the girl had last looked at, but it had lost its likeness to the haughty, the proud, the satisfied Mrs. Bertram of Catherine's knowledge. Its expression now betokened a kind of inward scare or fright.

"Mother, you have something to worry you, " said Kate, "I see that by your face. I am sorry. I am truly sorry. Sit down, mother. What can I do for you? "

"Nothing, my dear, except to be an attentive daughter—attentive and affectionate and obedient. Sometimes, Catherine, you are not that. "

"Oh, never mind now, when you are in trouble, I'd do anything in the world for you when you are in trouble. You know that. "

Mrs. Bertram had seated herself. Catherine knelt now, and took one of her mother's hands between her own. Insensibly the cold hand was comforted by the warm steadfast clasp.

"You are a good child, Kate, " said her mother in an unwonted and gentle voice. "You are full of whims and fancies; but when you like you can be a great support to one. Do you remember long ago when your father died how only little Kitty's hand could cure mother's headaches? "

"I would cure your heartache now. "

"You can't, child, you can't. And besides, who said anything about a heartache? We have no time, Kate, to talk any more sentimentalities. I have had a letter, my dear, and it obliges me to go to town to-night. "

"To-night? Surely there is no train? "

"There is. One stops at Northbury to take up the mails at a quarter to twelve. I shall go by it. "

"Do you want me to go with you? "

"By no means. Of what use would you be? "

"I don't know. Perhaps not of any use, and yet long ago when you had headaches, Kitty could cure them. "

There was something so pathetic and so unwonted in Catherine's tone that Mrs. Bertram was quite touched. She bent forward, placed her hand under the young chin, raised the handsome face, and printed a kiss on the brow.

"Kitty shall help her mother best by staying at home, " she said. "Seriously, my love. I must leave you in charge here. Not only in charge of the house, of the servants, of Mabel—but—of my secret. "

"What secret, mother? "

"I don't want any one here to know that I have gone to London. "

Catherine thought a moment.

"I know you are not going to give me your reasons, " she said, after a pause. "But why do you tell me there is a secret? "

"Because you are trustworthy. "

"Why do tell *me* that you are going to London? "

"Because you must be prepared to act in an emergency. "

"Mother, what do you mean? "

"I will tell you enough of my meaning to guide you, my love. I have had some news that troubles me. I am going to London to try and put some wrong things right. You need not look so horrified, Kate; I shall certainly put them right. It might complicate matters in certain quarters if it were known that I had gone to London, therefore I do it secretly. It is necessary, however, that one person should know where to write to me. I choose you to be that person, Catherine, but you are only to send me a letter in case of need. "

"If we are ill, or anything of that sort, mother? "

"Nothing of that sort. You and Mabel are in superb health. I am not going to prepare for any such unlikely contingency as your sudden illness. Catherine, these are the *only* circumstances under which you are to communicate with your mother. Listen, my dear daughter. Listen attentively. A good deal depends on your discretion. A stranger may call. The stranger may be either a man or a woman. He or she will ask to see me. Finding I am away this person, whether man or woman, will try to have an interview with either you or Mabel, and will endeavor by every means to get my address. Mabel, knowing nothing, can reveal nothing, and you, Kate, you are to put the stranger on the wrong scent, to get rid of the stranger by some means, and immediately to telegraph to me. My address is in this closed-up envelope. Lock the envelope in your desk; open it if the contingency to which I have alluded occurs, not otherwise. And now, my dear child, I must go upstairs and pack. "

Catherine roused herself from her kneeling position with difficulty. She felt cold and stiff, queer and old.

"Shall I help you, mother, " she asked.

"No, my dear, I shall ring for Clara. I shall tell Clara that I am going to Manchester. A train to Manchester can be taken from Fleet-hill Junction, so it will all sound quite natural. Go out to Mabel, dear. Tell her any story you like. "

"I don't tell stories, mother. I shall have nothing to say to Mabel. "

"Tell her nothing, then; only run away. What is the matter now? "

"One thing before you go, mother. I too had a letter to-night. "

"Had you, my dear? I cannot be worried about your correspondence now. "

"My letter was from Loftie. "

"Loftus! What did he write about? "

"He is coming here to-morrow night. "

Catherine glanced eagerly into her mother's face as she spoke. It did not grow any whiter or any more careworn.

She stood still for a moment in the middle of the drawing-room, evidently thinking deeply. When she spoke her brow had cleared and her voice was cheerful.

"This may be for the best, " she said.

Catherine stamped her foot impatiently.

"Mother, " she said, "you quite frighten me with your innuendoes and your half-confidences. I don't understand you. It is very difficult to act when one only half understands. "

"I cannot make things plainer for you, my dear. I am glad Loftie is coming. You girls must entertain him as well as you can. This is Wednesday evening. I hope to be back at the latest on Monday. It is possible even that I may transact my business sooner. Keep Loftus in a good temper, Kate. Don't let him quarrel with Mabel, and, above all things, do not breathe to a soul that your mother has gone to London. Now, kiss me, dear. It is a comfort to have a grown-up daughter to lean on. "

CHAPTER V.

THE USUAL SORT OF SCRAPE.

On the following evening Loftus Bertram made his appearance at Rosendale Manor. Catherine and Mabel were both waiting for him under the shade of the great oak tree which commanded a view of the gate. His train was due at Northbury at seven o'clock. He was to come by express from London, and the girls concluded that the express would not be more than five minutes late. Allowing for this, and allowing also for the probability that Loftus would be extremely discontented with the style of hackney coach which alone would await him at the little station and might in consequence prefer to walk to the Manor, the girls calculated he might put in an appearance on the scene at about twenty minutes past seven. They had arranged to have dinner at a quarter to eight, and sat side by side now, looking a little forlorn in the frocks they had grown out of, and a little lonely, like half-fledged chicks, without their mother's august protection.

"Loftie will wonder, " said Mabel, "at mother going off to Manchester in such a hurry. "

It was the cook who had told Mabel about Manchester, Clara having informed her.

"There's Loftus! " suddenly exclaimed Catherine. "I knew he'd walk. I said so. There's the old shandrydan crawling after him with the luggage. Come, Mabel. Let's fly to meet the dear old boy. "

She was off and away herself before Mabel had time to scramble to her feet. Her running was swift as a fawn's—in an instant she had reached her brother—threw herself panting with laughter and joy against him, and flung one arm round his neck.

"Here you are! " she said, her words coming out in gasps. "Isn't it jolly? Such a fresh old place! Lots of strawberries—glad you'll see it in the long days—give me a kiss, Loftie—I'm hungry for a kiss! "

"You're as wild an imp as ever, " said Loftus, pinching her cheek, but stooping and kissing her, nevertheless, with decided affection. "Why did you put yourself out of breath, Kitty? Catch May setting her precious little heart a-beating too fast for any fellow! Ah, here you come, lazy Mabel. Where is the mater? In the house, I suppose? I say, Kate, what a hole you have pitched upon for living in? I positively couldn't ride down upon the thing they offered me at the station. It wasn't even *clean*. Look at it, my dear girls! It holds my respectable belongings, and not me. It's the scarecrow or ghost of the ordinary station-fly. Could you have imagined the station-fly could have a ghost? "

"No, " retorted Mabel, "being so scarecrowy and ghost-like already. Please, driver, take Captain Bertram's things up to the house. He heard you speak, Loftie. These Northbury people are as touchy as if they were somebodies. Oh, Loftus, you will be disappointed. Mother has gone to Manchester. "

"To Manchester? " retorted Loftus. "My mother away from home! Did she know that I was coming? "

"Yes, " answered Kate, "I told her about your letter last night. "

"Did you show her my letter? "

"No. "

"Why didn't you? If she had read it she wouldn't have gone. I said I was in a scrape. I was coming down on purpose to see the mater. You might have sent me a wire to say she would not be at home, or you might have kept her at home by showing her my letter. You certainly did not act with discretion. "

"I said you'd begin to scold the minute you came here, Loftie, " remarked Mabel. "It's a way you have. I told Kitty so. See, you have made poor Kitty quite grave. "

Loftus Bertram was a tall, slim, young fellow. He was well-made, athletic, and neat in appearance, and had that upright carriage and bearing which is most approved of in her Majesty's army. His face was thin and dark; he had a look of Kate, but his eyes were neither so large nor so full; his mouth was weak, not firm, and his expression wanted the openness which characterized Catherine's features.

He was a selfish man, but he was not unkind or ill-natured. The news which the girls gave him of their mother's absence undoubtedly worried and annoyed him a good deal, but like most people who are popular, and Loftus Bertram was undoubtedly very popular, he had the power of instantly adapting himself to the exigencies of the moment.

He laughed lightly, therefore, at Mabel's words, put his arm round his younger sister's unformed waist, and said, in a gay voice:

"I won't scold either of you any more until I have had something to eat. "

"We live very quietly at the Manor, " remarked Mabel, "Mother wants to save, you know. She says we must keep up our refinement at any cost, but our meals are very—" she glanced with a gay laugh at Catherine.

"Oh, by Jove! I hope you don't stint in the matter of food, " exclaimed the brother. "You'll have to drop it while I'm here, I can tell you. I thought the mater would be up to some little game of this kind when she buried you alive in such an out-of-the-way corner. She makes a great mistake though, and so I shall tell her. Young girls of your age ought to be fed up. You'll develop properly then, you won't otherwise. That's the new dodge. All the doctors go upon it. Feed up the young to any extent, and they'll pay for it by-and-bye. Plenty of good English beef and mutton. What's the matter, Kate? What are you laughing in that immoderate manner for? "

"Oh, nothing, Loftie. I may laugh, I suppose, without saying why. I wish you would not put on that killing air, though. And you know perfectly there is no use in laying down the law in mother's house. "

The three young people were now standing in the hall, and Clara tripped timidly forward.

"We want dinner as quickly as possible, Clara, " said Mabel. "Come, Loftus, let us take you to your room. "

That night the choicely served repast was less meagre than usual. Caller herring graced the board in abundance, and even Loftus did not despise these, when really fresh and cooked to perfection. The hash of New Zealand mutton, however, which followed, was not so much to this fastidious young officer's taste, but quantities of fine strawberries, supplemented by a jug of rich cream, put him once more into a good humor. He did not know that Kate had spent one of her very scarce sixpences on the cream, and that the girls had walked a mile-and-a-half through the hot sun that morning to fetch it.

The decanters of wine did not only do duty as ornaments that evening, and as the black coffee which followed was quite to Loftus' taste, he forgot the New Zealand mutton, or, at least, determined not to speak on the subject before the next morning.

After Mabel went to bed that night Kate asked her brother what the fresh scrape was about. He was really in an excellent humor then; the seclusion and almost romance of the old place soothed his nerves, which were somewhat jaded with the rush and tear of a life not lived too worthily. He and Kitty were strolling up and down in the moonlight, and when she asked her question and looked up at him with her fine, intelligent, sympathetic face, he pulled her little ear affectionately, and pushed back the tendrils of soft, dark hair from her brow.

"The usual thing, Kitty, " he responded. "I'm in the usual sort of scrape. "

"Money? " asked Catherine.

"Confound the thing, yes. Why was money invented? It's the plague of one's life, Catherine. If there was no money there'd be no crime. "

"Nonsense, " answered Catherine, with shrewdness. "If there wasn't money there would be its equivalent in some form or other. Are you in debt again, Loftie? "

"How can I help it? I can't live on my pittance. "

"But mother gives you three hundred a year. "

"Yes—such a lot! You girls think that a fine sum, I suppose! That's all you know. Three hundred! It's a pittance. No fellow has a right to go into the army with such small private means. "

"But, Loftie, you would not accept Uncle Roderick Macleod's offer. He wrote so often, and said he could help you if you joined him in India. "

"Yes, I knew what that meant. Now, look here, Kate. We needn't rake up the past. My lot in life is fixed. I like my profession, but I can't be expected to care for the beggary which accompanies it. I'm in a scrape, and I want to see the mater. "

"Poor mother! I *wish* you weren't going to worry her, Loftie. "

"It doesn't worry a mother to help her only son. "

"But she has helped you so often. You know it was on account of you that we came down here, because mother had given you so much, and it was the only way left to us to save. It wasn't at all a good thing for Mabel and me, for we had to leave our education unfinished. But mother thought it best. What's the matter, Loftie? "

"Only if you're going on in this strain I'm off to bed. It is hard on a fellow when he comes once in a while to see his sisters to be called over the coals by them. You know I'm awfully fond of you, Kitty, and somehow I thought you'd be a comfort to me. You know very little indeed of the real worries of life. "

Loftus spoke in a tone of such feeling that Catherine's warm heart was instantly touched.

"I won't say any more, " she answered. "I know it isn't right of me. I always wished and longed to be a help to you, Loftie. "

"So you can. You are a dear little sis when you like. You're worth twenty of May. I think you are going to be a very handsome girl, Kate, and if you are only fed up properly, and dressed properly, so that the best points of your figure can be seen—well—now what's the matter? "

"Only I won't have you talking of me as if I were going to be put up to auction. "

"So you will be when you go to London. All girls are. The mothers are the auctioneers, and the young fellows come round and bid. Good gracious, what a thunder-cloud! What flashing eyes! You'll see what a famous auctioneer mother will make! What is the matter, Kitty? "

"Nothing. Good-night. I'm going to bed. "

"Come back and kiss me first. Poor little Kit! Dear, handsome, fiery-spirited little Kit! I say though, *what* a shabby frock you've got on! "

"Oh, don't worry me, Loftie! Any dress will do in the country. "

"Right, most prudent Catherine. By the way, when did you say mother would come back? "

"Perhaps on Monday. "

"What did she go to Manchester for? "

"I can't tell you. "

"Well, I trust she will be back on Monday evening, for I am due at the Depot on Tuesday. Lucky for me I got a week's leave, but I didn't mean to see it out. It will be uncommonly awkward if I cannot get hold of the mater between now and Tuesday, Kate. "

"Loftus—*are* you going to ask her to give you much money? "

"My dear child, you would think the sum I want enormous, but it isn't really. Most fellows would consider it a trifle. And I don't want her really to give it, Kate, only to lend it. That's altogether a different matter, isn't it? Of course I could borrow it elsewhere, but it seems a pity to pay a lot of interest when one's mother can put one straight. "

"I don't know how you are to pay the money back, Loftus. "

Loftus laughed.

"There are ways and means, " he said. "Am I going to take all the bloom off that young cheek by letting its owner into the secrets of Vanity Fair? Come Kitty, go to bed, and don't fret about me, I'll manage somehow. "

"Loftus, how much money do you want mother to lend you? "

"What a persistent child you are. You positively look frightened. Well, three fifty will do for the present. That oughtn't to stump anyone, ought it? "

"I suppose not, " answered Kate, in a bewildered way.

She put her hand to her forehead, bade her brother good-night, and sought her room.

"Three hundred and fifty pounds! " she murmured. "And mother won't buy herrings more than eightpence a dozen! And we scarcely eat any meat, and lately we have begun even to save the bread. Three hundred and fifty pounds! Well, I won't tell Mabel. Does Mabel really know the world better than I do, and is it wrong of me in spite of everything to love Loftus? "

CHAPTER VI.

FOR MY PART, I AM NOT GOING TO TAKE ANY NOTICE OF
THE BERTRAMS.

But notwithstanding all worries, the world in midsummer, when the days are longest and the birds sing their loudest, is a gay place for the young. Catherine Bertram stayed awake for quite an hour that night. An hour was a long time for such young and bright eyes to remain wide open, and she fancied with a wave of self-pity how wrinkled and old she would look in the morning. Not a bit of it! She arose with the complexion of a Hebe, and the buoyant and gladsome spirit of a lark.

As she dressed she sang, and when she ran downstairs she whistled a plantation melody with such precision and clearness that Loftus exclaimed, "Oh, how shocking! " and Mabel rolled up her eyes, and said sagely, that no one ever could turn Kate into anything but a tom-boy.

"Girls, what are we to do after breakfast? " asked the brother.

"Have you any money at all in your pocket, Loftie? " demurely asked Mabel, "for if so, if so—" her eyes danced, "I can undertake to provide a pleasant day for us all. "

"Well, puss, I don't suppose an officer in her Majesty's Royal Artillery—is quite without some petty cash. How much do you want? "

"A few shillings will do. Let us pack up a picnic basket. Kate, you needn't look at me. I have taken Mrs. Masters into confidence, and there's a cold roast fowl downstairs—and—and—but I won't reveal anything further. We can have a picnic—we can go away an hour after breakfast, and saunter to that place known as the Long Quay, and hire the very best boat to be had for money, and we can float about on this lovely harbor, and land presently on the shore over there where the ruins of the old Port are; and we can eat our dinners there and be jolly. Remember that we have never but once been on the water since we came. Think how we have pined for this simple pleasure, Loftie, and fork out the tin. "

"My dear Mabel, I must place my interdict on slang. "

"Nonsense. When the cat's away. Oh, don't look shocked! Are we to go? "

"Go! of course we'll go. Is there no pretty girl who'll come with us? It's rather slow to have only one's sisters. "

"Very well, Loftus. We'll pay you out presently, " said Kate.

"And there is a very pretty girl, " continued Mabel, "At least Catherine considers her very pretty—only—" her eyes danced with mischief.

"Only what? "

"The mother doesn't like her. There's a dear old Rector here, and he introduced the girl to Kitty, and mother was wild. Mother sounded the Rector the next day and heard something which made her wilder still, but we are not in the secret. Kate fell in love with the girl. "

"Did you, Kate? When a woman falls in love with another woman the phenomenon is so uncommon that a certain amount of interest must be roused. Describe the object of your adoration, Kitty. "

"Her name, " responded Kate, "is Beatrice Meadowsweet. I won't say any more about her. If ever you meet her, which isn't likely, you can judge for yourself of her merits. "

"Kitty is rather cross about Beatrice, " said Mabel; then she continued, "Loftie, what do you think? Mother has cut all the Northbury folk. "

"Mabel, you talk very wild nonsense. "

It was Kate who spoke. She rose from the breakfast-table with an annoyed expression.

"Wild or not—it is true, " replied Mabel. "Mother has cut the Northbury people, cut them dead. They came to see us, they came in troops. Such funny folk! The first lot were let in. Mother was like a poker. She astonished her visitors, and the whole scene was so queer and uncomfortable, although mother was freezingly *polite*, that Kate and I got out of the room. The next day more people came—and more, and more every day, but Clara had her orders, and we weren't 'at home. ' Kitty and I used to watch the poor Northburians from behind the summer-house. One day Kitty laughed. It was awful, and I am sure they heard.

"Another day a dreadful little woman with rolling eyes said she would leave a tract on *Lying* in the avenue—I wish she had. But I suppose she thought better of it.

"Then there came a bazaar, a great bazaar, and the Rector invited us, and said all the Northburians would be there. What do you think mother did? She returned their calls on that day. She knew they'd be out, and they were. Wasn't that a dead cut, Loftie? "

"Rather, " responded Loftus.

He rose slowly, looked deliberately at Kate, and then closed his lips.

"Mother is away, so we won't discuss her, " said Kate. "Run and pack the picnic basket, Mabel, and then we'll be off. "

The picturesque little town of Northbury was built on the slope of a hill. This hill gently descended to the sea. Nowhere was there to be found a more charming, landlocked harbor than at Northbury. It was a famous harbor for boating. Even at low tide people could get on the water, and in the summer time this gay sheet of dark blue sparkling waves had many small yachts, fishing smacks, and row-boats of all sizes and descriptions skimming about on its surface. In the spring a large fishing trade was done here, and then the steamers whistle? and shrieked, and disturbed the primitive harmony of the place. But by midsummer the great shoals of mackerel went away, and with them the dark picturesque hookers, and the ugly steamers, and the inhabitants were once more left to their sleepy, old-fashioned, but withal pleasant life.

Rosendale Manor was situated on high ground. It was surrounded by a wall, and the wide avenue was entered by ponderous iron gates. It was about eleven o'clock when the girls and their brother started gayly off for their day on the water. Loftus carried a couple of rugs, so that the fact of Mabel lugging a heavy picnic basket on her sturdy left arm did not look specially remarkable. They went down a steep and straggling hill, passed through an old-fashioned green, with the local club at one side, and a wall at the other which seemed to hang right over the sea.

They soon reached the Long Quay, and made their bargain for the best boat to be had. A man of the name of Driver kept many boats for hire, and he offered now to accompany the young party and show off the beauties of the place.

This, however, Mabel would not hear of. They must go alone or not at all. Loftus did not like to own to his very small nautical experience; the sea was smooth and shining, and apparently free from all danger, and the little party embarked gayly, and put out on their first cruise in high spirits.

Miss Peters and Mrs. Butler watched them with intense interest from their bay window. Miss Peters had possession of the spy-glass. With this held steadily before her eyes, she shouted observations to her sister.

"There they go! No, Dan Driver is *not* going with them! Any one can see by the way that young man handles the oar that he doesn't know a great deal about the water. Good gracious, Martha, they're taking a sail with them! Now I do call that tempting Providence. That young man has a very elegant figure, Martha, but mark my words he knows nothing at all about the management of a boat. The girls know still less. "

"Put down your spy-glass for a moment, and let me speak to you, Maria, " exclaimed Mrs. Butler in an exasperated voice. "I never knew such a tongue as yours for clap, clap, clapping. Did you say those two Bertram girls were going out alone with a *man*! Well, I have known what to think for some time! Alone on the water with a *young man*. Surely, Maria, you must have made a mistake. "

"It's just like you, Martha, you never believe in any one's eyes but your own. Here's the glass, look for yourself. If that isn't a man, and a young man, and a stylish, handsome man, my name isn't Maria Peters. "

"You'd be very glad if your name wasn't Peters, " replied the irate sister. "But I fear me there's little likelihood of your changing it now. Ah, here's Beatrice Meadowsweet. Good-morning, Bee, my dear. How's your dear mother? Is her poor precious cough any better? "

"Come here, Bee, " said Miss Peters. "Come over to the window this minute, and use your young eyes. Who are those people in Dan Driver's boat? There, you tell Martha, she wont believe me. "

"Those are the Bertrams, " exclaimed Beatrice.

She put up her hand to shade her eyes, and took a long steadfast look over the shining water.

"Those are the Bertrams, and of course, their brother. "

"Oh, my dear Bee, how you have relieved me! " exclaimed Mrs. Butler.

She re-seated herself on a settee which stood near, and took her handkerchief to wipe out some wrinkles of anxiety from her stout face.

Beatrice stared in astonishment.

"I don't quite understand, " she said.

"My dear! I feared something improper was going on. A young man, not a relation, out alone on the water with two girls! That's the kind of thing we don't allow, in Northbury, Bee. Now, what's the matter? "

"Look, " said Beatrice, "look! They are putting up the sail, and they are not doing it right. They oughtn't all three to stand up in the boat together. It will capsize! Oh, I must fly to them. Good-bye, Mrs. Butler. Mother would like to see you at tea, to-night. Good-bye, Miss Peters. "

She rushed away, and the next moment was down on the quay. Three moments later she was speeding with swift long strokes across the harbor in her own beautifully appointed row-boat.

Her dress was of dark blue serge, with white collar and cuffs. Her hat was a simple sailor one. The exercise brought the color into her cheeks, and her big somewhat pathetic gray eyes were bright.

"There she goes! " exclaimed Miss Peters. "Never saw such a girl. Doesn't she handle her oars with a touch? Oh, of course she is off to the rescue of those poor bunglers. And I daresay they don't think her good enough to speak to. "

"Good enough! " exclaimed Mrs. Butler. "She's twice too good for any one of them. Didn't her dress fit neat, Maria? Well, I hope she won't get let in by their fine ways. For my part, I'm not going to take any notice of the Bertrams. The way they behaved was past enduring. Not at homing when I called, and then leaving their cards on the day when I was at the bazaar. Highty-tighty, says I, who's Mrs. Bertram that she should look down on us in this fashion? Isn't the widow of a good honest butter merchant who paid his way, and left a comfortable fortune behind him, fit to associate with any lady of the land? Mrs. Bertram, indeed! A nice way she has treated us all. It isn't every newcomer we Northbury folks would take up. We hold ourselves high, that we do. Now, what's the matter, Maria? "

"We didn't hold ourselves high about Mrs. Bertram, " replied Miss Peters. "It isn't fair to say that we did. We all rushed up to call before she had the carpets well down. I did say, Martha, and you may remember too that I said it, for you were helping me to the tail of the salmon at the time, and I remarked that there was little or nothing to eat on it, you'll remember that I said to you: 'let them put their carpets straight at least. ' But you wouldn't—you were all agog to be off, when you saw that Mrs. Gorman Stanley had gone up there in her new bonnet, with the red and yellow poppies—the bonnet you know that she said she got from London. "

"Which she didn't, " snapped Mrs. Butler; "for I saw those identical poppies in Perry's shop on the quay. Well, well, Maria, I may have been a bit hasty in rushing after those who didn't want me, but the result would have been all the same. Maria, there's only one solution of the way we have been treated by that proud, stuck-up, conceited body. Maria, she doesn't pay her way. "

Miss Peters rolled her eyes with a quick dart at her sister.

"They do say she's very close in the kitchen, " she remarked; "and the butcher told Susan that they only go in for New Zealand. "

Mrs. Butler rose from her seat, to express more markedly her disgust for colonial viands.

"Ugh! " she said. "Catch me putting a morsel of that poisonous stuff inside my mouth. Well, well, you'll see I'm right, Maria. She don't pay her way, so she's ashamed, and well she may be, to look honest folk in the face. "

"Beatrice has got up to the other boat, " interrupted Miss Peters. Give me the glass, quickly, Martha. My word, the two boats are touching. And—would you believe it? —one of the young ladies is getting into Bee's boat, Martha. She's towing Driver's boat after her own! Well, well, that will be nuts to Mrs. Bertram. I declare, Martha, I shouldn't be one bit surprised if that young jackanapes of a brother fell in love with our Bee. "

"He won't get her for his pains, " retorted Mrs. Butler. "Those who don't pay their way won't touch Beatrice Meadowsweet's fortune. But, there, I'm sick of the subject. Let's talk of something else. Isn't that Mrs. Gorman Stanley coming down the street? Open the window and call out to her, Maria. Ask her if she wants me to send her round one pound of butter, or two from the farm? "

CHAPTER VII.

REPLY FOR US, KATE.

Beatrice Meadowsweet and the Bertrams spent a delightful day together. The Bertrams frankly owned their inability to manage a boat. They welcomed her timely assistance, and thanked her for offering it, and then the young folk laughed and joked together, the Bertrams secretly finding Beatrice all the more interesting and fascinating because they knew that their mother would not quite approve of their being found in her society.

Beatrice told them about the harbor, took Kate into her boat, instructed Loftus how to manage his sail, and showed him the difference between rowing on a river and on the sea. Finally, she frankly accepted their suggestion that she should join their impromptu picnic. They landed on the green banks of that part of the coast which contained the ruins of an ancient Danish fort. There they kindled a fire, boiled a kettle of water, made tea, enjoyed bread-and-butter, cold chicken and strawberries, and had an exceedingly festive time.

When the meal was over Bertram asked Miss Meadowsweet to show him over the fort. She complied at once, in that easy, unconcerned manner which gave her a certain charm, and which in itself was the perfection of good-breeding. Mabel was about to follow, but Kate caught hold of her skirt.

"Help me to wash up, " she said.

When the girls were alone, Mabel burst into a peal of laughter.

"Oh, what a time the little mice are having! " she exclaimed. "What a time! I only wish that nice Beatrice of yours had a couple of brothers as charming as herself. Then our state would approach perfection. "

"May, you oughtn't to talk in that silly fashion. No one hates leading-strings as I do, and I'm determined that mother shall allow me to make Miss Meadowsweet my friend. But this meeting seems like taking advantage of mother's absence; it does really, and although we could not help ourselves, I am sorry about it. "

"Well, I'm not. We have had a delicious time, and I think, too, we owe our lives to Miss Bee. Loftie was making an awful mess of that sail, and you know, Kate, none of us can swim. Now look at Loftie, do look at him! See how he's bending towards Miss Meadowsweet. He is quite taken with her, I can see. Oh, what a flirt he is. Doesn't she hold herself nicely, Kate? And hasn't she an independent sort of way? "

"Yes, " responded Catherine. "I think even mother must own that Beatrice is in good style. I knew that the moment she spoke to me. "

"They are coming back, " said Mabel. "Just toss me over that towel, please, Kate. Don't you think I provided a very nice little lunch? Mrs. Masters and I managed it between us, and you none of you knew, no none of you, how very ancient that chicken was. "

"Didn't I? " replied Kate. "I had one of the drumsticks. That chicken has woke me in a very lusty manner more than once in the morn. 'Up, Up! ' cries the crowing cock. Oh, Mabel, it was cruel of you to deprive us of his clarion note. "

"Never mind. I saw that Loftie and Miss Meadowsweet had the breast to eat. I nearly died when I saw you attacking the drumstick, but I knew you wouldn't split. Now, do look up, Kate? Doesn't Loftus look radiant? Isn't he a handsome fellow when he is pleased? What can Miss Meadowsweet be saying to him? How he does laugh! "

"Miss Meadowsweet has a good deal of fun in her, " responded Kate. "I think it is a certain tone in her voice. Well, here they come. How did you like the ruins, Loftus? "

"Very much—I mean as much as I care for any ruins. And I have had a capital guide. Miss Meadowsweet wants to propose something to you girls. "

"Yes, " said Beatrice, in her bright, quick way. "It will be so nice if you can do it. Captain Bertram says he is fond of tennis, and we have four very good courts at home. Will you all come and have supper this evening? Mother will be delighted to see you—Do come, Miss Bertram. "

She looked sympathetically and eagerly at Catherine. Catherine in her shabby, ill-fitting dress was not nearly such a distinguished figure as Miss Meadowsweet, whose serge costume fitted her like a glove. Yet Catherine drew herself up as if the invitation half offended her.

"I? " she began. She looked at Loftus. Her color came and went.

"Catherine is overpowered, " remarked the brother, with a smile at Miss Meadowsweet, but a certain expression about his mouth which Kate too well interpreted. "Catherine is overpowered. She and this little woman, " taking Mabel's hand, "have had very few invitations lately. Never mind, Kate, I'll support you, and if we hurry home now, you can polish up your rusty tennis powers at Rosendale. We must make a proper court there, Miss Meadowsweet. In the meantime, we are all delighted to accept your kind invitation. "

"Be with us at seven, " said Beatrice. "Mother doesn't like supper to be later than half-past-eight, but if you are with us by seven we shall have time for a good game first. And now, I think I must go home, or my mother will wonder what has become of me. "

Mabel picked up the luncheon basket. Loftus flung the rugs over his shoulder, and the four young people went down to the boats.

Loftus and Mabel lingered a little behind. Catherine and Beatrice led the way.

"You don't want to come to-night, " suddenly said Beatrice to her companion.

Catherine started and colored.

"Why do you say that? I—I am glad to come. "

"Don't come if you don't want to. I shall understand. "

They had reached the boats. The Bertrams seated themselves in their own. Miss Meadowsweet advised them not to put up the sail, but thought if she kept within easy distance, they might manage the oars. Loftus and Mabel rowed. Kate sat in the stern and steered. Beatrice Meadowsweet applauded, and rowed her own boat with skill. She reached the shore before them, and called out in her clear voice:

"I sha'n't wait now. I shall see you all at seven this evening. "

"Reply for us, Kate, " whispered Loftus. "Reply for us all, quickly. "

"Yes—we'll come, " called Catherine across the water.

Beatrice smiled. Her smile was of the sunniest. It flashed back a look of almost love at Catherine. Then she turned to walk up the steep steps which led from the quay to the little High Street.

"We ought not to go, " instantly began Catherine.

Loftus stopped rowing, bent forward and put his hand across her mouth.

"Not another word, " he said. "I'll undertake to conciliate the mother, and I think she can trust to my ideas of good-breeding. "

Meanwhile Beatrice walked quickly home. The Meadowsweets lived at the far end of the town in a large gray stone house. The house stood back a little from the road, and a great elm tree threw its protecting shade over the porch and upper windows. It was, however, an ordinary house in a street, and looked a little old-fashioned and a little gloomy until you stepped into the drawing-room, which was furnished certainly with no pretension to modern taste or art, but opened with French windows into a glorious, big, old-world garden.

The house was known by the name of the Gray House, and the old garden as the Gray Garden, but the garden at least bore no resemblance to its neutral-tinted name. It had green alleys, and sheltering trees, and a great expanse of smoothly kept lawn. It possessed flower-beds and flower borders innumerable. There was more than one bower composed entirely of rose-trees, and there were very long hedges of sweet briar and Scotch roses.

The tennis-courts were kept to perfection in the Gray Garden, and all the lasses and boys of Northbury were rejoiced when an invitation came to them to test their skill at a tournament here. There was no girl in Northbury more popular than Beatrice. This popularity was unsought. It came to her because she was gracious and affectionate, of a generous nature, above petty slanders, petty gossips, petty desires. Life had always been rich and plentiful for her, she possessed abundant health, excellent spirits, and a sunny temper not easily ruffled; she was sympathetic, too, and although, in mind and nature she was many steps above the girls with whom she associated, she was really unconscious of this difference and gave herself no superior airs. A companion who would have been her equal, whose intellect would have sharpened hers, whose spirit would have matched her own, whose refinement would have delighted and whose affection would have been something to revel in, she had never hitherto known.

Unconscious of her loss she had not deplored it. It was not until she and Catherine Bertram had flashed a look of delight and sympathy at one another that she first felt stirring within her breast the wings of a new desire. For the first time she felt unsatisfied and incomplete. She scarcely knew that she thirsted for Catherine, but this was so. Catherine awakened all sorts of new emotions in her heart. She had spent a delightful day with the Bertrams, and hurried home now in the highest spirits.

In the High Street she met three girls, whose names were Matty, Alice, and Sophy Bell. Their father was a retired coal merchant. There was scarcely any active trade down in Northbury, almost all the inhabitants having retired to live there on their fortunes. The Bells were small, rather thickly-made girls, with round faces and round eyes. They always dressed alike, and one was never seen without the other two. They generally walked through the streets with their arms linked, and each one echoed the sentiments of the other, so that the effect produced was a sense of medley and multiplicity.

To such an extent was this felt that the three girls were spoken of by the wits of the town as the "four-and-twenty Miss Bells. " They adored Beatrice, and bore down upon her now in a neat phalanx.

"Delighted to see you, Bee! " exclaimed Matty.

"Delighted! " echoed Alice.

"Lighted! " exclaimed Sophy.

"Where have you been? " began Matty, again.

Beatrice told. While she spoke, three pairs of lips were raised for a salute.

People kissed in the streets or anywhere at Northbury.

"You were with those Bertrams! Those *rude* Bertrams! Oh, fascinating—"

"Fascinating—"

"Nating, " burst from the three.

"Tell us about them, darling! " exclaimed one.

"Tell us! " said the other.

" —Us" —gasped the third.

Beatrice narrated her morning adventure with some spirit, praised her new friends, defended them from any score of rudeness, and altogether conjured up an interesting picture of them.

The Bells turned to walk with her. Matty hung on one arm, Alice on another, Sophy hopped backwards in front. Before she quite knew that she meant to do so, Beatrice had asked the Bells to join the tennis party that evening. They accepted the invitation rapturously.

"Might Polly and Daisy Jenkins come too, and might Polly's brother come, and if they met Mr. Jones, the curate—Mr. Jones did so love tennis—might *he* come? "

"Is the brother an officer in the real army? " inquired Matty.

"Real army—"

"Army—" echoed the others

Beatrice was able to assure them that Captain Bertram had nothing spurious about him.

"I'll see you at seven, " she added, nodding to her companions. "Yes, you can bring the Jenkinses and the boys, and Mr. Jones. I really must hurry home now. "

She reached the Gray House, found her mother nodding, as usual, in her great easy-chair, and told her what she had done.

"I met the Bertrams on the water, and had lunch with them, and they are coming to tennis to-night, and to supper afterwards, mother, " she said.

Mrs. Meadowsweet always approved of her daughter's doings. She approved now, nodding her kind old head, and raising her face with a smile.

"Quite right, Trixie, " she said. "How many Bertrams are there? Is Mrs. Bertram coming? If so, I had better put on my cap with the Honiton lace. "

"Mrs. Bertram is not coming, mother, but you must put on your best cap all the same. Mrs. Bertram is from home. It was the girls I met this morning—the girls, and their brother, Captain Bertram. "

"Oh, well, child, if they are all young folk the cap with Maltese lace will do. I don't wear Honiton, except for those who know. "

"Mother, I thought we might have supper in the garden. The weather is so lovely now, and it is quite light at half-past eight. Shall I give the order, and take all the trouble off you? "

Mrs. Meadowsweet rose with a slight effort to her feet.

"Do you think I am going to let you be worried, child? " she said. "No, no, what good is the old mother if she can't manage a thing of that sort? Of course you shall have supper in the garden, and a good supper, too. I am glad you have asked your friends, Bee. How well and bright you look. I am very glad you have made nice friends at last, child. "

"All my friends are nice, mother, at least I think so. By the way, I met the little Bells, and they were dying to come, so I asked them, and they said perhaps they would bring the Jenkinses, and Mr. Jones, and of course, the boys will drop in. "

"My word, child, but that's quite a party! I had better send out at once for a salmon, and two or three lobsters and some crabs. There's cream enough in the house, and eggs, and plenty of stuff in the garden for salads. Oh, I'll manage, I'll manage fine. I got in a couple of chickens and a pair of ducks this morning; I'll warrant that your grand friends have enough to eat, Trixie. But now I must go and have a talk with Jane. "

CHAPTER VIII.

NOBODY ELSE LOOKED THE LEAST LIKE THE BERTRAMS.

It was the fashion to be punctual at Northbury, and when Catherine, Mabel and Loftus Bertram arrived about ten minutes past seven at the Gray House they found the pleasant old drawing-room already full of eager and expectant guests.

Beatrice would have preferred meeting her new friends without any ceremony in the garden, but Mrs. Meadowsweet was nothing if she was not mistress of her own house, and she decided that it would be more becoming and *comme il faut* to wait in the drawing-room for the young visitors.

Accordingly Mrs. Meadowsweet sat in her chair of state. She wore a rose-colored silk dress, and a quantity of puffed white lace round her neck and wrists; and a cap which was tall and stiff, and had little tufts of yellow ribbon and little rosettes of Maltese lace adorning it, surmounted her large, full-blown face. That face was all beams and kindliness and good-temper, and had somehow the effect of making people forget whether Mrs. Meadowsweet was vulgar or not.

She sat in her chair of state facing the garden, and her visitors, all on the tip-toe of expectation, stationed themselves round her. The Bells had taken possession of the Chesterfield sofa. By sitting rather widely apart they managed to fill it; they always looked alike. To-night they so exactly resembled peas in a pod that one had a sense of ache and almost fatigue in watching them. This fatigue and irritation rose to desperation when they spoke. The Bells were poor, and their dresses bore decided signs of stint and poverty. They wore white muslin jackets, and pale green skirts of a shining substance known as mohair. Their mother fondly imagined that the shine and glitter of this fabric could not be known from silk. It was harsh, however, and did not lie in graceful folds, and besides, the poor little skirts lacked quantity.

The Bells had thin hair, and no knack whatever with regard to its arrangement. They looked unprepossessing girls, but no matter. Beatrice thought well of them. Mrs. Meadowsweet bestowed one or two broad glances of approval upon the inseparable little trio, and their own small hearts were dancing with expectation.

Would Bee, their darling, delightful, beautiful Bee, introduce them to Captain Bertram? Would he speak to them and smile upon them? Would he tell them stories of some of his gallant exploits? The Bells' round faces seemed to grow plumper, and their saucer eyes fuller, as they contemplated this contingency. What supreme bliss would be theirs if Captain Bertram singled them out for attention? Already they were in love with his name, and were quite ready to fall down in a phalanx of three, and worship the hero of many imaginary fights.

Standing by the open window, and with no shyness or stiffness whatever about them, Daisy and Polly Jenkins were to be seen. Daisy was a full-blown girl with a rather loud voice, and a manner which was by some considered very fascinating; for it had the effect of instantly taking you, as it were, behind the scenes, and into her innermost confidence.

Daisy was rather good-looking, and was the adored of Albert Bell, the little round-faced girls' brother. She was dressed in voluminous muslin draperies, and was a decidedly large and comfortable-looking young woman.

Polly was a second edition of her sister, only not so good-looking. She had made up her mind to marry Mr. Jones, the curate, who for his part was deeply in love with Beatrice.

"They are frightfully late, aren't they? " exclaimed Daisy Jenkins, giving a slight yawn, and looking longingly out at the tennis courts as she spoke. "I suppose it's the way with fashionable folk. For my part, I call it rude. Mrs. Meadowsweet, may I run across the garden, and pick a piece of sweet brier to put in the front of my dress? Somehow I pine for it. "

"I'll get it for you, " said Albert Bell, blushing crimson as he spoke.

He was a very awkward young man, but his heart was as warm as his manners were uncouth.

"I'll get it for you, Daisy, " he said. His dull eyes had not the power of shining or looking eloquent. He stepped from behind the sofa where his sisters sat, and stumbled over Mrs. Meadowsweet's footstool.

"I think, my dears, we'll just wait for our guests, " said the old lady. "We'll all just be present, please, when they come. It's my old-fashioned ideas, my loves, just for us all to be ready to give them a right-down, good welcome. "

"Bother! " exclaimed Miss Daisy. She flounced her full skirts, cast a withering glance at young Bell, and once more looked out of the open window.

"Come here, Beatrice, " exclaimed Polly.

Mr. Jones was talking to Beatrice, and Polly hoped they would both approach the window together.

"Come and tell us about that Adonis you went rowing with to-day, " called the girl in her shrill, half-jealous voice.

It was just at that moment that the door was flung open by Jane, and the Bertrams made their appearance.

Catherine and Mabel wore the simplest white washing-dresses. Their girlish waists were encircled by sashes of pale gold. Catherine's thick dark hair was coiled tightly round her head — Mabel's more frizzy and paler locks fell in wavy curls round her forehead and on her shoulders. Nobody else looked the least like the Bertrams. Their dresses were as cheap as any other girl's dresses in the room. Daisy and Polly Jenkins had really much handsomer and finer hair, but somehow the effect produced by the Bertrams was altogether different.

Mrs. Meadowsweet addressed them in a deferential tone as "Miss, " and it went like an electric flash through the minds of all the other visitors that the old lady was quite right when she thought it her duty to receive them in state.

Bertram was in flannels, and these were cut not exactly after the pattern of those worn by young Bell, who looked with a sort of despair at his true love, Daisy, whose eyes, in company with the three pairs of eyes of the Bells, were directed full upon the aristocratic face of Captain Bertram.

"Come into the garden, " said Beatrice, stepping forward in her usual bright way, forgetting herself completely, and in consequence putting every one else at their ease. "We are very punctual people at Northbury, " she continued, "and we are all wild to begin our game Captain Bertram, these are my friends, the Bells. May I introduce you? This is Miss Matty, and this is Miss Alice, and this is Miss Sophy. Matty, I put Captain Bertram into your charge. Albert, " she continued, looking at young Bell, "will you and Daisy arrange a set for tennis? "

How Albert Bell did bless Beatrice! In a moment or two all the visitors were perambulating about the garden. Mr. Jones was escorted on one side by Polly Jenkins, on the other, he, in his turn, tried to escort Mabel Bertram, who did not talk a great deal and seemed somewhat out of her element. Catherine and Beatrice walked together, and Mrs. Meadowsweet, still sitting in her arm-chair, smiled as she saw them.

"That's a nice girl, and a fine looking girl, " she murmured, "and very good company for my Bee. Very good company for her. Yes, the Bertrams are stylish but not of our set. My word, not a bit of our set. Bee, of course, might talk to anybody, but the rest of us—no, no, I'm the first to see the fitness of things, and the Bertrams don't belong to us nor we to them. Bee takes after her father, poor man, but the rest of us, we have no right to know the Bertrams. Now, do look at that young captain. Why, he's making the little Bells laugh themselves into fits. Dear me, I'd better go out. These girls don't know manners, and their heads will be turned by that fine young spark. They are certain to believe any rubbish he talks to them. "

Mrs. Meadowsweet rose with difficulty, stepped out of the open window, and sailed in her rose-colored satin across the grass.

"Now, what's up? " she said. "Fie, fie, Matty, your laugh is for all the world like a hen cackling. "

"He, he! " exclaimed the younger girls.

"Now, there you are off again, and all three of you this time! "

"It's Captain Bertram, ma'am, " began Matty.

"Captain Bertram! " echoed Alice.

"Bertram, " sighed Sophy.

"He says, " continued Matty, "that we are all alike, and he doesn't know one from the other, and we are trying to puzzle him. It is such delicious fun. "

"Delicious fun! " said Alice.

"Fun! " gasped Sophy, through her peals of mirth.

"Now, " continued Alice, "he shall begin again. He shall go through his catechism. Here we three stand in a row. Which is Matty, which is Alice, which is Sophy? "

Captain Bertram pulled his mustache, swept his dark eyes over the little eager palpitating group, and in a languid tone pronounced the wrong one to be Matty.

The cackling rose to a shriek.

"You shall pay a forfeit, you bad man, " said the real Matty. She shook her little fat finger at him. "Oh, yes, Mrs. Meadowsweet, he really shall—he *must*. This really is too sweetly delicious, —fancy his not knowing me from Alice—I call it ungallant. Now what shall the forfeit be, Alice and Sophy. Let's put our fingers on our lips and think. "

"He shall tell us, " exclaims Alice, "he shall describe at full length his—"

She looked at her sisters.

"His first battle, " prompted Matty.

"No, no, better than that, better than that—" came from Sophy's girlish lips. "Captain Bertram shall tell us about his—his first love. "

It may have been rude, but at this remark Captain Bertram not only changed color but turned in a very marked way from the Misses Bell, and devoted himself to his hostess.

He was attacked by a complaint somewhat in vogue in high life—he had a sudden fit of convenient deafness. He said a few words in a cold voice to Mrs. Meadowsweet, crushed the little Bells by his icy manner, and took the first opportunity of finding more congenial society.

An eager game of tennis was going on, and Beatrice, who did not play, stood by to watch. Northbury was accustomed to Beatrice, and did not therefore observe, what was very patent to Captain Bertram, that this girl was as perfectly well-bred as his own sisters. She wore a long, gray cashmere dress, slightly open at her throat, with ruffles of soft, real lace.

As she watched the game, her sensitive and speaking face showed interest, sympathy, keen appreciation. She heard Captain Bertram's step, and turned to welcome him with a smile.

"Would not you like to play? "

"Will you be my partner? "

"When they make up a fresh set I will, with pleasure; although, " she added, looking down at her long dress, "I did not expect to play to-night, and did not dress for it. "

"Thank goodness. I hate tennis dresses. All girls should wear trains. "

Beatrice raised her bright eyes to his face. Their open expression said plainly, "It is a matter of indifference to me what you think about my dress. " Aloud she said:

"What have you done with my friends, the Bells? "

"I am afraid, Miss Meadowsweet, that long intercourse with those young ladies would be too severe a strain on my intellect. "

"Captain Bertram, you don't mean what you are saying. "

"I do, on my honor. They are too intellectual for me. "

"They are not! You are laughing at them. "

Beatrice stepped back a pace, and looked at him with a heightened color coming into her face.

Captain Bertram began to explain. Before he could get in a word she said, abruptly:

"Pardon me, " and flew from his side.

Her movement was so fleet and sudden that he had not realized her departure before the impulsive girl was standing by the despised Matty, talking to her in a cheery and affectionate voice, and making fresh arrangements for the pleasure and satisfaction of all three.

"By Jove, she's a fine creature! " thought the captain. "I don't mind how much I see of her—but as to the rest of this motley herd, my mother is quite right in not letting the girls have anything to do with them. I suppose I put my foot in it bringing them here to-night. Well, that can't be helped now. I hope Miss Beatrice will soon come back. Her eyes flashed when I said even a word against those terrible little friends of hers. I should like her eyes to flash at me again. I suppose she'll soon return. She promised to be my partner in the next set at tennis. That girl doesn't care a bit for fine speeches. She won't take a compliment even when it is offered to her—won't stretch out her hand for it or touch it. Cool? I should think she is cool. Might have been through two or three London seasons. What a queer lot surround her! And how unlike them she is. There's the old mother— I had better go and talk to her. She's quite as vulgar as the rest, but somehow she doesn't jar on a man's nerves like those charming Miss Bells. Positively, I should have a fever if I talked much longer to them. My first love, too! I'm to tell them about *her*. Oh, yes, that's so likely. "

Again the angry flame mounted to Captain Bertram's thin cheek. He strolled across the grass, and joined his hostess.

"Now I call this a shame! " exclaimed the good lady, "you don't tell me that you are all by yourself, captain, and no one trying to make themselves agreeable to you! Oh, fie! this will never do—and you, so to speak, the lion of the party. "

"Pray don't say that, Mrs. Meadowsweet, I hate being a lion. "

"But you can't help it, my good young sir. You, who represent our Gracious Sovereign Lady's Army. Now, where's that girl of mine? Beatrice! Trixie! Bee! "

Captain Bertram was amazed at the shrill and far-sounding quality of Mrs. Meadowsweet's voice. It distressed him, for anything not ultra refined jarred upon this sensitive young officer's nerves; but he trusted that the result would be satisfactory, and that Beatrice, whose motions he began to liken to a poem, would put in a speedy appearance.

She was talking to Mr. Jones, however, and when her mother called her, she and the curate approached together.

"Beatrice, this poor young man—Captain Bertram, the hero of the evening, is all alone. Not a soul to amuse him or entertain him. "

"Mother, you mistake, " answered Beatrice, "Captain Bertram is being entertained by you. "

"Hoots, child! What should an old lady have to say to a gay young lad? "

"Plenty, I assure you. I am being delightfully amused, " replied the captain.

He gave Beatrice an angry look which she would not see.

"I want to talk to Jane about the supper, " said the young lady in a calm voice. "Captain Bertram, may I introduce you to Mr. Jones? "

Again she flew lightly away, and the captain owned to himself that the tennis party at the Gray House was a very dull affair.

Supper, however, made amends for much. The incongruous elements were not so apparent. Everybody was hungry, and even the most fastidious had to acknowledge the fare of the best. Captain Bertram quite retrieved his character in Beatrice Meadowsweet's eyes, so well did he help her in serving her guests. Matty, Alice and Sophy Bell forgave him for his abrupt departure earlier in the evening from the charms of their society, when he helped them each twice to lobster salad.

Captain Bertram was not at all averse to the charms of a small flirtation. He was forced to remain for a few days in the remote little world-forgotten town of Northbury, and it occurred to him as he helped the Bells to lobster salad, and filled up Miss Matty's glass more than once with red currant wine, that Beatrice could solace him a good deal during his exile from a gayer life. He was absolutely certain at the present moment that the best way to restore himself to her good graces was once again to endure the intellectual strain of the Bells' society. Accordingly when supper was over, and people with one consent, and all, as it were, moved by a sudden impulse, joined first in a country dance, then formed into sets for quadrilles, and finally waltzed away to the old-fashioned sound of Mrs. Meadowsweet's piano, played with vigor by the good lady herself, Captain Bertram, with a beseeching and deprecatory glance at Beatrice, who took care not to see it, led out Miss Matty Bell as his partner.

How much that young lady giggled! How badly she danced — with what rapture she threw up her round eyes at her partner's dark face, this chronicle need not record; so *naïve* was she, into such ecstasies did every word spoken by the captain throw her, that he quite feared for the result.

"It is awful when a girl falls in love in five minutes! " he mentally soliloquized. "I wonder if I have satisfied Miss Meadowsweet now? I do honestly think I have done my duty by Miss Matty Bell. "

So he conveyed the gushing young person back to her sisters, and sought for Beatrice who was once more frank and friendly, but gave him excellent reasons for not dancing with him.

At this moment Catherine came up and touched her brother. Her cheeks had a bright color in them, she looked animated and happy.

"Loftus, it is close on twelve o'clock. We must go home. Look at Mabel, " she added, seeing her brother hesitate, "she is frightfully sleepy. Mother never allows her to be up so late. We have had a happy evening, " continued Catherine, looking full into Miss Meadowsweet's face, "and we are very much obliged to you. Now I must go and say good-night to your mother. "

She tripped away, and Beatrice looked after her with affectionate eyes.

"It is unkind of you not to give me one dance, " said the captain.

She had forgotten his presence.

"It is not unkind, " she said. "The dancing is altogether an impromptu affair, and I had to attend to my guests. I was talking to your sister, Catherine, who did not care to dance. "

"Very ungenerous to me, " pursued the captain. "A poor return for all my efforts to please you. "

"Your efforts—pray, what efforts? "

"Did you not observe me with your friend, Miss Matty Bell? I assure you she and I are now excellent friends. "

"I do not suppose in my mother's house you would be anything else, Captain Bertram. "

Her tone irritated the captain. His manner changed.

"Do you think I *wanted* to dance with her? "

"I don't think about it. Here is your sister. I will help you to find your wraps, Catherine. "

She linked her hand through Catherine Bertram's arm, and went with her into the hall. A few moments later the brother and sisters were walking quickly home.

"So you have come to Christian names already, Catherine, " said Loftus.

"Yes, " replied Catherine. "She is the very dearest girl. Have we not had a delightful evening? "

"Delightful, truly. How did you enjoy yourself, Mab? "

"Middling, " replied Mabel. "I was with Mr. Jones, and he talked about vestments, and deplored the Rector's decision against High Church practices. He thought we were kindred souls, but we weren't, and I told him so. Then he turned crusty. I waltzed twice with Mr. Bell, and he kicked my ankle, and hurt me very much. I don't think I cared much for the party, Catherine, the people were so queer. "

"Were they? " answered Catherine. "I didn't notice anything the matter with them. I talked for a short time with Mrs. Meadowsweet, and found her most interesting. She told me a lot about Beatrice. She thinks Beatrice the noblest creature in the world. As I very nearly agreed with her we got on capitally. "

"What a romantic puss you are, Kate, " said her brother.

She was leaning on him, and he gave her arm a playful pinch.

"You met Miss Meadowsweet on Tuesday, wasn't it? This is Friday, and she is the 'very dearest girl in the world, ' and already you are Catherine and Beatrice to one another. Upon my word, hearts move rapidly towards each other in certain quarters. "

"In more quarters than one, " replied Kate, with an arch smile. "How you did flatter that poor little Miss Bell, Loftie. Her cheeks were like peonies while you talked to her. You certainly had an air of great tenderness, and I expect you have turned the poor little thing's head. "

"Yes, Loftus, " interrupted Mabel. "I remarked you, too, with Miss Bell. What a little fright she is—I never could have supposed she was in your style. "

"Good gracious, " began Loftus, "you didn't think—"

But Catherine in her sedate voice interrupted him.

"Beatrice and I were watching you. I laughed when I saw that expression of tenderness filling your glorious dark eyes, but I think Bee was vexed. "

"Vexed? No, Kate, surely not vexed? "

"I think so, Loftus. She said to me—'I hope your brother is not laughing at my little friend, Matty Bell. ' Then she added, 'I know Matty is not beautiful nor specially attractive, but she has the kindest heart. ' I said perhaps you were flirting, and that I knew you could flirt. She did not make any answer, only she looked grave, and turned away when you and Miss Bell came near us. "

"That accounts, " began Loftus. He did not explain himself further and by-and-by the little party reached the Manor.

There was an old tumble-down lodge at the gates. It was inhabited by a very poor man, who, for the sake of getting a shelter over his head, now and then undertook to clean up and do odd jobs in the Rosendale gardens. Mrs. Bertram thought it well to have some one in the lodge, and she was pleased with the economical arrangement she had made with David Tester.

One of his duties was to lock the old gates at night. There was a small and a large gate leading into the avenue, and it was one of Mrs. Bertram's special whims that both should be locked at night. Old Tester thought his mistress foolishly particular on this point, and wondered at so close a lady going to the expense of new locks, which were sent down from London, and were particularly good and expensive.

The small gate was furnished with a latch-lock as well. This arrangement was made for Tester's convenience, so that if Mrs. Bertram and her daughters chose to be absent from home a little later than usual, he could still close the gate and go to bed.

When the girls and their brother left home that evening Catherine had not forgotten the latch-key.

"We may be late, " she said, "so I will put it in my pocket. "

They were late, and as they approached the old gates Catherine gave the key to Mabel, who hastened to fit it into the lock of the side gate.

To her surprise it opened at a touch.

"Kate! " exclaimed the young girl, "Tester has been very careless; he has never closed the side gate. "

"I will call him up and speak to him now, " said Catherine, who had a certain touch of her mother's imperious nature. "He shall do it now. Mother is always most particular about the gates, and she ought not to be disobeyed in her absence. "

Catherine was running across the avenue to wake old Tester when Loftus laid his hand on her arm.

"You really are too absurd, Kitty, " he said. "I simply won't allow that poor, infirm, old man to be got out of his bed for such a ridiculous reason. Who cares whether the gates are locked, or not locked? "

"Mother cares, " said Catherine, her eyes flashing.

"Now, Kate, you must use your common-sense. That fad about locking the gates is a pure and simple whim on the mother's part. Of course we'll humor it, but not to the extent of waking up old Tester. Come, Kitty, you shall give the old man any amount of blowing up in the morning, only now you really must leave him alone. "

"I'm going on, " said Mabel; "I can scarcely keep my eyes open. Will you come with me, Loftie? If Kate likes to stay by herself with the dark trees and the ghosts, why, let her. I'm off to bed. "

She ran laughing and singing up the old avenue.

Loftus turned to resume his argument with Catherine, Mabel's gay voice echoed more faintly as she ran on. Suddenly it stopped. Patter, patter, came back the swift feet, and, trembling and shivering, she threw herself into Loftus's arms.

"I heard something—there's something in the avenue! "

The moon was shining, and showed Mabel's face as white as a sheet.

"You silly child, " said Loftus, "you heard a rabbit scuttling home. Here, take my arm, and let us all get home as fast as we can. Why, you are trembling from head to foot. You are tired out, that's it. Take her other arm, will you, Kate? "

"They say Rosendale is haunted, " panted Mabel.

"Folly! Don't listen to such rubbish. Your rabbit was hurrying to bed, and was as much afraid of you as you of it. "

"It—it wasn't a rabbit, " said Mabel. "Rabbits don't sigh. "

"Oh—sighs only belong to ghosts? "

"I don't know. Don't laugh at me, Loftie. I heard a real sigh and a rustle, and something white flashed. "

"Then you flashed back to us. Never talk of being a brave girl again, May. "

"Let us walk very quickly, " said Mabel. "It was just there I saw it. Just by that great clump of Lauristinus. Don't let us speak. There, that's better. I own I'm frightened, Loftie. You needn't laugh at me. "

Loftus Bertram had many faults, but he was not ill-natured. He took Mabel's little cold hand, and pressed it between his warm fingers, and ceased to laugh at her, and walked quickly, and was even silent at her bidding. By degrees, Mabel leaned all her weight on Loftus, and took no notice of Kate, who, for her part, held herself erect, and walked up the avenue with a half-aggrieved, half-scornful look on her face, and with some anxiety in her heart.

CHAPTER IX.

THE GHOST IN THE AVENUE.

Rosendale Manor had heaps of rooms. It was an old house, added to at many times; added to by builders, who had little or no knowledge of their craft, who were prodigal of space, and illiberal in all matters of convenience.

The Manor was the sort of house which might best be described as inadequate for the wants of ordinary people. For instance, its drawing-rooms were large out of all proportion, whereas its dining-room, morning-room and library were ridiculously small. It had a spacious hall and wide landings, but its stairs were steep and narrow, and there was not even one decent-sized bedroom in the house. All the rooms had low ceilings and were small. Their only virtue was that there were such a number of them.

Catherine and Mabel liked the bedrooms at the Manor, because being rather distinct in their tastes, and decidedly given to quarrel over the arrangements of their separate properties, it was impossible for them to sleep together. Each girl had a room of her own, and these rooms did not even touch, for Mabel slept near her mother, and Catherine away in a wing by herself. This wing could only be reached by a spiral staircase, and was pronounced by the timid Mabel to be odiously lonely.

Catherine, however, knew no fears, and enjoyed the privacy of her quaint little bedroom with its sloping roof and lattice window.

She bade her brother and sister good-night, and went up to it, now.

"You'll go to bed at once, won't you, Kitty? " said Mabel, whose eyes were half-shut. "Perhaps it *was* only a rabbit I heard. Only why did it flash white, and why did it sigh? Well, I won't think of it any more. Good-night, Kitty, how wide awake you look. "

Catherine kissed her sister and sought her distant chamber. She waited until all was silent in the house, then slowly and cautiously she unbarred her door and went downstairs.

The Honorable Miss: A Story of an Old-Fashioned Town

In the large square entrance hall she took a white shawl from a stand. She hung it across her arm, and still walking very softly reached the hall door, drew back its bolts, removed its chain, opened it, and went out into the porch.

Her mother had stood in that porch two nights fgo. Catherine thought of her now. The remembrance of her mother's face caused her to sigh and shiver as if she had been struck with sudden cold. Leaving the hall door ajar she wrapped the white shawl about her shoulders, and then walked a little way across the wide gravel sweep in front of the house.

Her footsteps crunched the gravel, but her brother and sister slept in distant bedrooms and could hear nothing. The moon was riding full and high in the heavens, and its reflection caused intense light and dark shadows. Catherine's own shadow stalked heavy and immense by her side.

She walked a little way down the avenue, listening intently. Even the crunching of the gravel disturbed her, so she stepped on the grass, and walked noiselessly on its velvet path.

Suddenly she stopped, threw up her head, flung her shawl off, and with a movement quick as lightning, put out her hand and caught something.

She was holding a girl's slender and round arm. She drew her forward, pushed back her somewhat tawdry hat, and looked into her face.

"What are you doing here? What is your name? Speak at once. Tell me the truth. "

The girl had queer, half-wild eyes. She looked down and began to mutter something indistinct. The next instant she went on her knees, caught Catherine's white dress and pressed it to her lips.

"Don't, " said Miss Bertram, with a movement both of decision and repulsion. "You aren't even clean. Don't touch my dress. What are you doing here? "

70

"I have travelled a long way. I am only dirty because I am travel-sore. I have come to see the lady, your mother. I have come from far to see her. I have a message for her. Is she at home? "

"Would she see you, if she were at home, at this hour? Tell me your name first, and then go away. You cannot see my mother. "

"You are Miss Bertram, are you not? "

"Yes—and Rosendale Manor is my home. It is not yours. Go away. Never come back here again. You are not to see my mother. "

The girl rose to her feet. Her dress was dirty, her face was begrimed with the dirt of travel, but Catherine noticed that the dress was whole, not patched anywhere, also that her accent was pure, and almost refined.

"Miss Bertram, " she said, "I must see the lady, your mother. I have an important message for her; I am not a spy, and I don't come in any unkindness, but I must see the lady who lives here, and who is your mother. I have waited for hours in the avenue, hours and hours. I will wait until morning. The nights are not cold, and I shall do very well. Let me see your mother then. "

"You cannot. She is from home. It was you then, who bribed Tester to keep the lodge gate open? "

"I gave the man a shilling. Yes, I confess it. I am doing no harm here. Put yourself in my place. "

"How dare you? How can you? " said Catherine, stepping away from the travel-stained figure.

"Ah, you are very proud, but there's a verse of Scripture that fits you. 'Let him that thinketh he standeth take heed lest he fall. ' I know your age—you are just seventeen, I'm only nineteen, just two years older than you. You have no feeling for me. Suppose I had none for you? "

The refinement of the girl's voice became more and more apparent to Catherine. There was a thrill and a quality in it which both repelled and fascinated. This queer waif and stray, this vagabond of the woodside, was at least as fearless as herself.

"I don't know what you mean, " she said, in a less imperious tone than she had hitherto used.

"I could explain what I mean, but I won't. I have too kind a heart to crush you. I could crush you. I could take that dainty white hand of yours, and feel it tremble in mine—and if you knew all that I could say you wouldn't leave me out here in the avenue, but you'd take me in, and give me the best to eat, and the softest bed to lie upon. Don't you think it's very kind of me when I could use such power over you that I don't use it? Don't you think it's noble of me? Oh, you are a dainty girl, and a proud, but I could bring you and yours to the very dust. "

"You must be mad, " said Catherine. "Absolutely mad. How can you possibly expect me to listen to this wild nonsense? You had better go away now. I'll walk with you as far as the gate, and then I'll wake up Tester to lock it after you. You needn't suppose that I'm afraid. "

"Don't taunt me, " said the girl. "If you do I'll use my power. Oh, I am hungry, and thirsty, and footsore. Why shouldn't I go into that house and sleep there, and eat there, and be rested? "

Her words were defiant, but just at the last they wavered, and Catherine saw by the moonlight that her face grew ghastly under its grimness, and she saw the slender young figure sway as if it would fall.

"You are hungry? " said Catherine, all her feelings merged in sudden pity. "Even though you have no right to be here, you sha'n't go hungry away. Sit down. Rest against that tree, and I will fetch you something. "

She ran into the house, returning presently with a jug of milk, and some thick bread and butter.

"Eat that, " she said, "and drink this milk, then you will be better. I slipped a cup into my pocket. It is not broken. I will pour you out a cup of milk. "

The girl seized the bread and butter, and began devouring it. She was so famished that she almost tore it as she ate. Catherine, who had quite forgotten her dignified r'le in compassion for the first real hunger she had ever witnessed, knelt on the grass by her side, and once, twice, thrice, filled the cup full of milk, and held it to her lips.

"Now you are better, " she said, when the meal had come to an end.

"Yes, thank you, Miss Bertram, much better. The horrible sinking is gone, and the ground doesn't seem to reel away when I look at it. Thank you, Miss Catherine Bertram, I shall do nicely now. I do not at all mind sleeping here on the cool grass till the morning. "

"But you are not to stay. Why are you obstinate when I am good to you? And why do you call me Miss Catherine Bertram? How can you possibly know my name? "

The girl laughed. Her laugh was almost cheerful, it was also young and silvery.

"You ask me a lot of questions, " she said. "I'll answer them one by one, and the least important first. How I know your name is my own secret; I can't tell that without telling also what would crush you. But I may as well say that I know all about you. I know your appearance, and your age, and even a little bit about your character; and I know you have a younger sister called Mabel, and that she is not so pretty as you, and has not half the character, and in short that you are worth two of her.

"Then you have a brother. His name is Loftus. He is like you, only he is not so fearless. He is in the army. He is rather extravagant, and your mother is afraid of him. Ah, yes, I know all about you and yours; and I know so much in especial about that proud lady, your mother, that if there were daylight, and I had pencil and paper, I could draw a portrait of her for you. There, have I not answered your first question? Now you want to know why I don't go away. If you had no money in your purse, and if you had walked between twenty and thirty miles to effect an object of the greatest possible importance to yourself, would you give it up at the bidding of a young girl? Would you now? "

"You are very queer, " said Catherine; "I fail to understand you. I don't know how you have got your extraordinary knowledge about us. You talk like a lady, but ladies don't starve with hunger, nor walk until they are travel-sore and spent. Ladies don't hide at midnight in shrubberies, in private grounds that don't belong to them. Then you say you have no money, and yet you gave Tester a shilling. "

"I gave him my last shilling. Here is my empty purse. Look at it. "

"Well, you are very, very queer. You have not even told me your name. "

"Josephine. I am called Josephine. "

"But you have another name. I am called Catherine, but I am also Bertram. What are you besides Josephine? "

"Ah, that's trenching into the darkness where you wouldn't like to find yourself. That's light for me, but dark ruin for you. Don't ask me what my other name is. "

"Listen, " said Catherine, suddenly, "you want to see my mother? "

"Yes, I certainly want to see her. "

"Listen again. I am absolutely determined that you shall not see her. "

"But I have a message for her. "

"You shall not see her. My mother is not well. I stand between my mother and trouble. I know you are going to bring her trouble; and you shall not see her. "

"How can you prevent me? "

"In this way. My mother is away from home. I will take care that she does not return until you have left this place. I am determined. "

"Is that true? " asked the girl. "Is she really away from home? "

"Am I likely to tell you a lie? My mother is from home. "

The strange girl had been sitting on the grass. Now she rose, pushed back her thick hair, and fixed her eyes on Catherine. Catherine again noticed the singular brightness, the half-wild light in her eyes. Suddenly it was quenched by great tears. They splashed down on her cheeks, and made clean channels where the dust had lain.

"I am deadly tired, " she said, with a half moan.

"Listen, Josephine, " said Catherine. "You shall not spend your night here. You shall not stay to see my mother. I will take you down to the lodge and wake up Tester, and his wife shall get a bed ready for you, and you shall sleep there, and in the morning you are to go away. You can have breakfast before you start, but afterwards you are to go away. Do you promise me? Do you agree to this? "

The girl muttered something, and Catherine took her hand and led her down to the lodge.

CHAPTER X.

THE REASON OF THE VISIT.

On the evening of the next day Mrs. Bertram came home. She looked very tired and worn, but her manner to her children was less stern, and more loving than usual. Loftus, in especial, she kissed with rare tenderness; and even for one brief moment laid her head on her tall son's broad shoulder, as if she wanted to rest herself there.

On the evening of her mother's return Catherine was particularly bright and cheerful. As a rule, Catherine's will and her mother's were two opposing elements. Now they were one. This conjunction of two strong wills gave an immense sense of rest and harmony to the whole establishment. No one knew particularly why they felt peaceful and satisfied, but this was the true cause.

After dinner, Mrs. Bertram saw Catherine by herself. She called her into the big drawing-room; and while Loftus and Mabel accurately measured out a new tennis-court, asked her daughter many and various questions.

"She has really gone away, mother, " said Catherine in conclusion. "I went to the lodge early this morning, and Tester told me that she got up early, and took a bit of bread in her pocket; but she would not even wait for a cup of tea. Tester said she was out of the house by six o'clock. She washed herself well first, though, and Mrs. Tester said that she came out of her bath as fair as a lily, and her hair shining like red gold. I thought last night, mother, " concluded Catherine, "that Josephine must be a pretty girl. I should like to have seen her this morning when her hair shone and her face was like a lily. "

"You are full of curiosity about this girl, are you not, Catherine? " asked her mother.

"It is true, mother. I conjecture much about her. "

"I can never gratify your curiosity, nor set your conjectures right. "

"You know about her then, mother? "

"Yes, I know about her. "

"Is Josephine an impostor? "

Mrs. Bertram paused.

"She is an impostor, " she said then, in a slow, emphatic voice.

"Mother, " said her daughter, suddenly. "You look very ill. "

"I have gone through a bad time, Kate. I have been worried. My dear child, be thankful you are not a middle-aged woman with many cares. "

"The thing I should be most thankful for at this moment, mother, would be to share in all your worries. "

"God forbid, child. Heaven forbid that such a lot should be yours. Now, my dear, we will keep our secret. It is only yours and mine. And—come here—kiss me—you have acted well, my darling. "

The rare caress, the unwonted word of love, went straight to Catherine Bertram's deep heart. She put her firm young arm round her mother's neck, and something like a vow and a prayer went up to God from her fervent soul.

"Come out, " said Mrs. Bertram. "The others will wonder what we are doing. Look as usual, Kitty, and fear nothing. I have been in peril, but for the present it is over. "

When Mrs. Bertram appeared Loftus went up to her at once. She took his arm, and they paced slowly under the trees. If Mrs. Bertram loved her daughters, and there is no doubt she had a very real regard for them, Loftus Bertram was as the apple of her eye. She adored this young man, she was blind to his faults, and she saw his virtues through magnifying glasses.

Loftus could always talk his mother into the best of humors. He was not devoid of tact, and he knew exactly how to manage her, so as to bring her round to his wishes. Having two ends in view to-night he was more than usually fascinating. He wanted money to relieve a pressing embarrassment, and he also wished to cultivate his acquaintance with Beatrice Meadowsweet. He was not absolutely in love with Beatrice, but her cool indifference to all his fascinations piqued him. He thought it would be pleasant to see more of her, delightful to make a conquest of her. He was not the sort of man to thwart his own inclinations. Beatrice had contrived to make Northbury interesting to him, and he thought he could easily manage to get leave to visit it soon again.

That evening, therefore, Mrs. Bertram not only found herself arranging to put her hand to a bill, payable at the end of six months, for her son's benefit, but further, quite complacently agreeing to call the very next day on Mrs. Meadowsweet, the wife of the ex-shopkeeper.

Hence that visit which had aroused the jealous feelings not only of Mrs. Morris, of Mrs, Butler and Miss Peters, but more or less of the whole society of Northbury.

CHAPTER XI.

SOMEBODY ADMIRED SOMEBODY.

"Then, if that's the case, " said Mrs. Bell, "if that's really and truly the case, and no mistake about it, Matty must have some new frocks made up for her at once. I have no idea of a child of mine looking shabby or behind any one else, but you must tell me truly, Alice, if he really was attentive. Bless you, child, you know what I mean. Was there any hand-squeezing, and was he always and forever making an excuse to have a look at her. No one could have been more genteel than your father during courtship, but the way his eyes did follow me wherever I turned, over and over put me to the blush. "

"Don't say anything to Matty, " responded Alice Bell. "She'll be sure to giggle awfully when next they meet, if you do. She can't keep anything in, and she owned to Sophy and me that he had got her heart. Well, yes, I suppose he was particular with her. He danced with her, and he looked at her, only, I do think it was *she* squeezed *his* hand. "

"Oh, fie, Alice, to say such things of your sister. Well, anyhow the town is full of it. When I went out yesterday Mrs. Morris asked me point-blank if I hadn't news for her, and Miss Peters has taken so frightfully to rolling her eyes whenever Matty and Captain Bertram are seen together, that I'm quite afraid she will contract a regular squint. How long was he with Matty on the green last night, Alice? "

"About half-an-hour, I should say, " responded Alice. "They walked round the Green five times, with me and Sophy doing gooseberry behind. I don't think Matty stopped laughing for a single minute, and the captain he did quiz her frightfully. "

"Poor man, he was trying to wheedle her heart out of her! " remarked the gratified mother. "And he has all my sympathies, and what's more, we must have him to supper, and lobsters and crabs, and anything else he fancies. It isn't for me to be hard-hearted, and not give the poor fellow his opportunities; and no doubt Matty will relent by-and-bye. "

"Oh, dear me, mother, she has relented now. She's only waiting and dying for him to pop the question. "

"If I were you, Alice, I wouldn't make so light of your own sister. Of course she is gratified by being spoken to and appreciated, but if you think a girl of mine is going to let herself down cheap—well, she'll be very different metal from her mother before her. Three times Bell had to go on his knees for me, and he thought all the more of me for having to do it. If I'm not mistaken, there are some in this town who are jealous of Matty. Who would have thought that handsome friend of yours, Bee Meadowsweet, would be looked over and made nothing of, and my girl be the favored one? Well, I must own I'm pleased, and so will her father be, too. It's a nice genteel connection, and they say there's lots of money somewhere in the background. — Oh, is that you, Matty? —Goodness, child, don't get your face so burnt, —you shouldn't go out without a veil in the sun. Now come here, pet, sit down and keep cool, and I'll bring in some buttermilk presently to bathe your neck and cheeks. There's nothing like buttermilk for burns. Well, well, what were we talking about, Alice, when Matty came in? "

"About the person we're always talking about, " replied Alice, rather crossly. "About Captain Bertram. Good gracious, Matty, it isn't at all becoming to you to flame up in that sudden way. Lor' ma, look at her, she's the color of a peony. "

[It may be remarked in passing that the Bells did not echo one another when at home.]

"Never mind, never mind, " retorted Mrs. Bell, who, with true delicacy, would not look at her blushing daughter.

"I was thinking Matty, my love, that you wanted a new evening dress. I don't like you to be behind any one else, my dear, and that green skirt with the white jacket, though genteel enough, doesn't seem quite the thing. I can't tell what's the matter with it, for the mohair in the skirts cost nine-pence half-penny a yard, and the first day you wore those dresses, girls, they shone as if they were silk, and your father asked me why I was so extravagant, and said that though he would like it he hadn't money to dress you up in silk attire. Poor Bell has a turn for poetry, and if he had not lost his money through the badness of the coal trade, he'd make you look like *three poems*, that's what he said to me. Well, well, somehow the dresses are handsome, and yet I don't like them. "

"They're hideous, " said Matty, kicking out her foot with a petulant movement. "Somehow, those home-made dresses never look right. They don't sit properly. We weren't a bit like the other girls at Mrs. Meadowsweet's a fortnight ago. "

"No, " said Alice, "we weren't. The Bertrams had nothing but full skirts and baby bodies, and sashes round their waists, just like little girls. Mabel Bertram's dress was only down to her ankles—nothing could have been plainer—no style at all, and yet we didn't look like them. "

"Well, " said the mother, bristling and bridling, "handsome dresses or not, *somebody* admired *somebody* at that party, or I'm greatly mistaken. Well, Matty dear, what would you fancy for evening wear? If my purse will stand it you shall have it. I won't have you behind no one, my love. "

It was at this critical moment, when Matty's giggles prevented her speaking, and Alice was casting some truly sarcastic and sisterly shafts at her, that Sophy burst open the door, and announced, in an excited voice, that Mrs. Middlemass, the pedler, had just stepped into the hall.

"She has got some lovely things to-day, " exclaimed Sophy. "Shall we have her up, mamma? Have we anything to exchange? "

"It's only a week since she was here, " replied Mrs. Bell. "And she pretty nearly cleared us out then. Still it would be a comfort if we could squeeze a frock for Matty out of her. I could buy the trimmings easy enough for you, Matty, at Perry's, if I hadn't to pay for the stuff. Dear, dear, now what can we exchange? Look here, Sophy, run, like a good child, to your father's wardrobe, and see if there are a couple of pairs of old trousers gone at the knees, and maybe that great-coat of his that had one of the flaps torn, and the patch on the left sleeve. It was warm, certainly, but it always was a show, that great-coat. Maybe he wouldn't miss it, or at any rate he'd give it up to help to settle Matty. "

"Lor, ma, I really do think you are indelicate, when the man hasn't even proposed! " exclaimed Alice. "There's Matty, she's off giggling again. I do believe she'll soon laugh day and night without stopping. "

"Are we to have Mrs. Middlemass up or not, mother? " exclaimed Sophy.

"Yes, child, yes. Bring her up by all means. We'll contrive to make some sort of a bargain with her. "

Sophy disappeared, and a moment or two later she ushered Mrs. Middlemass into the bedroom where the above conversation had taken place.

The pedler was a very stout person, with a red face, and the bundle which she carried in front of her and propelled first into the room, was of enormous dimensions.

"Good-day, Mrs. Bell, " she said. "Good-day, young ladies. And what may I have the pleasure of serving you with to-day, Mrs. Bell? I've got some elegant goods with me, just the style for your beautiful young ladies. "

With this speech, which was uttered with great gravity, Mrs. Middlemass proceeded to open her bundle, and to exhibit the worst muslin, cashmere, French merino, and other fabrics, which she offered for the highest price.

"There, " she said, "there's a cashmere for you! Feel it between your finger and thumb, Mrs. Bell, mum, there's substance, there's quality. It would make up lovely. Shall I cut a length a-piece for the three young ladies, ma'am? "

"No, no, " said Mrs. Bell, "that cashmere is dark and heavy, and coarse, too. I don't expect it's all-wool. It's shoddy, that's what it is. "

"Shoddy, ma'am! That a lady whom I've served faithful for years should accuse me of selling shoddy! No, Mrs. Bell, may Heaven forgive you for trying to run down a poor widow's goods. This is as pure all-wool cashmere as is to be found in the market, and dirt cheap at three and elevenpence a-yard. Have a length for yourself, ma'am; it would stylish you up wonderful. "

"No, " said Mrs. Bell, "I don't want a dress to-day, and that cashmere isn't worth more than one and six. What we are wishing for—though I don't know that we really *want* anything—do we, girls? But what we might buy, if you had it very cheap, is a bit of something light and airy that would make up very elegantly for the evening. Do you care to have another evening-dress, Matty? I know you have a good few in your wardrobe. "

"I don't know, " said Matty, "until I see what Mrs. Middlemass has. I don't want anything common. I can get common things at Perry's; and perhaps I had better send for my best dress to London, ma. "

This remark of giggling Miss Matty's was really astute for she knew that Mrs. Middlemass held Perry, the draper, in the most sovereign contempt.

"Right you are, my dear, " said the pedler, a smile of gratified vanity spreading over her face, "you *can* get your common things, and very common things they'll be, at Perry's. But maybe old Auntie Middlemass can give you something as genteel as the London shops. You look here, my pretty. Now, then. "

Here Mrs. Middlemass went on her knees, and with slow and exasperating deliberation, unfastened a parcel carefully done up in white muslin. From the depths of this parcel she extracted a very thin and crackling silk of a shade between brick and terra-cotta, which was further shot here and there with little threads of pale blue and yellow. This texture she held up in many lights, not praising it by any words, for she guessed well the effect it would have on her company. She knew the Bells of old: they were proof against anything that wasn't silk, but at the glitter and sheen of real silk they gave way. They instantly, one and all, fell down and worshipped it.

"*It is* pretty, " said Matty at last, with a little sigh, and she turned away as one who must not any longer contemplate so dazzling a temptation.

Mrs. Bell's heart quite ached for her eldest-born at this critical juncture. It was so natural for her to wish for silk attire when the hero was absolutely at the gates. And such a hero! So tall, so handsome, such an Adonis—so aristocratic! But, alas! silk could not be had for nothing. It would be an insult to offer Bell's old coat and the two pairs of trousers gone at the knees for this exquisite substance.

"Sixteen yards, " solemnly pronounced Mrs. Middlemass, when the silence had been sufficiently long. "Sixteen yards for three pound ten. There! it's a present I'm making to you, Miss Matty. "

"I like it very much, " said Matty.

"Like it! I should think you do. It was the fellow of it I sold this morning to Lady Georgiana Higginbotham, of Castle Higgins. She who is to be married next month. 'Middlemass, ' she said, when she saw it, 'I'm in love with it. It has a sheen about it, and a quality. Cut me twenty yards, Middlemass; I do declare I'll wear it for my travelling dress, and no other. ' She'll do it, too, Miss Matty, you'll see. And beautiful she'll look. "

The three girls sighed. They sighed in unison. As there was a lover in the question, the two younger were willing that Matty should have a new frock. But a silk! Each girl wanted the silk for herself.

"It is exquisite, " said Matty.

"Exquisite, " repeated Alice.

"Quisite, " said Sophy.

"I'll put it away for you, miss, " said the pedler, beginning to pack up her other things. "There, take it, miss, " she said, flinging a long sweep of the glittering texture over Matty's arm. "Now, it does become you, my dear. Doesn't it, ma'am? " turning to the mother. "Well, now, I never noticed it before, but Miss Matty has a great look of Lady Georgiana. Remarkable likeness! You wouldn't be known from her, miss when you had that dress on. Their eyes! the complexion! the figure! all ditto, ditto, ditto. "

The girls smiled; but what amount of flattery will not one accept when judiciously offered? They were all pleased to hear Mrs. Middlemass compare one of their number to Lady Georgiana, although they knew perfectly that the pedler had never in the whole course of her life even spoken to that young lady, who was a head and shoulders taller than Matty, and as unlike her in all particulars as a girl could be.

"There! " said the pedler. "Three pound ten! Dirt-cheap. Going, you may say, for nothing, and because it's the last piece I have of it. Lady

84

Georgiana paid me seven pounds for the length I cut her this morning. I'd like to see you in this dress, Miss Matty, and, maybe, if all reports is true, you'll want me to sell you something different, and more—more—well, more, perhaps, bridal-like, by-and-bye, my pretty young lady. "

This last speech finished the fate of the silk. If rumor had reached down to the strata of pedlers, etc., it simply could not be disregarded. Mrs. Bell bargained and haggled for the best part of an hour. She stripped herself of many necessary garments, and even ransacked her very meagre little collection of jewelry. Finally the purchase was completed with the sale of the ring which Bell had given her on the day when he had gone down on his knees for the third and successful time. That ring, of a showy style, but made of real gold and real gems, was beloved by Mrs. Bell above all her worldly goods. Nevertheless, she parted with it to make up the necessary price for the shot silk; for, what will not a mother do for her child?

CHAPTER XII.

NINA, YOU ARE SO PERSISTENT.

"I wish you wouldn't worry me so, miss. "

"Well, answer my question. Has Mr. Hart come back? "

"Yes—no—I'm sure I can't say. Maybe he's in his room, maybe he's not. You do look dirty, miss, and tired—my word, awful tired. Now, where have you been, Miss Josephine, since early yesterday morning? After no good, I'll be bound. Oh, dear me, yes, after no good! You're a wild one, and you're a daring one; and you'll come to a bad end, for all your eyes are so bright, if you don't mind. "

Josephine's queer, restless eyes flashed with an angry gleam.

"Do you know what this is? " she said, doubling up her small hand, and thrusting the hard-looking fist within an inch or two of her irate landlady's nose. "I knocked a man down before now with this, and I have no respect for women. You'd better not anger me, Mrs. Timms. "

"Oh, dear no, miss, I'm sure I meant no disrespect! "

"That's right. Don't say what you don't mean in future. "

"I won't, Miss Josephine. Now I come to think of it, I expect Hart is at home; I heard him shuffling about overhead last night. "

"I'll go up and see, " said Josephine.

She nodded to Mrs. Timms, and walked slowly, as though she were dead tired, and every step was an effort to her, up the stairs. They were rickety stairs, very dirty and dark, and unkept. Josephine went on and on, until her upward ascent ended under a sloping attic roof. Here she knocked at a closed door.

"Come in, " said a voice.

She entered a long, low room, which did service as a sitting-room, kitchen and studio, all combined. A little, old man with a long, white beard and a bald head was bending over a stove, frying eggs.

"Is that you, Nina? " he said, without looking round. "If it is, you may as well fry these eggs while I lay the cloth for supper. "

"No, you can finish them yourself, " replied Josephine. "I'm dead tired. I'd rather eat no supper than cook it. "

She flung herself into a long, low wicker-work chair, folded her hands and closed her eyes. The old man turned the tail of one eye to glance at her. Then he resumed his cooking, attending to it very carefully, removing each egg, as it was browned, to a hot and clean dish which stood in readiness.

"There, " he said, at last, "supper's ready. Here's the vinegar, here's the pepper, here's the salt, here's the pewter jug with the beer, here's the bread and butter, and last, but not least, here's your tea, Josephine. You're nowhere without your tea, are you, child? "

"Pour it out for me, " said Josephine. "Put an egg on a plate and give it to me. I'll be better when I've eaten. I can't talk until I have eaten. I was taken this way last night—I'll be better presently. "

The old man gave her a long, curious glance; then he fetched a tray, piled it with refreshments, and brought it to her side. She ate and drank ravenously. The food acted on her like magic; she sat upright—her eyes sparkled, her pallor left her, and the slight shade of petulance and ill-humor which had characterized her when she entered the room gave place to a sunshiny and radiant smile.

"Well, Daddy, " she said, getting up, going to the old man and giving him a kiss. "So you have come back at last. I was pretty sick of being a whole fortnight by myself, with no one but that interesting Mrs. Timms for company. You never wrote to me, and however careful I was, that five shillings wouldn't go far. What did you do in London? And why didn't you write? "

"One question at a time, Nina. Don't strangle me, child. Sit down quietly, and I'll tell you my news. I'm a good grandfather to you, Josephine. I'm a very good and faithful grandfather to you. "

"So you tell me every day of my life. I'll retort back now—I'm a good grandchild to you—the best in the world. "

"Bless me, what have you ever done, chit, but eat my bread and drink my water? However, I have news at last. Now, how eager you look! You would like to be a fine lady and forget your old granddad. "

"I'd like to be a fine lady, certainly, " responded Josephine.

She said nothing further, but sitting still, with her small hands crossed in her lap, she absolutely devoured the old man's face with her eyes.

He was accustomed to her gaze, which glittered and shone, and never wavered, and was by some people thought uncanny. He finished his supper slowly and methodically, and until he had eaten the last mouthful, and drained off the last drop of beer in the pewter mug, he didn't speak.

Then with a sharp glance at the girl he said, suddenly:

"So you wanted to take me unawares? "

"What do you mean, Grandfather? "

"You know what I mean well enough. However, I'll tell you, you have been on the tramp; you have no money; but you thought your legs would carry you where your heart wanted to be. Shall I go on? "

"Oh, yes, you may say anything you fancy. Stay, I'll say it for you. Yesterday I walked to Northbury. Northbury is over twenty miles from here. I walked every step of the way. In the evening I got there—I was footsore and weary. I had one and sixpence in my purse, no more for food, no more for bribes, no more for anything. I went to Northbury to see the Bertrams—to see that fine lady, that beloved friend of mine, Mrs. Bertram. She was from home. You probably know where she really was. I bribed the gatekeeper, and got into the grounds of Rosendale Manor. I frightened a chit of a schoolgirl, a plain, little, unformed, timorous creature. She was a Bertram, coming home from a late dissipation. She spoke of her fright, and gave her sister the cue. About midnight Catherine Bertram came out to seek me. What's the matter, Grand-dad? "

"Good heavens! Nina, that glib tongue of yours has not been blabbing. Catherine! What is Miss Bertram's Christian name to you? "

"Never mind. Her Christian name, and she herself also, are a good deal to me. As to blabbing, I never blab; I saw her, she spoke to me; I slept at the lodge; I returned home to-day. "

"You walked home? "

"Yes, and I am dead tired; I want to go to bed now. "

"You can't for a few minutes. I have a few words to say first. Josephine, I have always been a good grandfather to you. "

"Perhaps you have done your best, Grand-dad, but your best has not been much. I am clothed after a fashion, and fed after a style, and educated! " she filliped her slender fingers scornfully; "educated! I belong to the self-taught. Still, after your lights, you have been a good Grand-dad. Now, what is all this preamble about? I can scarcely keep my eyes open. If you are not quick your words will soon fall unregarded, for I shall be in the arms of that god of delight, Morpheus. "

"I have something very important to say, child. I want to lay a command upon you. "

"What is that? "

"You are not to act the spy on the Bertrams again. "

"The spy? What do you mean? "

"What I say. You are not to do it. I have made arrangements, and the Bertrams are to be unmolested. I have given my oath, and you must abide by it. "

"What if I refuse? "

"Then we part company. You go one way, I another. You are truly a beggar, and can take up no other position without my aid. You have a story to tell which no one will believe, for I alone hold the proofs. Talk much about your fine secret, and what will be the result? People will think you off your head. Be guided by me, and all comes right in the end and in the meantime we share the spoils. "

"The spoils, " said Josephine, "what do you mean?

"I can give you a practical answer, Nina. I have made a good bargain, a splendid bargain; seeing that I have only put on the first screw, my success has largely anticipated my wildest hopes. Josephine, my poor girl, you need no longer suffer the pangs of hunger and neglect. You and I are no longer penniless. What do you say to an income? What do you say to four hundred a year? "

Josephine put up her thin, white hand to her forehead.

"Four hundred a year? " she repeated, vaguely. "I don't quite know what it means. What have we now? "

"Anything or nothing. Sometimes a pound a week, sometimes two pounds, sometimes five shillings. "

"And we have in the future? "

"Didn't I tell you, child? Four hundred a year. One hundred pounds paid regularly every quarter. Got without earning, got without toiling for. Ours whether we are sick or well; ours under any circumstances from this day forward; ours just for keeping a little bit of a secret to ourselves. "

"A secret which keeps me out of my own. "

"We have no money to prove it, child, at present. In the meantime, this is a certainty. Whenever we get our proofs complete we can cease to take this annuity. "

"This bribe, you mean. I scorn it. I hate it. I won't touch it. "

Josephine's eyes again gleamed with anger.

"I hate bribes, " she repeated.

"All right, child. You can go on starving. You can go your own way, I mine. For myself, at least, I have accepted the annuity; and if you anger me any more, I'll burn the documents tonight, which give you the shadow of a claim. "

Josephine turned pale. There were moments when, fearless as she was, she feared this queer old man. The present was one of them. She sat quite still for a moment or two, during which she thought deeply. Then she spoke in an altered tone.

"Grandfather, if I consent to make no fuss, to say nothing, to reveal nothing by word or action, will you give me half your annuity? "

"Why so, Nina? Had we not better live together? When all is said and done, I'd miss you, Grandchild, if you left me. "

"You'd get over that, Grand-dad. These are not the days when people are especially affectionate. Will you give me two hundred a year, and let me live away from you? "

The old man looked down at the floor, and up at the ceiling; then furtively into his granddaughter's face, then away from her.

"It's late now, we'll talk of it to-morrow, " he said.

"No, I am not sleepy any longer. Two hundred a year is worth staying awake for. Will you give it to me? You can promise to-night as well as tomorrow. "

"This is an important thing. I can't make up my mind all in a minute. I've got to think. "

"You can think now. I'll give you half-an-hour. I'll shut my tired eyes, and you can think hard for half-an-hour. "

"Nina, you are so persistent. "

"Exactly, I am so persistent. Now my eyes are shut. Please begin to think. "

CHAPTER XIII.

THE WHITE BOAT AND THE GREEN.

About a fortnight after the events mentioned in the last chapter, the landlady of the Blue Lion, the little slatternly village inn where Mr. Hart and his granddaughter had their quarters, was somewhat disappointed, somewhat puzzled, and certainly possessed by the demon of curiosity when Hart told her that he and his granddaughter intended to take their departure that evening. Hart often went away; Mrs. Timms was quite accustomed to his sudden exits, but his granddaughter was always left as a hostage behind. Hart with his queer ways, his erratic payments, was perhaps not the most inviting lodger for an honest landlady to count upon, but Mrs. Timms had grown accustomed to him. She scolded him, and grumbled at him, but on the whole she made a good thing out of him, for no one could be more generous than old Hart when he was at all flush of cash.

He came down, however, this morning, and told her he was going.

"For a fortnight or so? " responded Mrs. Timms. "You'll leave Miss Josephine behind as usual? I'll take good care of her. "

"No, Miss Josephine is also going. Make out our bills, my good Timms, I can pay you in full. "

That evening there arrived at Northbury by the seven o'clock train a single first-class passenger—a girl dressed in a long gray cloak, and a big, picturesque shady hat stepped on to the platform. She was the only passenger to alight at Northbury, and the one or two sleepy porters regarded her with interest and admiration. She was very graceful, and her light-colored eyes had a peculiar quick expression which made people turn to watch her again.

The strange girl had scarcely any luggage—only a small portmanteau covered with a neat case of brown holland, and a little trunk to match.

She asked one of the porters to call a cab, did not disdain the shaky and ghastly-looking conveyance which Loftus Bertram had been too proud to use; sprang lightly into it, desired the porter to put her luggage on the roof, and gave the address of Rosendale Manor.

"Oh, that accounts for it, " said the man to his mate. "She's one of them proud Bertram folk. I thought by the looks of her as she didn't belong to none of the Northbury people. "

The other laughed.

"She have got an eye, " he said. "My word, don't it shine? Seems to scorch one up. "

"There's the 7.12 luggage train signalled, Jim! " exclaimed the other.

The men forgot the strange girl and returned to their duties.

Meanwhile, she sat back in her cab, and gazed complacently about her. She knew the scene through which she was passing—she had looked on it before. Very travel-stained and weary she had been then; very fresh and keen, and all alive she felt now.

She threw open the windows of the close cab, and took a long breath of the delicious sea air. It was a hot evening towards the middle of July, but a slight breeze rippled the little waves in the harbor, and then travelled up and up until it reached the girl in the dusty cab.

The Northburians were most of them out on the water. No one who knew anything of the ways of Northbury expected to see the good folk in the streets on an evening like this. No, the water was their highway, the water was their pleasure-scene. Each house owned a boat, each garden ended in steps against which the said boat was moored. It was the tiniest walk from the supper room or the high tea-table to the little green-painted boat, and then away to float over the limpid waves.

All the girls in Northbury could row, steer—in short, manage a boat as well as their brothers.

There was a view of the straggling, steep little High Street from the water; and the Bells now, in a large white boat with four oars, and occupied at the present moment by Mrs. Bell, fat and comfortable in the stern, Alice and Sophy each propelling a couple of oars, and the blushing, conscious Matty in the bow, where Captain Bertram bore her company, all saw the old cab, as it toiled up the hill in the direction of Rosendale Manor.

"Do look at Davis's cab! " exclaimed Matty. "Look, Captain Bertram, it's going in your direction. I wonder now, if any one has come by the train. It's certainly going to the Manor. There are no other houses out in that direction. Do look, Captain Bertram. "

"Lor, Matty, you are so curious! " exclaimed her sister Sophy, who overheard these remarks from her position as bow oar. "As if Captain Bertram cared! You always do so fuss over little things, Matty. Even if there are visitors coming to the Manor, I'm sure the captain doesn't care. He is not like us who never see anybody. Are you, Captain Bertram? "

"I beg your pardon, " said the captain, waking put of a reverie into which he had sunk. "Did you speak, Miss Bell? " he continued, turning with a little courteous movement, which vastly became him, towards the enamored Matty.

"I said a cab was going up the hill, " said Matty.

"Oh, really! A cab *is* an interesting sight, particularly a Northbury cab. Shall I make a riddle for you on the spot, Miss Bell? What is the sole surviving curiosity still to be found out of Noah's ark? "

Matty went off into her usual half-hysterical laughter.

"Oh! I do declare, Captain Bertram, you are too killingly clever for anything, " she responded. "Oh, my poor side—I'll die if I laugh any more. Oh, do have mercy on me! To compare that poor cab to Noah's ark! "

"I didn't; it isn't the least like the ark, only I think it must once have found a shelter within that place of refuge. "

"Oh! oh! oh! I am taken with such a stitch when I laugh. You are too witty, Captain Bertram. Sophy, you must hear what the captain has said. Oh, you killing, funny man—you must repeat that lovely joke to Sophy. "

"Excuse me, it was only meant for Miss Matty's ears. "

Matty stopped laughing, to blush all over her face, and Sophy thought it more decorous to turn her back on the pair.

"Does not that green boat belong to Miss Meadowsweet? " interrupted Bertram. "Look, Miss Bell, I am sure that is Miss Meadowsweet's boat. "

(He had seen it for the last ten minutes, and had been secretly hoping that Mrs. Bell would unconsciously steer in that direction; she was going the other way, however, and he was obliged to speak.)

"Yes, that's Beatrice, " said Matty, in an indifferent tone. "She generally goes for a row in the evening. "

"All alone like that? "

"Yes, Mrs. Meadowsweet is such a coward. She is afraid of the water. "

"Poor Miss Meadowsweet, how sad for her to be by herself! "

Matty gave a furtive and not too well-pleased glance at her captain.

"Bee likes to be alone, " she said.

"I should never have thought it. She seems a sociable, bright sort of girl. Don't you want to talk to her? I know you do. I see it in your face. You think it will be irksome for me, but, never mind, we need not stay long. I must not be selfish nor indulge in the wish to keep you all to myself. I know you want to talk to Miss Meadowsweet, and so you shall, —I *won't* have you balked. "

Here he raised his voice.

"Mrs. Bell, will you steer over to Miss Meadowsweet's boat? Miss Matty, here, has something to say to her. "

Not an earthly thing had Matty to communicate to her friend, but the captain had managed to put the matter in such a light that she could only try to look pleased, and pretend to acquiesce.

"Oh, yes, she had always lots to say to her darling Bee, " she murmured. And then, somehow, her poor little silly spirits went down, and she had a sensation of feeling rather flat.

As will be seen by the foregoing remarks, Captain Bertram had a rare gift for making killing and funny speeches.

Matty had over and over pronounced him to be the most brilliantly witty person she had ever in the whole course of her life encountered. But his talent as a supposed wit was nothing at all to the cleverness with which he now managed to keep the large white boat by the side of the small green one for the remainder of the evening. It was entirely managed by the superior will of one person, for certainly none of the Bells wished for this propinquity.

Mrs. Bell, who like a watchful hen-mother was apparently seeing nothing, and yet all the time was tenderly brooding over the little chick whom she hoped was soon about to take flight from the parent nest, saw at a glance that her chick looked nothing at all beside that superior chicken of Mrs. Meadowsweet's. For Matty's little nose was sadly burnt, and one lock of her thin limp hair was flying not too picturesquely in the breeze. And her home-cut jacket was by no means remarkably becoming, and one of her small, uncovered hands — why *would* Matty take her gloves off? —was burnt red, not brown by the sun. Beatrice, on the contrary, looked as she always did, trim and neat, and bright and gracious. She had on the gray cashmere dress which she had worn when Captain Bertram first began to lose his heart to her, and over this, tonight, she had twisted a long bright crimson scarf. Into her white hat, too, she had pinned a great bunch of crimson roses, so that, altogether, Beatrice in her pretty green boat made a beautiful picture. She would have made this in any case, for her pose was so good, and her figure fine, but when, in addition, there was a sweet intelligent face without one scrap of self-consciousness about it, and two gray eyes full of a tender and sympathetic light, and when the rosy lips only opened to make the pleasantest and most appropriate speeches, and only to give utterance to words of tact and kindness, Mrs. Bell was not very far wrong when she felt a sense of uneasiness for her own poor chick.

Shuffle, however, as she would up in the stern, viciously pull the rudder string so as to incline the boat away from Beatrice, the captain's will still kept the green boat and the white together. Was he likely to give in or to succumb to a woman like Mrs. Bell? Had he not planned this meeting in his own mind from an early hour that morning? For had he not met Beatrice and incidentally gathered that she would be sure to be on the water that night? And after receiving this information, had he not carefully made his plans, wandering about on the quay just when the Bells were getting into their boat, accepting the invitation eagerly given that he should go on the water with them, and afterwards come home to supper.

"Sophy, " Mrs. Bell had gasped, at that critical and triumphant moment in a whisper, pulling her youngest daughter aside, "fly up to Gibb's at the corner, and order in two lobsters for supper. The captain loves lobsters with the coral in them. Be sure you see that they have the coral in them, Sophy. Fly, child. We'll wait for you here. "

And Captain Bertram had overheard this whisper, and mentally determined that Beatrice Meadowsweet should also eat lobster with coral in it for supper. Was it likely, therefore, that he would now yield to that impatient tug of Mrs. Bell's rudder? On the contrary, he put out his hand in apparently the most unconscious way, and held the little green boat to the side of the white. In his way he was a diplomat, and even Matty did not suspect that he wanted to do anything but show her a kindness by keeping her in such close conversation with her friend.

"It's getting quite chill, " suddenly exclaimed Mrs. Bell. "Girls, it's time for us to be getting home. Your father likes his supper punctually. Well, Bee, my dear, there's no use in asking you to supper, I suppose? Of course, more than welcome you'd be if you would come, lovey, but you're such a daughter—one in a thousand. I assure you, Captain Bertram, I can hardly ever get that girl to leave her mother alone in the evening. "

Beatrice laughed.

"It so happens, " she said, "that my mother is having tea and supper to-night at Mrs. Butler's. So if you really care to have me, Mrs. Bell, I shall be delighted to come. "

Beatrice, the popular, the beloved of all in the town, never knew, never to her dying day, that on a certain memorable occasion, good-humored, fat, pompous Mrs. Bell would have given half a sovereign to box her ears. The astute captain, however, guessed her feelings, and chuckled inwardly. He had also found out during his brief morning's conversation that Mrs. Meadowsweet was going to sup from home.

"How delightful you look, Miss Bell! " he said, suddenly, fixing his dark eyes on Matty.

Their glance caused her to start and blush.

"Mrs. Bell, " he said, raising his voice again, "Miss Matty has been so anxious to have Miss Meadowsweet's company this evening. And now we are all happy, " he added, gayly. "Shall I give you another riddle, Miss Matty? "

Mrs. Bell's anxious brows relaxed, and she smiled inwardly.

"Poor man! He is over head and ears in love, " she murmured. "I suppose he thinks Beatrice will play gooseberry with the other girls, and leave him more chance to be alone with little Matty. She does *not* look her best, that I will say for her; but, poor fellow, he sees no faults, that's evident. How beautiful the love-light in his eyes is—ah, dear me, it reminds me of the time when I was young, and Bell used to go on his knees to me—Bell hadn't eyes like Captain Bertram though. Dear, dear, he is attentive, poor man, and how close he bends over Matty. I'll help him, so I will. I'll take Beatrice and the other girls away when once we get out of the boat. We four will walk up to the house together, and let Captain Bertram and his little girl follow. Why, of course, she's his little girl; bless her, the dear child! Then when we get in, I'll get Bee and Alice and Sophy to come upstairs by way of consulting how Matty's new dress is to be made, so the two poor things can have the drawing-room to themselves. I shouldn't be a bit surprised if he popped there and then. Well, I am gratified. Bertram is a pretty name—Matilda Bertram! She won't like to be known as Matty, then. 'Mrs. Captain Bertram'—it sounds very stylish. I wonder how much money pa will allow for the trousseau. And how am I to manage about the breakfast? None of our rooms are big, and all the town's people will want to be asked. It isn't for me to turn my back on old friends; but I doubt if the Bertrams will like to meet every one, of course, they are the first to be considered. Lor, Sophy, how you startled me; what's the matter, child? "

"You're in a brown study, ma. How much longer are you going to stay in the boat? We have all landed. "

"Good gracious! mercy mother! Help me out quick, Sophy, quick! Bee, Beatrice, come and lend me your hand. You are bigger than my girls, and my legs are always a little unsteady in a boat. Oh, not you, Captain Bertram, I beg, I pray. You just go on with Matty to the house, and we'll follow presently. Go on like a good man, and don't bother yourself. "

Here she winked broadly at Beatrice, who started and colored.

"I don't want to keep him back, " she said, in a broad whisper to the young lady, who was helping her to alight on the steps. "He's over head and ears, and I thought we would give them their chance. You stay close to me, lovey. What a fine strong arm you have! There! Alice hasn't a bit of gumption—as if Matty wanted Alice to walk with her! Alice, come back and help your mother. I'm quite giddy from the motion of the water. Come back, child, I say! "

But it was not Alice who turned. Captain Bertram, with the most gracious gallantry, proffered his arm to the fat old lady, and while he helped her to the house looked again and again at Beatrice.

CHAPTER XIV.

AT HER GATES.

Mr. Bell was as thin as his wife was fat, and as quiet and unassuming as she was bumptious and talkative. On the occasion of this memorable supper he very nearly drove his better half into fits by his utter want of observation.

"It's that that worries me in Bell, " the good woman was often heard to say. "When a thing is as plain as the nose on his face he won't see it. And not all my hints will make him see it. Hints! —You might hint forever to Bell, and he wouldn't know what you were driving at. "

These remarks Mrs. Bell had made, times without number, concerning her spouse, but never had ehe more cause to give utterance to them than on the present occasion. For just when the whole party were seated at supper, and she by the boldest manoeuvres had placed Captain Bertram next to herself by the coffee-tray, and had planted Matty at his other side, so that he was in a measure hemmed in, and if he did not talk to Matty had no one to fall back on but herself, who, of course, would quickly, using the metaphor of battledore and shuttlecock, toss him back to her daughter—having arranged all this, what should Bell do but put his foot in it?

"Captain Bertram, " he called in his thin voice across the table, "I hope you enjoyed your row, and I'm proud to see you at my humble board. But come up here, my good young sir; you're quite smothered by the missis and the teacups. We have fine room at this end, haven't we, Beatrice? You come away up here, Captain Bertram, where you'll have room to use your elbows; the missis mustn't keep you to herself altogether, that ain't fair play. "

"Oh, we're as comfortable as possible, Peter, " almost screamed Mrs. Bell.

But in vain. The captain was too acute a person not to seize this opportunity. He said a courteous word or two to Mrs. Bell, apologized for having already crowded her, smiled at Matty, and then with a light heart seated himself beside Beatrice.

After this, matters seemed to go wrong as far as the Bells were concerned. It is true that after supper Beatrice called Matty to her side, and looked over a photographic album with her, and tried hard to draw her into the gay conversation and to get her to reply to the light repartee which Captain Bertram so deftly employed. But, alas for poor Matty she had no conversational powers; she was only great at interjections, at ceaseless giggling, and at violent and uncontrollable fits of blushing. Even Beatrice felt a sense of repulsion at the very open way in which Matty played her innocent cards. Matty was in love, and she showed it by voice, look and gesture. Beatrice tried to shield her, she was mortified for her, and felt a burning sense of resentment against the captain.

In spite, however, of the resentment of the one girl, and the too manifest admiration of the other, this hero managed to have pretty much his own way. Beatrice had to reply to his sallies, she was forced to meet his eyes; now and then even he drew a smile from her.

When the time came for Miss Meadowsweet to go home, Albert Bell was eagerly summoned to accompany her.

"This is unnecessary, " said the captain; "I will see Miss Meadowsweet back to the Gray House. "

"Oh, now, Captain! Bee, don't you think it's really too much for him? "

"Of course I don't, dear Mrs. Bell, " said Beatrice, stopping the good lady's lips with a kiss; "but Albert shall come too, so that I shall be doubly escorted. "

She nodded and smiled to her hostess, and Mrs. Bell felt a frantic desire to send Matty with her brother, but some slight sense of decorum prevented her making so bare-faced a suggestion.

Albert Bell was very proud to walk with Beatrice, and Captain Bertram felt proportionately sulky. To Albert's delight, who wanted to confide his own love affairs to Bee, the captain said good-night at the top of the High Street.

"As you have an escort I won't come any further, " he said. "When are we to see you again? Will you come to the Manor to-morrow? "

101

"I don't know, " said Beatrice, "I've made no plans for to-morrow. "

"Then come to us; Catherine told me to ask you. Our tennis court is in prime order. Do come; will you promise? "

"I won't quite promise, but I'll come if I can. "

"Thanks; we shall look out for you. "

He shook hands, gave her an earnest glance, nodded to Bell and turned away. His evening had been a partial success, but not a whole one. He left Beatrice, as he almost always did, with a sense of irritation. It was her frank and open indifference that impelled him to her side. Indifference when Captain Bertram chose to woo was an altogether novel experience to so fascinating an individual. Hitherto it had been all the other way. He had flirted many times, and with success. Once even he had fallen in love; he owned to himself that he had been badly hit, but there had been no doubt at all about his love being returned, it had been given back to him in full and abundant measure. He sighed to-night as he thought of that passionate episode. He remembered ardent words, and saw again a face which had once been all the world to him. Separation had come, however; his was not a stable nature, and the old love, the first love, had given place to many minor flirtations.

"I wonder where my old love is now, " he thought, and then again he felt a sense of irritation as he remembered Beatrice. "She is quite the coolest girl I have ever met, " he said to himself. "But I'll win her yet. Yes, I'm determined. Am I to eat the bread of humiliation in vain? Faugh! Am I to make love to a creature like Matty Bell in the vain hope of rousing the envy or the jealousy of that proud girl? I don't believe she has got either envy or jealousy. She seemed quite pleased when I spoke to that wretched little personage, although she had the grace to look a trifle ashamed for her sex when Miss Matty so openly made love to me. Well, this is a slow place, and yet, when I think of that haughty—no, though, she's not haughty—that imperturbable Beatrice Meadowsweet, it becomes positively interesting.

"Why has the girl these airs? And her father kept a shop, too! I found that fact out from Matty Bell to-day. What a spiteful, teasing little gnat that same Matty is, trying to sting her best friend. What a little mock ridiculous air she put on when she tried to explain to me the social status of a coal merchant (I presume Bell is a coal merchant) *versus* a draper. "

As Bertram strolled along, avoiding the High Street, and choosing the coast line for his walk, he lazily smoked a pipe, and thought, in that idle indifferent way with which men of his stamp always do exercise their mental faculties, about his future. His past, his present, his possible future rose up before the young fellow. He was harassed by duns, he was, according to his own way of thinking, reduced to an almost degrading state of poverty. His mother had put her hand to a bill for a considerable amount to save him. He was morally certain that she would have to meet that bill, and when she met it that she would be half ruined. Nevertheless, he felt gay, and light at heart, for men of his class are seldom troubled with remorse.

Presently he reached the lodge gates. His mother's fad about having them locked was always religiously kept, and he grumbled now as he sought for a latch-key in his waistcoat-pocket.

He opened the side gate and let himself in; the gate had a spring, and was so constructed that it could shut and lock itself by the same act. Bertram was preparing to walk quickly up the avenue when he was startled by a sudden morement; a tall slim apparition in gray came slowly out of the darkness, caused by the shadow of the lodge, to meet him.

"Good God! " he said; and he stepped back, and his heart thumped hard against his breast.

"It's me, Loftus—I'm back again—I'm with you again, " said a voice which thrilled him.

The girl in gray flung her arms around his neck, and laid her head of red gold on his breast.

"Good God! Nina! Josephine! Where have you come from? I was thinking of you only tonight. It's a year since we met. Where have you sprung from? Out of the sky, or the earth? Look at me, witch, look in my face! "

He put his hand under her chin, raised her very fair oval face; (the moonlight fell full on it—he could see it well); he looked long and hungrily into her eyes, then kissed her eagerly several times.

"Where have you come from? " he repeated. "My God! to think I was walking to meet you in such a calm fashion this evening. "

"You never were very calm, Loftie, nor was I. Feel my heart—I am almost in a tempest of joy at meeting you again. I knew you'd be glad. You couldn't help yourself. "

"I'm glad and I'm sorry. You know you intoxicate me, witch—I thought I had got over that old affair. What: don't flash your eyes at me. Oh, yes, Nina, I am glad, I am delighted to see you once again. "

"And to kiss me, and love me again? "

"Yes, to kiss you and love you again. "

"How soon will you marry me, Loftie? "

"We needn't talk about that to-night. Tell me why you have come, and how. Where is your grandfather? Do you still sing in the streets for a living? "

"Hush, you insult me. I am a rich girl now. "

"You rich? What a joke! "

"No, it is a reality. Riches go by comparison, and Josephine Hart has an income—therefore she is rich compared to the Josephine who had none. When will you marry me, Loftie? "

"Little puss! We'll talk of that another day. "

He stroked her cheek, put his arm around her waist and kissed her many times.

"You have not told me yet why you came here, " he said.

She laughed.

"I came here because my own sweet will directed me. I have taken rooms here at this lodge. The man called Tester and his wife will attend on me. "

"Good gracious! at my mother's very gates Is that wise, Nina. "

"Wise or unwise I have done it. "

"To be near me? "

"Partly. "

"Nina, you half frighten me. You are not going to do me an injury? It will prejudice my mother seriously if she finds out my—my—"

"Your love for me, " finished Josephine.

"Yes. "

"Why will it prejudice her? "

"Need I—must I tell you? My mother is proud; she—she would almost disown me if I made a *mésalliance*. "

Nina flung back her head.

"You talk like a boy, " she said. "When you marry me you save, not degrade, yourself. Ah, I know a secret. Such a secret! Such a blessed, blessed, happy secret for me. It is turning me into a good girl. It causes my heart to sing. When I think of it I revel in delight; when I think of it I could dance: when I remember it I could shout with exultation. "

"Nina, what do you mean? "

"Nothing that you must know. I rejoice in my secret because it brings me to you, and you to me. You degrade yourself by marrying me? You'll say something else some day. Now, goodnight. I'm going back to Tester. He's stone deaf, and he's waiting up for me. Good-night—good-night. No, Loftus, I won't injure you. I injure those I hate, not those I love. "

She kissed her hand to him. He tried to catch the slim fingers to press them to his lips, but with a gay laugh she vanished, shutting the lodge door after her. Loftus Bertram walked up the avenue with the queerest sensation of terror and rejoicing.

CHAPTER XV.

JOSEPHINE LOOKED DANGEROUS.

In those days after her mysterious and secret visit to London Mrs. Bertram was a considerably altered woman. All her life hitherto she had enjoyed splendid health; she was unacquainted with headaches; neuralgia, rheumatism, gout, the supposed banes of the present day, never troubled her.

Now, however, she had absolutely an attack of the nerves. Mabel found her mother, on coming to wish her good-morning one day, shivering so violently that she could not complete her dressing. Loftus was not at home. He had rejoined his regiment for a brief spell, so Catherine and Mabel had to act on their own responsibility.

They did not hesitate to send for the local doctor.

Dr. Morris, who was calmly shaving in his bedroom was very much excited when his wife rushed in to tell him that he was summoned in haste to the Manor.

"And you might peep into the Manor drawing-room on your way downstairs, doctor, " whispered the good lady, in her muffled tone, "and find out if the carpet is really felt. Mrs. Gorman Stanley swears that it is, but for my part I can scarce give credence to such an unlikely story, for surely no woman who could only afford a felt covering for the floor of her best sitting-room would give herself the airs Mrs. Bertram has done. "

"Just see that my black bag is ready, Jessie, " was the husband's retort to this tirade. "And you might hurry John round with the pony-chaise. "

Dr. Morris felt intensely proud as he drove off to see his august patient. He drew up his rough pony once or twice to announce the fact to any stray passer-by.

"Good-day, Bell, —fine morning, isn't it? I'm just off to the Manor. Mrs. B. not quite the thing. Ah, I see Mrs. Jenkins coming down the street. I must tell her that I can't look in this morning. "

He nodded to Mr. Bell, and drove on until he met the angular lady known by this name.

"Good-morning, good-morning, " he called in his cheery tones, and scarcely drawing in the pony at all now. "I meant to look round in the course of the forenoon to see how the new tonic agrees with Miss Daisy; but I may be a little late; I'm summoned in haste to the Manor. "

Here he touched his little pony's head with the whip, and, before Mrs. Jenkins could utter a word of either astonishment or interest, had turned the corner and was out of sight.

The fashionable disease of nerves had not yet become an epidemic at Northbury, and Dr. Morris was a little puzzled at the symptoms which his great patient exhibited. He was proud to speak of Mrs. Bertram as his "great patient, " and told her to her face in rather a fulsome manner that he considered it the highest possible honor to attend her. He ordered his favorite tonic of cod liver oil, told her to stay in bed, and keep on low diet, and, having pocketed his fee drove away.

Mrs. Bertram was outwardly very civil to the Northbury doctor, but when he departed she scolded Catherine and Mabel for having sent for him, tore up his prescription, wrote one for herself, which she sent to the chemist to have made up, and desired Catherine to give her a glass of port wine from one of a treasured few bottles of a rare vintage which she had brought with her to Rosendale.

"It was a few days after her visit to the Meadowsweets that Mrs. Bertram had been taken ill. She soon became quite well again, and then rather astonished Catherine by telling her that she had herself seen Beatrice Meadowsweet; that she had found her daughter's judgment with regard to her to be apparently correct, and that, in consequence, she did not object to Beatrice visiting at the Manor.

"You may make Miss Meadowsweet your friend, " she said to both girls. "She may come here, and you may sometimes go to see her. But remember, she is the only Northbury young lady I will admit into my society. "

A few days afterwards, Loftus, who had again managed to obtain leave of absence from his military duties, reappeared on the scenes.

As has been seen, Loftus would admit of no restrictions with regard to his acquaintances, and after the remarkable fashion of some young men, he tried to secure an interest in the affections of Beatrice by flirting with Matty Bell.

Mrs. Bertram knew nothing of these iniquities on the part of her son. It never entered even into her wildest dreams that any son or daughter of her could associate with people of the stamp of the Bells. Even had she been aware of it, however, she knew better than to try to coerce her captain.

She had quite worries enough of her own, poor woman, and not the least of them, in the eyes of the girls, was the fresh mania she took for saving. Meals had never been too plentiful at Rosendale. Now, the only remark that could be made in their favor was that they satisfied hunger. Healthy girls will eat any wholesome food, and when Loftus was not at home, Catherine and Mabel Bertram made their breakfast off porridge.

Mabel ate hungrily, and grumbled not a little. Catherine was also hungry, but she did not grumble. She was never one to care greatly for the luxuries of life, and all her thoughts now were taken up watching her mother. The effect of her mother's sudden confidence in her, the effect of the trouble which had undoubtedly come to her mother had altogether an extraordinary influence over Catherine. She ceased to be a wild and reckless tom-boy, she ceased to defy her mother in small matters; her character seemed to gain strength, and her face, always strong in its expression and giving many indications of latent power of character, looked now more serious than gay, more sweet and thoughtful than fastidious and discontented.

Catherine had plenty of tact, and she watched her mother without appearing to watch her. She was loyal, too, in heart and soul, and never even hinted to others of the confidence reposed in her.

It was a lovely summer's morning. Catherine and Mabel were up early; they were picking raspberries to add to the meagre provisions for breakfast. It was always difficult to manage a pleasant breakfast hour when Loftus was at home. Mrs. Bertram used to flush up painfully when Loftus objected to the viands placed before him, and Catherine was most anxious to spare her mother by satisfying the fastidious tastes of her brother.

"Why should Loftus have all the raspberries? " angrily queried Mabel. "I should like some myself, and so would you, Kate. Why should Loftus have everything? "

"Nonsense, May, he's not going to have everything. This plate of special beauties is for mother. "

"Well, that's quite right. Loftus and you and I can divide the rest. "

"May, I'm going to whisper a secret to you. Now, don't let it out, for the lords of creation would be so angry if they knew. But I do think in little things girls are much greater than men. Now what girl who is worth anything cares whether she eats a few raspberries or not. While as to the men—I consider them nothing but crybabies about their food. Here, Mab, race me to the house. "

Mabel puffed and panted after her more energetic sister. It was a very hot morning, and it really was aggravating of Kate to fly on the wings of the wind, and expect her to follow.

"Kate has no thought, " she muttered, as she panted along. "I shall feel hot and messy for the day now, and there's nothing nice for me to eat when I do get in. It's all very fine to be Kate, who, I don't think, is mortal at all about some things, but I expect I'm somewhat of a cry-baby too, when I see all the nice appetizing food disappearing down a certain manly throat. Hullo, what's the matter now, Kitty? "

Catherine was standing by the window of the breakfast-room waving an open note in her hand.

"Three cheers for you, Mabel! You may be as greedy as you please. The knight of the raspberry plantation has departed. Read this; I found it on my plate. "

Catherine was about to toss the note to Mabel, when a hand was put quietly over her shoulder, and Mrs. Bertram took Loftus's letter to read.

"Mother, I didn't know you were down. "

"I just came in, my dear, and heard you speaking to Mabel. What is this? "

She stood still to read the brief lines:

"Dearest Sis, —I have had a sudden recall to Portsmouth. Will write from there. Love to the mother and Mab. —Your affectionate brother,

"Loftus. "

Mrs. Bertram looked up with a very startled expression in her eyes.

"Now, mother, there's nothing to fret you in this, " said Kate, eagerly. "Was not Loftie always the most changeable of mortals? "

"Yes, my dear, but not quite so changeable as not to know anything at all about a recall in the afternoon yesterday, and to have to leave us before we are out of bed in the morning. Did anybody see Loftus go? Had he any breakfast? "

Catherine flew away to inquire of Clara, and Mabel said in an injured voice:

"I dare say Loftie had a telegram sent to him to the club. Anyhow, he has all the excitement and all the pleasure. I watched him through the spy-glass last night. He was in the Bells' boat, and Beatrice was all alone in hers. Beatrice was talking to Loftus and the boats were almost touching. Mother, I wish we could have a boat. "

"Yes, dear, I must try and manage it for you at some future time. Well, Catherine, have you heard anything? "

"No, mother. Loftus must have gone away very, very early. No one saw him go; he certainly had no breakfast. "

Mrs. Bertram was silent for a few moments; then, suppressing a sigh, she said, in a would-be cheerful tone:

"Well, my loves, we must enjoy our breakfasts, even without the recreant Loftus. Mabel, my dear, what delicious raspberries! They give me quite an appetite. "

"Kitty picked them for you, mother, " said Mabel. "She has been treasuring a special bush for you for a week past. "

Mrs. Bertram looked up at her eldest daughter and smiled at her. That smile, very much treasured by Kate, was after all but a poor attempt, gone as soon as it came. Mrs. Bertram leant back in her chair and toyed with the dainty fruit. Her appetite was little more than a mockery.

"It was very thoughtful of Loftus not to waken any one up to give him breakfast, " said Catherine.

Her mother again glanced at her with a shadow of approval on her worn face. Artful Kitty had made this speech on purpose; she knew that any praise of Loftus was balm to her mother.

After breakfast Mrs. Bertram showed rather unwonted interest in her daughters' plans.

"It is such a lovely day I should like you to go on the water, " she said. "At the same time, I must not think of hiring a boat this summer. "

"Are we so frightfully poor, mother? " asked Mab.

Mrs. Bertram's brow contracted as if in pain, but she answered with unwonted calm and gentleness:

"I have a fixed income, my dear Mabel, but, as you know, we have come to Northbury to retrench. "

She was silent again for a minute. Then she said:

"I see nothing for it but to cultivate the Meadowsweets. "

"Mother! " said Catherine. The old fire and anger had come into her voice. Unusual as it may be with any girl brought up in such a worldly manner, Catherine hated to take advantage of people.

"You mistake me, Kate, " said her mother, shrinking back from her daughter's eyes, as if she had received a blow. "I want you to have the pleasure of Beatrice Meadowsweet's friendship. "

"Oh, yes, " replied Catherine, relieved.

"And, " continued the mother, her voice growing firm and her dark eyes meeting her daughter's fully, "I don't mean to be out in the cold, so I shall make a friend of Mrs. Meadowsweet. "

Mabel burst into a merry girlish laugh. Catherine walked across the grass to pick a rose. Mrs. Bertram took the rose from her daughter's hand, although she knew and Catherine knew that it was never intended for her. She smelt the fragrant, half-open bud, then placed it in her dress, with a simple, "Thank you, my dear. "

"I am going to write a note to Mrs. Meadowsweet, " she said, after a minute or two. "I know Beatrice is coming here this afternoon. It would give me pleasure if her mother accompanied her. "

"Shall we take the note to the Gray House, mother? " eagerly asked Mabel. "It is not too long a walk. We should like to go. "

"No, my dear. You and Kate can amuse yourselves in the garden, or read in the house, just as you please. I will write my note quietly, and when it is written take it down to Tester at the lodge. No, thank you, my loves, I should really like the walk, and would prefer to take it alone. "

Mrs. Bertram then returned to her drawing-room, sat down by her davenport, and wrote as follows:

"Rosendale Manor.

"Thursday.

"Dear Mrs. Meadowsweet, —Will you and Miss Beatrice join the girls and me at dinner this afternoon? Your daughter has already kindly promised to come here to play tennis to-day—at least I understand from Kate that such is the arrangement. Will you come with her? We old people can sit quietly under the shade of the trees and enjoy our tea, while the young folks exert themselves. Hoping to see you both,

"Believe me,

"Yours sincerely,

"Catherine de Clifford Bertram. "

Mrs. Bertram put this letter into an envelope, directed it in her dashing and lady-like hand, and then in a slow and stately fashion proceeded to walk down the avenue to the lodge. She was always rather slow in her movements, and she was slower than usual to-day. She scarcely owned to herself that she was tired, worried—in short, that the strong vitality within her was sapped at its foundation.

A man or a woman can often live for a long time after this operation takes place, but they are never the same again. They go slowly, with the gait of those who are halt, through life.

Mrs. Bertram reached the lodge, and after the imperious fashion of her class did not even knock at the closed door before she lifted the latch and went in.

It was a shabby, little, tumble-down lodge. It needed papering, and white-washing, and cleaning; in winter the roof let in rain, and the rickety, ill-fitting windows admitted the cold and wind. Now, however, it was the middle of summer. Virginia creeper and ivy, honeysuckle and jasmine, nearly covered the walls. The little place looked picturesque without; and within, honest, hard-working Mrs. Tester contrived with plentiful scouring and washing to give a clean and cosy effect.

Mrs. Bertram, as she stepped into the kitchen, noticed the nice little fire in the bright grate (the lodge boasted of no range); she also saw a pile of buttered toast on the hob, and the tiny kitchen was fragrant with the smell of fresh coffee.

Mrs. Bertram was not wrong when she guessed that Tester and his wife did not live on these dainty viands.

"I'm just preparing breakfast, ma'am, for our young lady lodger, " said good Mrs. Tester, dropping a curtsey.

"For your young lady lodger? What do you mean, Mrs. Tester? "

"Well, ma'am, please take a chair, won't you, Mrs. Bertram—you'll like to be near the fire, my lady, I'm sure. " (The Testers generally spoke to the great woman in this way—she did not trouble herself to contradict them.) "Well, my lady, she come last night by the train. It was Davis's cab brought her up, and set her down, her and her bits of things, just outside the lodge. Nothing would please her but that we should give her the front bedroom and the little parlor inside this room and she is to pay us fifteen shillings a week, to cover board and all. It's a great lift for Tester and me, and she's a nice-spoken young lady, and pleasant to look at, too. Oh, yes, miss—-I beg your pardon, miss. I was just a bringing of your breakfast in, miss. "

The door had been opened behind Mrs. Bertram. She started and turned, as a tall, slim girl with a head of ruddy gold hair, a rather pale, fair face, and big bright eyes, came in.

The girl looked at Mrs. Bertram quickly and eagerly. Mrs. Bertram looked back at her. Neither woman flinched as she gazed, only gradually over Mrs. Bertram's face there stole a greeny-white hue.

The girl came a little nearer. Old Mrs. Tester bustled past her with the hot breakfast.

"*You!* " said Mrs. Bertram, when the old woman had left the room, "you are Josephine Hart. "

"I am Josephine; you know better than to call me Hart. "

"Hush! that matter has been arranged between your grandfather and my solicitor. Do you wish the bargain undone? "

"I sincerely wish it undone. "

"I think you don't, " said Mrs. Bertram, slowly. She laughed in a disagreeable manner. "The old woman is coming back, " she said suddenly; "invite me into your parlor for a moment, I have a word or two to say to you. "

Josephine led the way into the little sitting-room; she offered a chair to Mrs. Bertram, who would not take it. Then she went and shut the door between the kitchen and the parlor, and standing with her back to the shut door turned and faced Mrs. Bertram.

"How did you guess my name? " she said, suddenly.

"That was not so difficult. I recognized you by the description my daughter gave of you. She saw you, remember, that night you hid in the avenue. "

"I did not know it was that, " said Josephine softly; "I thought it was the likeness. I am the image of *him*, am I not? "

She took a small morocco case out of her pocket and proceeded to open it.

Mrs. Bertram put her hand up to her eyes as if she would shut away a terrible sight.

"Hush, child! how dare you? Don't show me that picture. I won't look. What a wicked impostor you are! "

"Impostor! You know better, and my grandfather knows better. What is the matter, Mrs. Bertram? "

Mrs. Bertram sank down into the chair which at first she had obstinately refused.

"Josephine, " she said, "I am no longer a young woman; I have not got the strength of youth. I cannot bear up as the young can bear up. Why have you come here? What object have you in torturing me with your presence here? "

"I won't torture you; I shall live quietly. "

"But why have you come? You had no right to come. "

"I had perfect right to live where I pleased. I had all the world to choose from, and I selected to live at your gates. "

"You did very wrong. Wrong! It is unpardonable. "

"Why so? What injury am I doing you? I have promised to be silent; I will be silent for a little. I won't injure you or yours by word or deed. "

"You have a story in your head, a false story; you will spread it abroad. "

"I have a story, but it is not false. "

"False or true, you will spread it abroad. "

"No, the story is safe. For the present it is safe, my lips are sealed. "

"Josephine, I wish you would go away. "

"I am sorry, I cannot go away. "

"We cannot associate with you. You are not brought up like us. You will be lonely here, you will find it very dull, you had better go away. "

"I am not going away. I have come here and I mean to stay. I shall watch you, and your son, and your daughters; that will be my amusement. "

"I won't say any more to you, proud and insolent girl. My son, at least, is spared your scrutiny, he is not at Rosendale; and my daughters, I think, they can live through it. "

Mrs. Bertram turned and left the little parlor. She gave her note to Mrs. Tester, desired it to be taken at once to the Gray House, and then returned quietly and steadily to the Manor. When she got in she called Catherine to her.

"Kate, the girl you saw hiding in the avenue has come to live at the lodge. "

"Mother! "

"I have seen her and spoken to her, my dear daughter. She is nothing either to you or me. Take no notice of her. "

"Very well, mother. "

Meanwhile, in her little parlor, in the old lodge, Josephine stood with her hands clasped, and fiery lights of anger, disappointment, pain, flashing from her eyes. Were that woman's words true? Had Loftus Bertram gone away? If so, if indeed he had left because she had arrived, then—Her eyes flashed once more, and with so wicked a light that Mrs. Tester, who, unobserved, had come into the room, left it again in a fright. She thought Josephine Hart looked dangerous. She was right. No one could be more dangerous if she chose.

CHAPTER XVI.

A BRITISH MERCHANT.

Soon after four that afternoon, Davis's tumble-down cab might have been seen standing outside the gate of the Gray House. Immediately afterwards the door was opened, and Mrs. Meadowsweet, in her rose-colored satin, with a black lace shawl, and a bonnet to match made her appearance.

She stepped into the cab, and was followed by Beatrice, Jane, the little maid, handing in after them a small band-box, which contained the cap trimmed with Honiton lace.

Mrs. Meadowsweet's cheeks were slightly flushed, and her good-humored eyes were shining with contentment and satisfaction.

"Oh, there's Mrs. Morris! " she said to Beatrice. "I'd better tell her where we are going. She's always so interested in the Manor folks. Davis, stop the cab a minute! Call to him, Bee. Da-vis! "

The cap stopped, and Mrs. Morris, eager and bustling, drew nigh.

"How are you, dear? " she said. "How do you do, Beatrice? Isn't it bad for you, dear love, " turning again to the elder lady, "to have the window of the fly open? Although it is summer, and the doctor makes a fuss about the thermometer being over eighty in the shade, I know for a positive fact that the wind is east, and very treacherous. "

"I don't take cold easily, Jessie, " replied Mrs. Meadowsweet. "No, I prefer not to have the windows up, poor Bee would be over hot. We must think of the young things, mustn't we, Jessie? Well, you'll wonder why I am in my best toggery! Bee and I are off to the Manor, no less, I assure you. And to dinner, too! There's news for you. "

"Well, I'm sure! " responded Mrs. Morris. Envy was in every tone of her voice, and on every line of her face. As usual, when excited, she found her voice, which came out quite thin and sharp. "Well, I'm sure, " she repeated. "I wish you all luck, Lucy. Not that it's such a condescension, oh, by no means. The doctor said the bedrooms were very shabby in their furniture, and such a meal as those poor girls were eating for breakfast. He said his heart quite ached for them.

Nothing but stale bread, and the name of butter, and tea like water bewitched. He said he'd rather never have a child than see her put down to such fare. "

"Dear, dear, you don't say so, " answered Mrs. Meadowsweet. "Bee, my love, we must have those nice girls constantly to the Gray House, and feed them up all we can. I'm very sorry to hear your news, Jessie. But I'm afraid we can't wait to talk any longer now. Nothing could have been more affable than Mrs. Bertram's letter, sent down by special messenger, and written in a most stylish hand. "

"You haven't got it in your pocket, I suppose? " asked Mrs. Morris.

"To be sure I have. You'd like to see it; well, here it is. You can let me have it back to-morrow. Now, good-bye. Drive on, Davis. "

The cab jumbled and rattled over the paving stones, and Mrs. Meadowsweet lay back against the cushions, and fanned her hot face.

"I wonder if it's true about those poor girls being so badly fed, " she inquired of her daughter. "Dear, dear, and there's nothing young things want like generous living. Well, it's grievous. When I think of the quarts of milk I used to put into you, Bee, and the pounds and pounds of the best beef jelly—jelly that you could fling over the house, for thickness and solidity, and the fowls I had boiled down for you after the measles—who's that coming down the street, Bee? Look, my love, I'm a bit short-sighted. Oh, it's Miss Peters, of course. How are you, Miss Peters? Hot day, isn't it? Bee and I are off to the Manor—special invitation—letter—I lent it to Mrs. Morris. Oh, yes, to dinner. I have my best cap in this band-box. What do you say? You'll look in to-morrow—glad to see you. Drive on, Davis. "

"Really, mother, if you stop to speak to every one we won't get to the Manor to-night, " gently expostulated Beatrice.

"Well, well, my love, but we don't go to see the Bertrams every day, and when one feels more pleased and gratified than ordinary, it's nice to get the sympathy of one's neighbors. I do think the people at Northbury are very sympathetic, don't you, Bee? "

"Yes, mother, I think they are, " responded the daughter.

"And she took care not to tell her parent of any little lurking doubts which might come to her now and then with regard to the sincerity of those kind neighbors, who so often partook of the hospitality of the Gray House. "

When they reached the lodge, old Mrs. Tester came out to open the gates. She nodded and smiled to Beatrice who had often been very kind to her, and Mrs. Meadowsweet bent forward in the cab to ask very particularly about the old woman's rheumatism. It was at that moment that Beatrice caught sight of a face framed in with jasmine and Virginia creeper, which looked at her from out of an upper casement window in Mrs. Tester's little lodge. The face with its half-tamed expression, the eager scrutiny in the eyes, which were almost too bold in their brightness, startled Beatrice and gave her a sense of uneasiness. The face came like a flash to the window and then disappeared, and at that same moment Davis started the cab forward with a jerk. It was to the credit of both Davis and his sorry-looking steed that they should make a good show in the avenue. For this they had been reserving themselves, and they went along now in such a heedless and almost frantic style that Mrs. Meadowsweet had her bonnet knocked awry, and the band-box which contained the precious cap absolutely dashed to the floor of the cab.

Beatrice had therefore no time to make any remark with regard to Mrs. Tester's unwonted visitor.

"This is delightful, " said Mrs. Meadowsweet, as she clasped her hostess's hand, in the long, cool, refined-looking drawing-room. "I'm very glad to come, and it's most kind of you to invite me. Dear, dear, what a cool room! Wonderful! How do you manage this kind of effect, Mrs. Bertram? Dearie me—*very* pretty—*very* pretty indeed. "

Here Mrs. Meadowsweet sank down on one of the sofas, and gazed round her with the most genuine delight.

"Where's Bee? " she said. "She ought to look round this room and take hints from it. We spent a lot of money over our drawing-room, but it never looks like this. Where are you, Beatrice? "

"Never mind now, " responded Mrs. Bertram, whose voice, in spite of herself, had to take an extra well-bred tone when she spoke to Mrs. Meadowsweet. Miss Beatrice has just gone out with my girls, and I thought you and I would have tea here, and afterwards sit under the shade of that oak-tree and watch the children at their game. "

"Very nice, I'm sure, " responded Mrs. Meadowsweet. She spread out her fat hands on her lap and untied her bonnet-strings. "It's hot, " she said. "Do you find the dog-days try you very much, Mrs. Bertram? "

"I don't feel the heat particularly, " said Mrs. Bertram. She was anxious to assume a friendly tone, but was painfully conscious that her voice was icy.

"Well, that's lucky for you, " remarked the visitor. "I flush up a good deal. Beatrice never does. She takes after her father; he was wonderfully cool, poor man. Have you got a newspaper of any sort about, that you'd lend me, Mrs. Bertram? "

"Oh, certainly, " answered Mrs. Bertram, in some astonishment. "Here is yesterday's *Times*. "

"I'll make it into a fan, if you have no objection. Now, that's better. Dear, dear, what a nice room! "

Mrs. Bertram fidgetted on her chair. She wondered how many more times Mrs. Meadowsweet would descant on the elegancies of her drawing-room. She need not have feared. Whatever Mrs. Meadowsweet was she was honest; and at that very moment her eyes lighted on the felt which covered the floor. Mrs. Meadowsweet had never been trained in a school of art, but, as she said to herself, no one knew better what was what than she did; above all, no one knew better what was *comme il faut* in the matter of carpets. Meadowsweet, poor man, had been particular about his carpets. There were grades in carpets as in all other things, and felt, amongst these grades, ranked low, very low indeed. Kidderminster might be permitted in bedrooms, although Mrs. Meadowsweet would scorn to see it in any room in *her* house, but Brussels was surely the only correct carpet for people of medium means to cover their drawing-room floors with. The report that Mrs. Bertram's drawing-room wore a mantle of felt had reached Mrs. Meadowsweet's ears. She had emphatically declined to believe in any such calumny, and yet now her own eyes saw, her own good-humored, kind eyes, that wished to think well of all the world, rested on that peculiar greeny-brown felt, which surely must have come to its present nondescript hue by the aid of many suns. The whole room looked immediately almost sordid to the poor woman, and she felt no longer anxious for Beatrice to appreciate its beauties.

At that moment Clara appeared with the tea. Now, if there was a thing Mrs. Meadowsweet was particular about it was her tea; she revelled in her tea; she always bought it from some very particular and exclusive house in London. She saw that it was served strong and hot; she was particular to have it made with what she called the "first boil" of the water. Water that had boiled for five minutes made, in Mrs. Meadowsweet's opinion, contemptible tea. Then she liked it well sweetened, and flavored with very rich cream. Such a cup of tea, as she expressed it, set her up for the day. The felt carpet had given Mrs. Meadowsweet a kind of shock, but all her natural spirits revived when she saw the tea equipage. She approved of the exquisite eggshell china, and noted with satisfaction that the teapot was really silver.

"What a refreshment a cup of tea is! " exclaimed the good woman. "Nothing like it, as I dare say you know, Mrs. Bertram. "

Mrs. Bertram smiled languidly, and raising the teapot, prepared to pour out a cup for her guest. She was startled by a noise, which sounded something like a shout, coming from the fat lady's lips.

"Did you speak? " she asked.

"Oh, I beg your pardon, Mrs. Bertram, but don't—it's cruel. "

"Don't do what? "

"The tea isn't drawn. Let it rest a bit—why, it's the color of straw. "

"This peculiar tea is always of a light color, " replied Mrs. Bertram, her sallow face growing darkly red. "I hope you will appreciate it; but perhaps it is a matter of training. It is, however, I assure you, quite the vogue among my friends in London. "

Mrs. Meadowsweet felt crushed. She received the cup of flavorless, half-cold liquid presented to her in a subdued spirit, sipped it with the air of a martyr, and devoutly wished herself back again in the Gray House.

Mrs. Bertram knew perfectly well that her guest thought the tea detestable and the cake stale. It was as necessary for people of Mrs. Meadowsweet's class to go in for strong tea and high living as it was for people of Mrs. Bertram's class to aspire to faded felt in the matter of carpets, and water bewitched in the shape of tea. Each after her kind, Mrs. Bertram murmured. But as she had an object in view it was necessary for her to earn the good-will of the well-to-do widow.

Accordingly, when the slender meal came to an end, and the two ladies found themselves under the shelter of the friendly oak-tree, matters went more smoothly. Mrs. Bertram put her guest into an excellent humor by bestowing some cordial praise upon Beatrice.

"She is not like you, " continued the good lady, with some naïveté.

"No, no, " responded the gratified mother. "And sorry I'd be to think that Beatrice took after me. I'm commonplace. Mrs. Bertram. I have no figure to boast of, nor much of a face either. What *he* saw to like in me, poor man, has puzzled my brain a score and score of times. Kind and affectionate he ever was, but he couldn't but own, as own I did for him, that I was a cut below him. Beatrice features her father, Mrs. Bertram, both in mind and body. "

Mrs. Bertram murmured some compliment about the mother's kind heart, and then turned to a subject which is known to be of infallible interest to all ladies. She spoke of her ailments.

Mrs. Meadowsweet beamed all over when this subject came on the *tapis*. She even laid her fat hand on Mrs. Bertram's lap.

"Now, *did* you ever try Eleazer Macjone's Pills of Life? " she asked. "I always have a lot of them in the house; and I assure you, Mrs. Bertram, they are worth all the doctor's messes put together; for years I have taken the pills, and it's a positive fact that they're made to fit the human body all round. Headaches—it's wonderful what Macjone's pills do for headaches. If you have a low, all-overish feeling, Macjone's pills pick you up directly. They are wonderful, too, for colds; and if there's any infection going they nip it in the bud. I wish you would try them, Mrs. Bertram; I know they'd pull you round, I'll send for a box for you with pleasure when I'm having my next chest of tea down from London. I always get my tea from London. I think what they sell here is little better than dishwater; so I say to Beatrice, 'Bee, my love, whatever happens, we'll get our tea from town. "

"And your pills from town, too, " responded Mrs. Bertram. "I think you are a very wise woman, Mrs. Meadowsweet. How well your daughter plays tennis. Yes, she is decidedly graceful. I have heard of many pills in my day, and patent pills invariably fit one all round, but I have never yet heard of Eleazer Macjone's Life Pills. You look very well, Mrs. Meadowsweet, so I shall recommend them in future. For my part, I think the less drugs one swallows the better. "

"You are quite right, Mrs. Bertram, quite right. Except for the pills I never touch medicine. And now I'd like to give you a wrinkle. I wouldn't spend much money, if I were you, on Dr. Morris. He's all fads, poor man, all fads. He speaks of the Life Pills as poison, and his terms—I have over and over told his wife, Jessie Morris, that her husband's terms are preposterous. "

"Then I am afraid he will not suit me, " replied Mrs. Bertram, "I cannot afford to meet preposterous terms, for I, alas! am poor. "

"Dear, dear, I'm truly sorry to hear it, Mrs. Bertram. And with your fine young family, too. That lad of yours is as handsome a young fellow as I've often set eyes on. And your girls, particularly Miss Catherine, are specially genteel. "

"A great many people consider Catherine handsome, " replied her mother, who began to shiver inwardly under the infliction of Mrs. Meadowsweet's talk. She tried to add something about Loftus, but for some reason or other words failed her. After a moment's pause she resumed:

"Only those who know what small means are can understand the constant self-denial they inflict.

"And that's true enough, Mrs. Bertram. "

"Ah, Mrs. Meadowsweet, you must be only assuming this sympathetic tone. For, if all reports are true, you and Miss Beatrice are wealthy. "

Mrs. Meadowsweet's eyes beamed lovingly on her hostess.

"We have enough and to spare, " she responded. "Thank the good God we have enough and to spare. Meadowsweet saw to that, poor man. "

"Your husband was in business? " gently in quired Mrs. Bertram.

"He kept a shop, Mrs. Bertram. I'm the last to deny it. He kept a good, thriving draper's shop in the High Street. The best of goods he had, and he sold fair. I used to help him in those days. I used to go to London to buy the Spring fashions, and pretty things I'd buy, uncommonly pretty, and the prettiest of all, you may be sure, for little Beatrice. Ah! you could get a stylish hat in Northbury in those days. Poor man, he had the custom of all the country round. There was no shop like Meadowsweet's. Well, he made his fortune in it, and he died full of money and much respected. What could man do more? "

"And your daughter Beatrice resembles her father? "

"She does, Mrs. Bertram. He was a very genteel man—a cut above me, as I said before. He was fond of books, and but for me maybe he'd have got into trade in the book line. But I warned him off that shoal. I said to him, scores of times, 'Mark my words, William, dress will last, and books won't. People must be clothed, but they needn't read. ' He was wise enough to stick to my words, and he made his fortune. "

"I suppose, " said Mrs. Bertram, in a slow, meditative voice, "that a—um—merchant—in a small town like this, might, with care, realize, say, two or three thousand pounds. "

Mrs. Meadowsweet's eyes almost flashed.

"Two or three thousand! " she said, "dearie me, dearie me. When people talk of fortunes, in Northbury, they *mean* fortunes, Mrs. Bertram. "

"And your daughter will inherit? " asked the hostess of her guest.

"There's full and plenty for me, Mrs. Bertram, and when Beatrice comes of age, or when she marries with her mother's approval, she'll have twenty thousand pounds. Twenty thousand invested in the funds, that's her fortune, not bad for a shopkeeper's daughter, is it,

Mrs. Bertram? " Mrs. Bertram said that it was anything but bad, and she inwardly reflected on the best means of absolutely suppressing the memory of the shopkeeper, and how, by a little judicious training, she might induce Mrs. Meadowsweet to speak of her late partner as belonging to the roll of British merchants.

CHAPTER XVII.

THE WITCH WITH THE YELLOW HAIR.

A corner is a very pretty addition to a room, and a cleft-stick has been known to present a more picturesque appearance than a straight one. But to find oneself, metaphorically speaking, pushed into the corner or wedged into the cleft of the stick is neither picturesque nor pleasant.

This was Mrs. Bertram's present position. She had suddenly, and at a moment when she least expected it, been confronted with the ghost of a long ago past. The ghost of a past, so remote that she had almost forgotten it, had come back and stared her in the face. This ghost had assumed terrible dimensions, and the poor woman was dreadfully afraid of it.

She had taken a hurried journey to London in the vain hope of laying it. Alas! it would not be laid. Most things, however, can be bought at a price, and Mrs. Bertram had bought the silence of this troublesome ghost of the past. She had bought it at a very heavy cost.

Her money was in the hands of trustees; she dared not go to them to assist her, therefore, the only price she could pay was out of her yearly income.

To quiet this troublesome ghost she agreed to part with four hundred a year. A third of her means was, therefore, taken away with one fell swoop. Loftus must still have his allowance, for Loftus of all people must know nothing of his mother's anxieties. Mrs. Bertram and her girls would, therefore, have barely five hundred a year to live on. Out of this sum she would still struggle to save, but she knew she could save but little. She knew that all chance of introducing Catherine and Mabel into society was at an end. She had dreamed dreams for her girls, and these dreams must come to nothing. She had hoped many things for them both, she had thought that all her care and trouble would receive its fruition some day in Catherine's establishment, and that Mabel would also marry worthily. In playing with her grandchildren by-and-bye, Mrs. Bertram thought that she might relax her anxieties and feel that her labors had not been in vain. She must put these hopes aside now, for her girls would probably never marry. They would live on at this dull old Manor until their youth had left them, and their sweet, fresh bloom departed.

Mrs. Bertram thought of the girls, but no compunctions with regard to them caused her to hesitate even for a moment. She loved some one else much better than these bright-eyed lasses. Loftus was the darling of his mother's heart. It was bad to sacrifice girls, but it was impossible to sacrifice the beloved and only son.

Mrs. Bertram saw her solicitors, confided to them her difficulties, and accepted the terms proposed to her by the enemy, who, treacherous and awful, had suddenly risen out of the ashes of the past to confront her.

With four hundred a year she bought silence, and silence meant everything for her. Thus she saved herself, and one at least belonging to her, from open shame.

She received Catherine's telegram, and was made aware that Josephine Hart had come down to spy out the nakedness of the land. She felt herself, however, in a position to defy Josephine, and she returned to the Manor fairly well pleased.

It was Loftus, for whom she had really sacrificed so much, who dealt her the final blow. This idle scapegrace had got into fresh debt and difficulty. Mrs. Bertram expostulated, she wrung her hands, she could almost have torn her hair. The young man stood before her half-abashed, half sulky.

"Can you help me, mother? That's the main point, " was his reiterated cry.

Mrs. Bertram managed at last to convince him that she had not a farthing of ready money left.

"In that case, " he replied, "nothing but ruin awaits me. "

His mother wept when he told her this. She was shaken with all she had undergone in London, poor woman, and this man, who could cringe to her for a large dole out of her pittance, was the beloved of her heart.

He begged of her to put her hand to a bill; a bill which should not become due for six months. She consented; she was weak enough to set him, as he expressed it, absolutely on his feet. All debts would be paid at once, and he would never exceed his allowance again; and as to his mother's difficulty, in meeting a bill for six hundred pounds, it was not in Loftus Bertram's nature to trouble himself on this score six months ahead.

That bill, however was the proverbial last straw to Mrs. Bertram. It haunted her by day and night; she dreamt of it, sleeping, she pondered over it, waking. Six short months would speedily disappear, and then she would be ruined; she could not meet the bill, exposure and disaster must follow.

Even very honorable people when they get themselves into corners often seek for means of escape which certainly would not occur to them as the most dignified exits if they were, for instance, not in the corner, but in the middle of the room.

Mrs. Bertram was a woman of resources, and she made up her mind what to do. She made it up absolutely, and no doubts or difficulties daunted her for an instant. Loftus should marry Beatrice Meadowsweet long before the six months were out.

Having ascertained positively not only from her mother's lips, but also from those of Mr. Ingram, that the young girl could claim as her portion twenty thousand pounds on her wedding day, Mrs. Bertram felt there was no longer need to hesitate. Beatrice was quite presentable in herself; she was handsome, she was well-bred, she had a gracious and even careless repose of manner which would pass muster anywhere for the highest breeding. It would be quite possible to crush that fat and hopelessly vulgar mother, and it would be easy, more than easy, to talk of the wealthy merchant's office instead of the obnoxious draper's shop.

Bertram, who had just moved with the *dépot* of his regiment to Chatham, on returning to his quarters one evening from mess saw lying on his table a thick letter in his mother's handwriting. He took it up carelessly, and, as he opened it, he yawned. Mother's letters are not particularly sacred things to idolized sons of Bertram's type.

"I wonder what the old lady has got to say for herself, " he murmured. "Can she have seen Nina? And has Nina said anything.

Not that she can seriously injure me in the mater's eyes. No one would be more lenient to a little harmless flirtation which was never meant to lead anywhere than my good mother. Still it was a great bore for Josephine to turn up when she did. Obliged me to shorten my leave abruptly, and see less of Miss Beatrice. What a little tiger Nina would be if her jealousy was aroused—no help for me but flight. Yes, Saunders, you needn't wait. "

Bertram's servant withdrew; and taking his mother's letter out of its envelope, the young man proceeded to acquaint himself with its contents. They interested him, not a little, but deeply. The color flushed up into his face as he read. He made one or two strong exclamations, finally he laughed aloud. His laugh was excited and full of good humor.

"By Jove! the mother never thought of a better plot. Beatrice—and fortune. Beatrice, and an escape into the bargain from all my worries. Poor mater! She does not know that that six hundred of hers has only just scraped me through my most pressing liabilities. But a small dip out of Beatrice Meadowsweet's fortune will soon set me on my feet. The mater's wishes and mine never so thoroughly chimed together as now. Of course I'll do it. No fear on that point. I'll write off to the dear old lady, and set her heart at rest, by this very post. As to leave, I must manage that somehow. The mother is quite right. With a girl like Beatrice there is no time to be lost. Any fellow might come over to Northbury and pick her up. Why, she's perfectly splendid. I knew I was in love with her—felt it all along. Just think of my patrician mother giving in, though. Well, nothing could suit me better. "

Bertram felt so excited that he paced up and down his room, and even drank off a brandy and soda, which was not in his usual line, for he was a sober young fellow enough.

As he walked up and down he thought again of that night when he had last seen Beatrice. How splendid she had looked in her boat on the water; how unreserved, and yet how reticent she was; how beautiful, and yet how unconscious of her beauty. What a foil she made to that dreadful little Matty Bell!

Bertram laughed as he remembered Matty's blushes and affected giggles and simpers. He conjured up the whole scene, and when he recalled poor Mrs. Bell's frantic efforts to get the white boat away from the green, his sense of hilarity doubled. Finally he thought of his walk home, of the meditations which had occupied his mind, and last of all of the girl in the gray dress who had put her arms round his neck, laid her head on his breast, and whose lips he had passionately kissed. That head! He felt a thrill now as he remembered the sheen of its golden locks, and he knew that the kisses he had given this girl had been full of the passion of his manhood. He ceased to laugh as he thought of her. A growing sense of uneasiness, of even fear, took possession of him, and chased away the high spirits which his mother's acceptable proposal had given rise to.

He sat down again in his easy chair and began to think.

"It is not, " he said to himself, "that I have got into any real scrape with Nina. I have promised to marry her, of course, and I have made love to her scores and scores of times, but I don't think she has any letters of mine, and in any case, she is not the sort of girl to go to law with a fellow. No, I have nothing really to fear on that score. But what perplexes and troubles me is this: she has got a great power over me. When I am with her I can't think of any one else. She has an influence over me which I can't withstand. I want her, and her only. I know it would ruin me to marry her. She has not a penny; she is an uneducated poor waif, brought up anyhow. My God, when I think of how I first saw you, Nina! That London street, that crowd looking on, and the pure young voice rising up as it were into the very sky. And then the sound stopping, and the shout from the mob. I got into the middle of the ring somehow, and I saw you, I saw you, my little darling. Your hand was clenched, and the fellow who had dared to insult you went down with that blow you gave him to the ground. Didn't your eyes flash fire, and the flickering light from that fishmonger's shop opposite lit up your hair and your pale face. You looked half like a devil, but you were beautiful, you were superb. Then you saw me, and you must have guessed that I felt with you and for you. Our souls seemed to leap out to meet one another, and you were by my side in an instant, kissing my hand, and raining tears on it. We loved each other from that night; our love began from the moment we looked at each other, and I love you still—but I mustn't marry you, little wild, desperate, bewitching Nina, for that would ruin us both. My God! I wish I had never met you; I am afraid of you, and that is the fact. "

Perhaps it was the unwonted beverage in which he had just indulged, which gave rise to such eager and impetuous thoughts in the breast of Captain Bertram. It is certain when he had slept over his mother's letter he felt much more cool and collected. If he still feared Josephine Hart, he was absolutely determined not to allow his fears to get the better of him. He ceased even to say to himself that he was in love with this pretty witch of the yellow hair, and his letter to his mother was as cool and self-possessed as the most prudent among parents could desire.

Bertram told his mother that he thought he could manage to exchange with a brother officer, so as to secure his own leave while the days were long and the weather fine. He said that if all went as he hoped, he would be at the Manor by the end of the following week, and he sent his love to his sisters, and hoped the mater was quite herself again.

Not once did he mention the name of Beatrice, but Mrs. Bertram read between the lines. She admired her son for his caution. Her heart leaped with exultation, her boy would not fail her.

If she had known that the old postman Benjafield had left a letter by the very same post for Miss Hart at the lodge, and that this letter in a disguised hand bore within the undoubted signature of her own beloved captain, her rejoicing would not have been so keen. But as people are very seldom allowed to see behind the scenes Mrs. Bertram may as well have her short hour of triumph undisturbed.

CHAPTER XVIII.

"WHEN DUNCAN GRAY CAME HOME TO WOO. "

Most people go away for change of air in the month of August, but this was by no means the fashion in the remote, little old-world town of Northbury. In November people left home if they could, for it was dull, very dull at Northbury in November, but August was the prime month of the year.

It was then the real salt from the broad Atlantic came into the limpid waters of the little harbor. August was the month for bathing, for yachting, for trawling. Some denizens of the outside world even came to Northbury in August; the few lodging-houses were crammed to overflowing; people put up with any accommodation for the sake of the crisp air, and the lovely deep blue water of the bay. For in August this same water was often at night alight with phosphorescent substances, which gave it the appearance in the moonlight of liquid golden fire. It was then the girls sang their best, and the young men said soft nothings, and hearts beat a little more quickly than ordinary, and in short the mischievous, teasing, fascinating god of love was abroad.

In preparation for these August days Perry the draper did a roaring trade, for all the Northbury girls had fresh ribbons put on their sailor hats, and fresh frills in their blue serge dresses, and their tan leather gloves had to be neat and new, and their walking shoes trim and whole, for the entire little world would be abroad all day and half the night, in company with the harvest moon and the glittering golden waves, and all the other gay, bright things of summer.

This was therefore just the most fitting season for Captain Bertram to come back to Northbury, on wooing intent. More than one girl in the place rejoiced at his arrival, and Mrs. Bertram so far relaxed her rigid hold over Catherine and Mabel as to allow them to partake, in company with their brother and Beatrice Meadowsweet, of a certain portion of the general merry-making.

Northbury was a remarkably light-hearted little place, but it never had entered into quite so gay a season as this memorable August when Captain Bertram came to woo.

It somehow got into the air that this gay young officer had taken his leave for the express purpose of getting himself a wife. Nobody quite knew how the little gossiping whisper arose, but arise it did, and great was the commotion put into the atmosphere, and severe the flutterings it caused to arise in more than one gentle girl heart.

Catherine and Mabel Bertram were in the highest possible spirits during this same month of August. Their mother seemed well once more, well, and gay, and happy. The hard rule of economy, always a depressing *régime*, had also for the time disappeared. The meals were almost plentiful, the girls had new dresses, and as they went out a little it was essential for them in their turn to entertain.

Mrs. Bertram went to some small expense to complete the tennis courts, and she even endured the sight of the Bells and Jenkinses as they struggled with the intricacies of the popular game.

She herself took refuge in Mr. Ingram's society. He applauded her efforts at being sociable, and told her frankly that he was glad she was changing her mind with regard to the Northbury folk.

"Any society is better than none, " he said. "And they really are such good creatures. Not of course in the matter of finish and outward manner to compare with the people you are accustomed to, Mrs. Bertram, but—"

"Ah, I know, " interrupted Mrs. Bertram in a gay voice. "Rough diamonds you would call them. But you are mistaken, my dear friend; there is, I assure you, not a diamond in this motley herd, unless I except Miss Beatrice. "

"I never class Beatrice with the other Northbury people, " replied Mr. Ingram; "there is something about her which enables her to take a stand of her own. I think if she had been born in any rank, she would have kept her individuality. She is uncommon, so for that matter is Miss Catherine. "

The two girls were standing together as Mr. Ingram spoke. They were resting after a spirited game, and they made a pretty picture as they stood under the shelter of the old oak tree. Both were in white, and both wore large drooping hats. These hats cast picturesque shadows on their young faces.

Mrs. Bertram looked at them with a queer half-jealous pang. Beatrice was the child of a lowly tradesman, Catherine the daughter of a man of family and some pretension; and yet Mrs. Bertram had to own that in any society this tall, upright, frank, young Beatrice could hold her own, that even Catherine whose dark face was patrician, who bore the refinement of race in every point, could scarcely outshine this country girl.

"It is marvellous, " said Mrs. Bertram after a pause; "Beatrice is one of nature's ladies. There are a few such, they come now and then, and no circumstances can spoil them. To think of that girl's mother! "

"One of the dearest old ladies of my acquaintance, " replied Mr. Ingram. "Beatrice owes a great deal of her nobleness of heart and singleness of purpose to her mother. Mrs. Bertram, I have never heard that woman say an unkind word. I have heard calumny of her, but never from her. Then, of course, Meadowsweet was quite a gentleman. "

"My dear friend! A draper a gentleman? "

"I grant the anomaly is not common, " said the Rector. "But in Meadowsweet's case I make a correct statement. He was a perfect gentleman after the type of some of those who are mentioned in the Sacred Writings. He was honest, courteous, self-forgetful. His manners were delightful, because his object ever was to put the person he was speaking to completely at his ease. He had the natural advantage of a refined appearance, and his accent was pure, and not marred by any provincialisms. He could not help speaking in the best English because he was a scholar, and he spent all his leisure studying the classics. Therefore, although he kept a draper's shop, he was a gentleman. By the way, Mrs. Bertram, do you know anything of the young girl who has been staying at your lodge? You—you are tired, my dear lady? "

"A little. I will sit on this bench. There is room for you too, Rector. Sit near me, what about the girl at my lodge? "

"She is no longer at your lodge. She has left. Do you happen to know anything about her? "

"Nothing. "

"Ah, that seems a pity. She is the sort of young creature to excite one's sympathy. I called to see her a week ago, and she talked prettily to me and looked sorrowful. Her name, she says, is Hart. "

"Really? I—I confess I am not interested. "

"But you ought to be, my dear friend, you ought to be. The girl seems alone and defenceless. She is reserved with regard to her history, won't make confidences, although I begged of her to confide in me, and assured her that I, in my position, would receive what she chose to tell under the seal of secrecy. Her eyes filled with tears, poor little soul, but her lips were dumb. "

"Oh, she has nothing to confide. "

"Do you think so? I can't agree with you. Although my lot has been cast in this remote out-of-the-world town, I have had my experiences, Mrs. Bertram, and I never yet saw a face like Miss Hart's which did not conceal a history. "

"May I ask you, Mr. Ingram, if you ever before saw a face like Miss Hart's? "

"Well, no, now that you put it to me, I don't think that I ever have. It is beautiful. "

"Ugly, you mean. "

"No, no, Mrs. Bertram. With all due deference to your superior taste I cannot agree with you. The features are classical, the eyes a little wild and defiant, but capable of much expression. The hair of the admired Rossetti type. "

"Oh, spare me, Rector, spare me. I don't mean this low girl's outward appearance. It is that which I feel is within which makes her altogether ugly to me. "

"Ah, poor child—women have intuitions, and you may be right. It would of course not be judicious for your daughters to associate with Miss Hart. But you, Mrs. Bertram, you, as a mother, might get at this poor child's past, and counsel her as to her future. "

"She has gone away, has she not? " asked Mrs. Bertram.

"I regret to say she has, but she may return. She promised me faithfully to come to church on Sunday, and I called at the lodge on my way up to leave her a little basket of fruit and flowers, and to remind her of her promise. Mrs. Tester said she had left her, but might return again. I hope so, and that I may be the means of helping her, for the poor child's face disturbs me. "

"I trust your wish may never be realized, " murmured Mrs. Bertram, under her breath. Aloud she said cheerfully, "I must show you my bed of pansies, Rector. They are really quite superb. "

CHAPTER XIX.

THE RECTOR'S GARDEN PARTY.

A few days after the tennis party at the Manor, at which Bertram had talked a good deal to Beatrice, and in a very marked way snubbed Matty Bell, the Rector gave his customary annual treat. He gave this treat every year, and it was looked upon by high and low alike as the great event of the merry month of August. The treat lasted for two days, the first day being devoted to the schools and the humble parishioners, the second to the lads and lasses, the well-to-do matrons and their spouses, who formed the better portion of his parishioners.

Every soul in the place, however, from the poorest fisherman's child to the wealthy widow, Mrs. Meadowsweet, wag expected to come to the Rectory to be feasted and petted, and made much of, at Mr. Ingram's treat.

With the small scholars and the fishermen and their wives, and all the humbler folk of the place, this story has nothing to do. But it would not be a true chronicle of Northbury if it did not concern itself with the Jenkinses and their love affairs, with Mrs. Gorman Stanley and her furniture, with Mrs. Morris and her bronchitis, with Mrs. Butler and her adorable sister, Miss Peters, and last, but not least, with that young, *naïve*, and childish heart which beat in the breast of Matty Bell.

There are the important people in all histories, and such a place in this small chronicle must the Bertrams hold, and the Meadowsweets. But Matty, too, had her niche, and it was permitted to her to pull some not unimportant wires in this puppet show.

It is not too strong a word to say that Matty, Alice and Sophy Bell, received their invitation to play tennis at the Manor with a due sense of jubilation. Matty wore the shot silk which had been partly purchased by the sale of good Mrs. Bell's engagement ring. This silk had been made, at home, but, with the aid of a dressmaker young Susan Pettigrew, who had served her time to the Perrys. Susan had made valuable suggestions, which had been carried into effect, with the result that the shot silk was provided with two bodies—a high one for morning wear, and one cut in a modest, demi-style for evening festivities. The evening body had elbow-sleeves, which were furnished with raffles of coffee-colored lace, and, when put on, it revealed the contour of a rather nice plump little throat, and altogether made Matty Bell look nicer than she had ever looked in anything else before.

The wonderful Miss Pettigrew had also supplied the dress with a train, which could be hooked on with safety hooks and eyes for evening wear, and removed easily when the robe was to act as a tennis or morning costume. Altogether, nothing could have been more complete than this sinning garment, and no heart could have beat more proudly under it than did fair Matty's.

When the captain went suddenly away this little girl and her good mother had both owned to a sense of depression; but his speedy return was soon bruited abroad, and at the same time that little whisper got into the air with regard to the gallant captain, that, like Duncan Gray, he was coming back to woo. It did not require many nods of Mrs. Bell's head to assure all her acquaintances whom she considered the favored young lady. Matty once more blushed consciously, and giggled in an audible manner when the captain's name was mentioned. The invitation to play tennis at the Manor completed the satisfaction of this mother and daughter.

"There's no doubt of it, " said Mrs. Bell; "I thought my fine lady would have to come down from her high horse. I expect the captain makes his mother do pretty much what he wishes, and very right, too, very right. He wants to show his little girl to his proud parent, and, whether she likes it or not, she'll have to make much of you, my love. Sophy and Alice, it's more than likely Matty will be asked to dine and spend the evening, at the Manor, and I think we'll just make up the evening body of her silk dress and her train in a bit of brown paper, and you can carry the parcel up between you to the Manor. Then, if it's wanted, it will come in handy, and my girl won't be behind one of them. "

"Lor, ma, what are we to do with such a bulky parcel? " objected Sophy, who was not looking her best in a washed-out muslin of two years' date. "What can we do with the parcel when we get to the Manor? "

"Take it up, of course, to the house, child, and give it to the servant, and tell her it's to be kept till called for. She'll understand fast enough; servants always guess when there's a sweetheart in the question. Most likely she'll place the things ready for Matty in one of the bedrooms. I'll put in your best evening shoes too, Matty, love, and my old black lace fan, in case you should flush up dreadful when the captain is paying you attention. And now, Sophy, you'll just be good-natured, and leave the parcel with the parlor maid, so your sister will be prepared for whatever happens. "

Sophy, having been judiciously bribed by the loan of a large Cairngorm brooch of her mother's, which took up a conspicuous position at her throat, finally consented to carry the obnoxious parcel. Alice was further instructed, in case Mrs. Bertram so far failed in her duty as to neglect to invite Matty to stay to dine at the Manor to try and bring Captain Bertram back with them to supper.

"You tell him that I'll have a beautiful lobster, and a crab done to a turn ready for him, " whispered the mother. "You'll manage it, Alice, and look sympathetic when you speak to him, poor fellow. Let him know that I'll give him his chances, whether that proud lady, his mother, does or not. Now then, off you go, all three of you. Kiss me, Matty, my pet. Well, to be sure, you do look stylish. "

The three little figures in their somewhat tight shoes toddled down the street. In the evening they toddled back again. The brown paper parcel tossed, and somewhat torn, was tucked fiercely under Sophy's arm, and Alice was unaccompanied by any brave son of Mars.

Sophy was the first to enter her expectant mother's presence.

"There, ma, " she said, flinging the paper parcel on the table. "I hope we have had enough of those Bertrams and their ways. The fuss I had over that horrid parcel. I thought I'd never get it back again. In the end I had to see Mrs. Bertram about it, and didn't she crush me just! She's an awful woman. I never want to speak to her again all my life, and as to the captain caring for Matty! "

"Where is Matty? " here interrupted Mrs. Bell. "She was not asked to stay behind after all, then? "

"*She* asked to stay behind? You speak for yourself, Matty. For my part, I think it was very unfair to give Matty that silk. We might all have had nice washing muslins for the price of it. Where are you, Matty? Oh, I declare she has gone upstairs in the sulks! "

"You're in a horrid bad temper, Sophy; that I can see, " expostulated the mother. "Well, Alice, perhaps you can tell me what all this fuss is about? I hope to goodness you gave the captain my message, child. "

"I didn't see him to give it, mother, " answered Alice. "He never spoke once to us the whole time. He just shook hands when we arrived, but even then he didn't speak. "

"Captain Bertram never spoke to Matty during the entire evening? " gasped Mrs. Bell. "Child, you can't be speaking the truth, you must be joking me. "

"I'm not, truly, mother. Captain Bertram didn't even look at Matty. He was all the time following Beatrice Meadowsweet about like a shadow. "

Mrs. Bell gave her head a toss.

"Oh, that's it, is it? " she said. "I didn't think the captain would be so artful. Mark my word, girls, he behaved like that just as a blind to put his old mother off the scent. "

But as Mrs. Bell spoke her heart sank within her. She remembered again how Beatrice had looked that evening in the green boat, and she saw once more Matty's tossed locks and sunburnt hands.

After a time she went upstairs, and without any ceremony entered her daughter's room.

Matty had tossed off the gaudy silk, and was lying on her bed. Her poor little face was blistered with tears, and, as Mrs. Bell expressed it, it "gave me a heart-ache even to look at her. " She was not a woman, however, to own to defeat. She pretended not to see Matty's tears, and she made her tone purposely very cheerful.

"Come, come, child, " she said, "what are you stretched on the bed for, as if you were delicate? Now, I wouldn't let this get to Captain Bertram's ears for the world. "

"What do you mean, mother? " asked the astonished daughter.

"What I say, my love. I wouldn't let the captain know that you were so tired as to have to lie down after a game of tennis, for a ten pound note. Nothing puts a man off a girl so soon as to hear that she's delicate. "

"Oh, he—he doesn't care, " half sobbed Matty.

"Oh, doesn't he, though? I never knew anything more like caring than for him to be too shy to come near you. Things have gone pretty far when a man has to blind his mother by pretending to be taken up with another girl. I knew the captain was in love, Matty, but I did not suppose he was deep enough to play his cards after that fashion. You get up now, lovey, and come down, and have a nice hot cup of tea. It will revive you wonderfully, my pet. "

Matty allowed her mother to coax her off the bed, and to assist her on with her every-day brown holland frock. She was a good deal comforted and inclined to reconsider the position which had seemed so hopeless half-an-hour ago.

"Only he did neglect me shamefully, " she said, with a little toss of her head. "And I don't see why I should take it from him. "

"That's right, my girl. You show Captain Bertram you've got a spirit of your own. There's nothing brings a man to the point like a girl giving him a little bit of sauce. Next time he speaks to you, you can be as stand-off as you please, Matty. "

"Yes, mother, " said Matty, in a languid tone.

She knew, however, that it was not in her nature to be stand-off to any one, and beneath all the comfort of her mother's words she could not help doubting if Captain Bertram would care how she behaved to him.

The next morning the Rector's invitation came for the annual treat, and the hopes of the Bells once more rose high. On this occasion Mrs. Bell was to accompany her daughters. Bell would also be present, but, as he was never of much account, this small fact scarcely rested on any one's mind. All the town was now in state of ferment. The Rector's party was the only thing spoken about, and many were the prognostications with regard to the weather.

The day of festival came at last; the sun arose gloriously, not a cloud was in the sky, all the merry-makers might go in their best, and all

141

hearts might be jubilant. It was delightful to see Northbury on this day, for so gay were the costumes worn by its inhabitants that as they passed through the narrow old streets they gave the place of their birth a picturesque and even a foreign appearance.

The Rectory was just outside the town, and, of course, all the footsteps were bending thither. The Rector had invited his guests to assemble at three o'clock, and punctually at a quarter to that hour Miss Peters seated herself in her bay window, armed with a spy-glass to watch the gathering crowd.

Miss Peters was already arrayed in her festive clothes, but she and Mrs. Butler thought it ungenteel not to be, at least, an hour late. "The Bertrams will be sure to be late, " remarked the good lady to her sister, "and we, too, Martha, will show that we know what's what. "

"Which we don't, " snapped Mrs. Butler. "We are sure and certain to be put in the wrong before we are half-an-hour there. However, I agree with you, Maria; we won't be among the hurryers. I hate to be one of those who snap at a thing. Now, what's the matter? How you do startle me! "

"It's Mrs. Gorman Stanley, " gasped Miss Peters; "she's in red velvet, with a beaded bodice—and—oh, do look at her bonnet, Martha! Positively, it's hideous. A straw-green, with blue forget-me-nots, and those little baby daisies dropping over her hair. Well, well, how that woman does ape youth! "

Mrs. Butler snatched the spy-glass from her sister, and surveyed Mrs. Gorman Stanley's holiday attire with marked disapproval. She threw down her glasses presently with a little sniff.

"Disgusting, " she said with emphasis. "That woman will never see fifty again, and she apes seventeen. For my part, I think, when women reach a certain age they should not deck themselves with artificial flowers. Flowers are for the young, not for poor worn-out, faded types of humanity. Now you, Maria— —"

"Oh, don't, " said Miss Maria, stepping back a few paces in alarm, and putting up her hand to her bonnet, "don't say that wallflowers aren't allowable, Martha; I always did think that wallflowers were so *passé*. That's why I chose them. "

The Honorable Miss: A Story of an Old-Fashioned Town

"Who's that now? " exclaimed Mrs. Butler. "My word, Maria, get quick behind the curtain and peep! Give me the spy-glass; I'll look over your head. Why, if it isn't—no—yes—it is, though—it's that young Captain Bertram, a *most* stylish young man! He looks elegant in flannels—quite a noble face—I should imagine him to be the image of Julius Caesar—there he comes—and Bee—Bee Meadowsweet with him. "

"Just like her name, " murmured Miss Peters; "just—just like her name, bless her! "

The poor, withered heart of the little old maid quite swelled with love and admiration as the beautiful girl, dressed simply all in white, with roses on her cheeks, and sparkles in her eyes, walked to the scene of the coming gayeties in the company of the acknowledged hero of the town.

"Poor Matty Bell, I pity her! " said Mrs. Butler. "Oh, it has been a sickening sight the way the mother has gone on lately, perfectly sickening; but she'll have her come down, poor woman, and I, for one, will say, serve her right. "

"We may as well be going, Martha, " said Miss Peters.

"Well, I suppose so, since our betters have led the way. Now, Maria, don't drag behind, and don't ogle me with your eyes more than you can help. I have made up my mind to have a seat next to Mrs. Bertram at the feast, and to bring her down a peg if I can. Now, let's come on. "

The ladies left the house and joined the group of holiday-seekers, who were all going in the direction of the Rectory. When they reached the festive scene, the grounds were already thronged. Mr. Ingram was very proud of his gardens and smoothly-kept lawns. He hated to see his velvet swards trampled on and made bare by the tread of many feet. He disliked the pet flowers in his greenhouses being pawed and smelt, and his trim ribbon borders being ruthlessly despoiled. But on the day of the annual treat he forgot all these prejudices. The lawns, the glass-houses, the flower-beds, might and would suffer, he cared not. He was giving supreme pleasure to human flowers, and for two days out of the three hundred and sixty-five they were free to do as they liked with the vegetable kingdom over which on every other day he reigned as monarch supreme.

Marquees now dotted the lawns, and one or two brass bands played rather shrill music. There were tennis-courts and croquet lawns, and fields set aside for archery. Luxurious seats, with awnings over them, were to be found at every turn, and as the grass was of the greenest here, the trees of the shadiest, and the view of the blue harbor the loveliest, the Rector's place, on the day of the feast, appeared to more than one enthusiastic inhabitant of Northbury just like fairyland.

Matty Bell thought so, as, accompanied by her sisters and mother she stepped into the enchanted ground. The girls were in white to-day, not well made, and very bunchy and thick of texture. But still the dresses were white, and round each modest waist was girdled a sash of virgin blue.

"It makes me almost weep to look at the dear children, " whispered Mrs. Bell to her husband. "They look so innocent and lamb-like, more particularly Matty. "

Here she sighed profoundly.

"I don't see why you should single out Matty, " retorted the spouse. "She's no more than the others, as far as I can see, and Sophy has the reddest cheeks. "

"That's all you know, " said Mrs. Bell. Here she almost shook herself with disdain. "Well, Peter, I often do wonder what Pas are for—not for observation, and not for smoothing a girl's path, and helping an ardent young lover. Oh, no, no! "

"Helping an ardent young lover, Tilly! Whatever are you talking about? Where is he? I don't see him. "

"You make me sick, Peter. Hold your tongue, do, and believe your wife when she says that's about all you are good for. Matty's on the brink, and that's the truth. "

Poor Bell looked as mystified as he felt. Presently he slunk away to enjoy a quiet smoke with some congenial spirits in the coal trade, and Mrs. Bell marshalled her girls to as prominent a position as she could find.

It was her object to get on the terrace. The terrace was very broad, and ran not only the length of the front of the house, but a good way beyond at either side. At each end of the terrace was a marquee, decorated with colored flags, and containing within the most refined order of refreshments. On the terrace were many seats, and the whole place was a blaze of gay dresses, brilliant flowers, and happy, smiling faces.

It was here the *élite* of the pleasure-seekers evidently meant to congregate, and as Mrs. Bell intended, on this occasion at least, to join herself to the select few, her object was to get on the terrace. She had not at first, however, the courage to mount those five sacred steps uninvited. The battery of eyes which would be immediately turned upon her would be greater than even her high spirit could support. Mr. Ingram had already spoken to her, she did not know Mrs. Bertram, although she felt that if Catherine or Mabel were near she might call to one of them, and make herself known as Matty's mother.

Catherine and Mabel were, however, several fields away engaged in a vigorous game of archery. Mrs. Bell raised her fat face, and surveyed the potentates of the terrace with anxiety.

"Keep close to me, Matty, " she said to her eldest daughter. "Don't go putting yourself in the background. It isn't becoming, seeing what will be expected of you by-and-by. Now I wonder where the captain is! Mr. Ingram is sure to make a fuss about those Bertrams, and that young man will be expected to be at the beck and call of everybody all day long. But never you mind, Matty, my pet. He shall have his chances, or my name is not Tilly Bell. "

"I wish ma wouldn't, " whispered Sophy to Alice. "I don't believe Captain Bertram cares a bit for Matty. Now, what are we all going to do! Oh, dear, I quite shake in my shoes. Ma is awfully venturesome, and I know we will be snubbed. "

"Come on, girls, " said Mrs. Bell looking over her shoulder. "What are you loitering for? I see Mrs. Gorman Stanley at the back there, by one of the big refreshment booths. I'm going to make for her. "

"Oh, ma, she doesn't care a bit for us. "

"Never mind, she'll do as an excuse. Now let's all keep close together. "

Amongst the select company on the terrace Mrs. Bertram of course found a foremost place. She was seated next to Lady Verney, whose daughter, the Lady Georgiana Higginbotham also stood near, languidly pulling a splendid gloire de Dijon rose to pieces. She was a tall, sallow-faced girl, with the true aristocratic expression of "I-won't-tell-you-anything-at-all" stamped on her face. She was to be married the following week, and had all the airs of a bride-elect.

This young lady raised her pince nez to watch the Bells as they ascended the steps.

"Who *are* those extraordinary people? " she whispered to her mother.

"I'm sure I don't know, my dear. How intolerably hot it is. Really our good Rector ought not to ask us to submit to the fierce rays of the sun during this intense weather. Georgiana, pray keep in the shade. Yes, Mrs. Bertram, you must find the absence of all society a drawback here. "

"I sha'n't stay here long, " responded Mrs. Bertram. "Catherine is still so young that she does not want society. Ah, there is Loftus. I should like to introduce him. Loftus, come here. "

Captain Bertram, raising his hat to the Bells as he passed, approached his mother's side. He was introduced in due form to Lady Verney and the Lady Georgiana, and the two young people, retiring a little into the background, began to chat.

"Who are those extraordinary folk? " asked Lady Georgiana of her companion.

She waved her fan in the direction of Mrs. Bell's fat back.

"Do you know them, Captain Bertram? "

His eyes fairly danced with mirth as he swept them over the little group.

"I must confess something, Lady Georgiana. I do know those young ladies and their mother. I have supped with them. "

"Oh, horrors! And yet, how entertaining. What were they like? "

"Like themselves. "

"That is no answer. Do divert me with an account of them all. I am sure they are deliciously original. I should like to sketch that mother's broad back beyond anything. "

It was at this moment that Beatrice and Catherine appeared together on the scene. Captain Bertram, who thought himself an adept in a certain mild, sarcastic description, was about to gratify Lady Georgiana with a graphic account of the Bells' supper-table, when his gaze met the kind, clear, happy expression of Beatrice Meadowsweet's eyes. He felt his heart stir within him. The Bells were her friends, and she was so good, bless her—the best girl he had ever met. No, he could not, he would not, turn them into fun, just to while away an idle five minutes.

Mrs. Bertram called Catherine over to introduce her to Lady Verney, and Bertram, in a moment, was by Beatrice's side.

"This is lucky, " he said. "I thought you had left me for the day. "

"Why should you think that? " she replied. "It would be impossible for people not constantly to come against each other in a small place like this. "

"May I come with you now? You seem very busy. "

"You can come and help me if you feel inclined. I always have a great deal to do at these feasts; I have been at them for years, and know all about them, and the Rector invariably expects me to keep the ball going. "

"What ball? "

"The ball of pleasure. Each hand must grasp it—everyone must be happy. That is the Hector's aim and mine. "

"I think it is your aim not only to-day, but every day. "

"Yes, if I can manage it. I can't always. "

"You could always make me very happy. "

Beatrice turned her eyes and looked at him. Her look made him blush.

"You are mistaken when you say that, " she responded, in a grave tone. "You are not the sort of person to be made happy by a simple country girl like me. The Northbury people only need small things, and many times it is within my power to supply their desires. But you are different. You would not be content with small things. "

"Assuredly not from you. "

Then he paused; and as she blushed this time, he hastened to add:

"You can help me not in a small, but in a big way, and if you grant me this help, you will save my mother, and—yes—and Catherine. "

"I love Catherine, " said Beatrice.

"I know it—you would like to save her. "

"Certainly; but I did not know she was in peril. "

"Don't whisper it, but she is. You can put things straight for her. May I talk to you? May I tell you what I mean? "

"You look very solemn, and this is a day of pleasure. Must you talk to me to-day? "

"I won't talk of anything to worry you today. But I may some time? "

"I suppose you may. At least it is difficult to reply in the negative to any one who wants my help. "

"That is all I need you to say. You will understand after I have spoken. May I come to see you to-morrow? "

"Yes, you may come to-morrow. I shall be at home in the morning. "

"Beatrice, " said a voice, "Bee—Trixie—I do think it's unkind to cut an old friend. "

Beatrice turned.

Mrs. Bell, puffed and hot, accompanied by Matty, who was also a little blown, and by the younger girls, looking very cross, had been chasing Captain Bertram and Miss Meadowsweet from one lawn to another. Mrs. Bell, after receiving a somewhat severe snubbing from Mrs. Gorman Stanley, had just retired into the marquee to refresh herself with strawberry ices, when Sophy, laying a hand on her mother's shoulder, informed her in a loud whisper that Captain Bertram and Bee Meadowsweet had gone down the steps of the terrace to the tennis lawn side by side.

"We'll make after them! " exclaimed the good lady. "Girls, don't finish your ices; come quick. "

Mrs. Bell took her eldest daughter's hand, and rushed out of the tent. Sophy and Alice stayed behind to have one parting spoonful each of their delicious ices. Then the whole family went helter-skelter down the five sacred steps and on to the lawn. They saw the objects of their desire vanishing through a gap in the hedge into a distant field. They must pursue, they must go hotly to work. Mrs. Bell panted and puffed, and Matty stopped once to breathe hard.

"Courage, child, " said the mother. "We'll soon be up with them. I'm not the woman to leave an innocent young man alone with that siren. "

"Mother! You call Beatrice a siren? "

"Well, and what is she, Matty, when she takes your lawful sweetheart away before your very eyes? But here, we're in hailing distance, now, and I'll shout. Beatrice—Bee—Trixie! "

Beatrice turned. She came up at once to Mrs. Bell, took her hand, and asked all four why they had run so fast after her.

"For I was coming back at once, " she said, in a *naïve* tone. "Captain Bertram was kind enough to walk with me to the archery field. Then I was coming to arrange some tennis sets. "

"My girls have had no tennis yet to-day, Beatrice, " said Mrs. Bell, fixing her eyes solemnly on Miss Meadowsweet. "And they are all partial to it, more especially Matty. You're a devotee to tennis too, aren't you, Captain Bertram? "

"Well, ah, no, I don't think I am, " said the captain.

"You'd maybe rather have a quiet walk, then. For my part I approve of young men who are prudent, and don't care to exercise themselves too violently. Violent exercise puts you into too great a heat, and then you're taken with a chill, and lots of mischief is done that way. Bee, lend me your arm, love. I'm more recovered now, but I did have to hurry after you, and that's a fact. "

Determined women very often have their way, and Mrs. Bell had the satisfaction of walking in front with Beatrice, while Captain Bertram brought up the rear in Matty's company.

Sophy and Alice Bell no longer belonged to the group. They had found matters so intolerably dull that they started off on their own hook to find partners for tennis.

Mrs. Bell, as she walked in front with Beatrice heard Matty's little and inane giggles, and her heart swelled within her.

"Poor young man, he is devoted, " she whispered to her companion. "Ah, dear me, Beatrice, I know you sympathize with me; when one has a dear child's fate trembling in the balance it's impossible not to be anxious. "

Mrs. Bell's face was so solemn, and her words so portentous, that Beatrice was really taken in. It was stupid of her to misunderstand the good woman, but she did.

"Is anything the matter? " she asked, turning to look at Mrs. Bell. "Whose fate is trembling in the balance? "

If it had been possible for light blue eyes of a very common shade and shape to wither with a look, poor Beatrice would never have got over that terrible moment.

Stout Mrs. Bell dropped her companion's arm, moved two or three paces away, and accompanied her scorching glance with words of muffled thunder.

"Beatrice Meadowsweet, you are either green with jealousy, or you are a perfect goose. "

CHAPTER XX.

YOU CAN TAKE ANY RANK.

Beatrice was not, in any sense of the word, a conventional girl. Her nature was independent, and from her earliest days she had been allowed a great deal of liberty. While her father lived he had trained her to love his tastes, to respond to his ideas; he had shared his thoughts with her, and as these thoughts happened to be original, and even slightly tinged with latent genius, the young girl had from the first taken a broad view of life. She was naturally intelligent; and to read and think for herself became a delight to her.

Mr. Meadowsweet died when Beatrice was twelve and then that further thing happened which so often makes an unselfish woman really noble. Beatrice had to support the burdens of another. Mrs. Meadowsweet was a most loving and affectionate character; but she was not as strong mentally as her daughter. She did not know that she leant on Beatrice, but she did. The effect of all this was that Miss Meadowsweet grew up something as the wild flowers do, with perfect liberty, and yet governed by the gracious and kindly laws which nature sets about her children.

Beatrice did not know what it was to be proud of her reputed wealth. When she looked at her sweet face in the glass she was not vain of it. Altogether, she was a very simple-hearted girl, as yet untouched by real trouble, for, except when her father died, its shadow had not approached her.

The passionate, childish sorrow for her father was no longer poignant. She revered his memory, she loved to dwell on his gentleness and goodness, and in her own manner she tried to plant her young footsteps in his.

On the morning after the Rector's feast, Beatrice sat at home and waited for Captain Bertram. She almost always wore white in the hot days, and she was in white now. She chose natural flowers as her invariable adornment, and two crimson roses were now daintily fastened into her girdle.

Beatrice could not help wondering what special thing Captain Bertram had to communicate. She was not particularly troubled or roused in any way by his admiration of her. He was certainly pleasant to talk to; she had never met a refined man of the world before, and Captain Bertram was handsome to look at, and had a charming way of saying charming nothings. Beatrice did not object to his talking to her, but her heart had never yet in the smallest degree responded to any beat of his.

More than one young man in Northbury had fallen in love with Beatrice. She had been very kind to these would-be lovers, and had managed skilfully to get rid of them. No man yet had secured even a small place in her affections.

"Are you going out this morning, Bee? " asked her mother. "It's very fine, and you are fond of a row on the water in the sunshine. It's wonderful to me how your skin never tans nor freckles, child. You might be out in all weathers without its doing you harm. "

Mrs. Meadowsweet was seated in her arm-chair. In her hand she held a piece of knitting. She was making a quilt for Beatrice's bed. This quilt was composed of little squares of an elaborate pattern, with much honey-combing, and many other fancy and delicate stitches ornamenting it. Mrs. Meadowsweet liked to feel her fingers employed over Beatrice's quilt.

"With each stitch I give her a thought, " she said to herself. "Beatrice will sleep soft and warm under this covering when it is finished, " the old mother used to say, "for every bit of it is put together with love. "

She was knitting Beatrice's quilt now, her chair drawn up as usual to face the sunny garden, and on the footstool at her feet her favorite tabby cat was curled.

"It is too hot for me to go out this morning, " replied Beatrice. "So for that reason I don't go, and also for another. Captain Bertram has promised to call. "

"Eh? " queried Mrs. Meadowsweet. To call, has he? Maybe you'd like to ask him to lunch, child? "

"No, mother, I don't think so. "

"You can if you like, Trixie. Say the word, and I'll have a spring chicken done to a turn, and a cream, and a jelly put in hand. "

"Oh, no, mother, he won't want to pay such a long call. "

"Well, he's a nice young man. I have nothing to say against him, he carries himself nearly as upright as your poor father did, and he has a pleasant, affable way with old and young alike. I haven't a word to say against the young man, not a word. When he comes I'll just step into the garden, for you two young things would rather have your chatter alone. Oh, you needn't tell me, Trixie, I know. I was young once, and I never cared to have my nonsense listened to. By the way, I might ask Captain Bertram to take a box of Eleazer's Life-pills to his poor mother. I was recommending them to her, and I'm convinced they are just the medicine for her complaint. And, Bee, I wish you'd remind me to tell Jane to send over a jug of buttermilk to the Bells. I did think that poor child Matty looked so frightfully burnt yesterday, and there's nothing like bathing the face and neck in buttermilk, to get rid of the ugly redness. My word, child, is that a ring at the hall door? Then I'll be off, but I'll be in the garden handy within call, in case you should want me, my pet. "

As Captain Bertram entered the drawing-room Mrs. Meadowsweet's trailing skirts might have been seen disappearing down the steps which led from the French window to the garden. Beatrice said to herself with an inward smile:

"From the dear old mother's way, any one would suppose I was going to receive a lover, " and then she raised her eyes, and a very lover-like gaze met hers.

The expression in Captain Bertram's dark eyes joined to the thought which had flown into her heart, made the young girl flush up almost painfully. This sudden blush caused the gallant wooer's heart to beat with rapture, and he instantly changed his tactics and resolved, instead of giving Beatrice a half confidence with regard to his troubles, to take the apparently unapproachable fortress by storm.

"I had a long story to tell you, but I find I can't tell it, " he said.

Then he looked at her again, as he knew how momentous were the words which must follow, he turned pale.

"Sit down, " said Beatrice. "Come over to the window and sit down. We have such a pretty view of the garden from here. Mother and I are very proud of our garden. "

"Are you? Miss Meadowsweet, I want to say something. Look at me, will you look at me? "

"Of course I will. I expected you to say something when you called this morning. You had some sort of trouble you wanted to confide in me. What is the matter? "

"I don't feel now as if I had any trouble to confide in you. I can only say one thing. "

Beatrice began to wish that her mother had not left the drawing-room. She moved forward as if to step through the open French window.

"And I must tell you this thing, " pursued the captain's voice.

Its tone arrested her.

"But I am mad to say it. "

"Don't say it then, " she began.

"I can't help myself. You must listen. I love you better than all the world. I won't marry any one but you. I will marry you, I am determined. "

"You are determined, " repeated Beatrice, slowly. "*You*— determined—and about me? I am obliged. "

Her lips took a scornful curl. She sat down. She was quiet enough now; the worst was over.

Beatrice, however, was only a country girl, and she had very little idea with whom she had to deal. No one could plead better his cause than Loftus Bertram. Defeat here meant the ruin of his worldly prospects as well as of his love. He was the kind of man with whom the present must always be paramount; for the time being he had absolutely forgotten Josephine Hart, for the time being he thought himself honestly, deeply in love with Beatrice.

So he talked and talked, until poor Beatrice felt both her head and heart aching.

"I am not in your rank of life, " she said at last, as her final thrust. "My set is not the same as yours; my people can never belong to yours—my dear old mother is a lady at heart, but she has not the outward polish of your mother. You want me to be your wife now, but by-and-bye you will remember the gulf which socially lies between us. "

"How can you talk such nonsense? You are one of nature's ladies. Ask my mother what she thinks of you. Ask Catherine. Don't you think Catherine would be happy to put her arms round you and call you sister? "

When Bertram mentioned Catherine a sweet light came for the first time into Beatrice's eyes.

"I love your sister Catherine, " she said.

"You will love me too. You will make me the happiest of men. "

"I have not even begun to love you. I have not a shadow of affection for you. "

"If you saw me very unhappy you would pity me. "

"Yes, I pity all unhappy people. "

"Then pity me, for I am miserable. "

"Pity won't do you any good; and you have no right to be miserable. "

"Still, pity me; for I am, I can't help it—I am wretched beyond words. "

His face had grown really haggard, for he was beginning to think she would never yield, and this look won her to say:

"Well, yes, if it comforts you to know it. I do pity you. "

"Pity is akin to love. You will love me next. "

"I don't see the smallest prospect; you mustn't delude yourself. "

"I do, I will. I will trust you. I know your heart. You will pity me and then you will love me. I am not a good fellow. "

His words and looks were the soul of sincerity now. He took her hand.

"I have never been a really good man. I have not been a dutiful son, and I have made my mother unhappy. If you were my wife I think I should become good, for you, Beatrice, you are very good. "

He was telling her the old, old story, and she was half believing him, half believing that it might be in her power to redeem him. Beatrice Meadowsweet was just the sort of woman to love such work, to glory in such martyrdom.

She did not withdraw her hand from his, and her gray eyes, already dark and misty with emotion, filled with tears.

"I have never been spoken to like this before, " she said.

Here she rose and stood before him.

"Your words trouble me. It is not right for a girl to marry without love, and yet most surely I pity you. "

"Carry your pity a little further, and believe that the love will come. You cannot receive all and give nothing in return—the love will come, Beatrice, believe me, do believe me. "

"I am not of your rank, " she said, going back to her old objection, which in itself was a sign of weakness.

"See what my mother says of your rank and of you. You can take any rank. Oh, Beatrice, how happy you will make my mother. "

She was not moved at all by this.

"And Catherine, I can see her eyes sparkle. "

At Catherine's name Beatrice clasped her hands before her, and began to pace slowly up and down the little enclosure which contained the wide French windows opening into the garden.

"And you will make me good, Beatrice. "

Captain Bertram was astute enough to see that he played his best card here.

Half an hour later he left her. She had apparently consented to nothing—but she had agreed to see him again the following day.

CHAPTER XXI.

WITH CATHERINE IN THE ROSE BOWER.

Mrs. Meadowsweet was not the least like Mrs. Bell. She was not constantly on the watch for lovers for her only daughter. She was naturally such a contented and easy-going woman that she never troubled herself to look far ahead. The time being was always more or less sufficient to her. No two people could be snugger or more absolutely comfortable together than she and her Bee. It was no use therefore worrying her head about the possible contingency that the girl might marry and leave her.

Mrs. Meadowsweet, as she walked about her old-fashioned garden on that summer's morning was not at all put about by the fact that her pretty daughter was having a solemn conference in the drawing-room with the handsomest and most elegant young man of their acquaintance. She was not curious nor anxious, nor perturbed in any way. She pottered round her plants, pulling up a weed here, and removing a withered bud there, in the most comfortable fashion, and only once she made a remark to herself with regard to the occupants of the drawing-room. This was her sole allusion to them.

"I hope that young man won't forget to take the box of Eleazer'ss Life-pills to his mother. I left it handy on the hall table, and I hope he'll remember to slip it into his pocket. "

Presently Mrs. Meadowsweet re-entered the house. There she noticed two things. The drawing-room was empty, and the box of pills lay untouched on the hall table.

She sighed a little over this latter circumstance, but reflecting that she could send Jane with them in the evening she went slowly up to her bedroom and busied herself putting on her afternoon gown, which was of a large check pattern, the coloring being different shades in terra-cotta.

Arrayed thus she came down to dinner, and then for the first time she was really startled by perceiving that Beatrice's place was empty. Jane immediately explained her young mistress's absence.

"Miss Bee has a headache and is lying down, ma'am. I'm to take her a cup of tea presently, but she doesn't want any dinner. "

"Dear, dear, " ejaculated Mrs. Meadowsweet.

"And the peas are lovely and tender to-day, and so for that matter is the chicken. What a pity! Jane, you tell Miss Bee that if she has a headache she had better take two of my pills immediately after she has had her tea. You'll find them in the bottle on my dressing-table, Jane, and you had better take her up some raspberry jam to swallow them in. "

Jane promised obedience, and Mrs. Meadowsweet ate her green peas and tender, young chicken in great contentment.

In the course of the afternoon Beatrice came downstairs again. She told her mother that her headache was quite gone, but the old lady was acute enough to observe a great change in the girl. She did not look ill, but the brightness had gone out of her face.

"Is anything wrong, dearie? " she asked. "Has any one been worrying you, my treasure? "

"I have got to think about something, " replied Beatrice. "And I am just a very little upset. I am going into the garden with a book, and you won't mind if I don't talk to you, mother dear? "

"Of course not, my pet. What is an old mother good for, but to humor her child? Go you into the garden, Trixie, and no one shall fret or molest you, I'll see to that. "

Beatrice kissed her mother, and book in hand went to the rose-bower, a secluded spot where no one could see her or take her unawares. Mrs. Meadowsweet sat upright in her chair, took out her knitting-bag, and proceeded to add a few stitches to Beatrice's quilt.

Presently there came a quick and somewhat nervous ring to the door-bell. Mrs. Meadowsweet often said that there were rings and rings. This ring made her give a little start, and took away the sleepiness which was stealing over her.

The next moment Catherine Bertram entered the room. Her eyes were glowing, and her face, usually rather pale, was effused with a fine color. She looked eager and expectant.

Mrs. Meadowsweet stretched out her two hands to her, and gave her a few warm words of welcome. The impulsive girl stooped down, and kissed the old lady on the forehead.

"You're just the person I'm glad to see, my dear, " said Mrs. Meadowsweet. "You'll take your mother back her pills. Poor dear, she must have thought I had forgotten all about her. "

"I have come to see Beatrice, " said Catherine. "It is important. Can I see her? "

"Well, my love, Bee is not quite herself. She is worried about something; I don't know what for it's my aim in life to make her lot smooth as velvet. She's in the garden with a book, and I said she shouldn't be disturbed. But you, my dear — —"

"I must see Beatrice, " repeated Catherine. "It's important. I've come here on purpose. "

"Well, my love, you and Bee are always great friends. You haven't a worrying way with you. She's in the rose-arbor. You can find her, child. You walk straight down that path, and then turn to your left. "

Catherine did not wait another instant. She had the quick and graceful motions of a young fawn, and when she reached Beatrice her eager face was so full of light and excitement that the other girl sprang to her feet, her unopened book tumbled to the floor, and in one moment the two friends had their arms round each other.

They did not kiss. This was not the moment for outward expressions of affection. They looked at one another, then Catherine said:

"Well, Beatrice? " and, taking her friend's hand, she sat down by her.

"You know what happened this morning, Catherine? " said Beatrice, looking at her sadly.

"Yes, I know. I have come about that. Loftus came home, and he told mother. I heard him talking to her, and I heard mother crying; I came into the room then, for I cannot bear the sound of my mother's sobs when she is in distress, and she at once looked up when she heard nay step, and she said:

"'It is all hopeless, Catherine; Beatrice Meadowsweet will not marry Loftus. '

"'Nay, mother, ' interrupted Loftus, 'there's a chance for me, she has consented to see me again to-morrow. '

"I flew up to mother when Loftus had done speaking, and I knelt by her and looked into her face and said, 'You make my heart beat so hard, I never, never thought of this. ' Mother went on moaning to herself. She did not seem to care about me nor to notice that I was with her.

"'It was my last hope, ' she said; 'the only chance to avert the trouble, and it is over. '

"She went on saying that until I really thought she was almost light-headed. At last Loftus beckoned me out of the room.

"'What is it, Loftus, what is wrong? " I asked.

"'Poor mother, ' he replied; 'she loves Beatrice, and she had set her heart on this. Her nerves are a good deal shaken lately. Poor mother! she has had a more troubled life than you can guess about, Catherine. '

"'Loftie, ' I answered, 'I have long guessed, I have long feared. '

"'If I could win Beatrice, ' said Loftus, 'my mother should never have another ache nor pain. '

"Then he went back into mother's room, and I stayed outside and thought. After a time I resolved to come to you. No one knows that I am here. "

"What have you come for, Catherine? " asked Beatrice.

"I have come to know what you mean to do. When you see Loftus to-morrow what will you say to him? "

"What would you say, Catherine? If you did not love a man at all, if he was absolutely nothing to you, would you give yourself to him? Yourself? That means all your life, all your days, your young days, your middle-aged years, your old age, always, till death parts you. Would you do that, Catherine? Speak for yourself; would you? "

"How old are you, Beatrice? " asked Catherine.

"I am nineteen; never mind my age, that has nothing whatever to say to the question I want you to answer. "

"I asked you about your age on purpose—because I can't answer your question. You are nineteen, I am seventeen. I feel like a child still; I don't understand anything about loving people as you talk of love; but I could be kind, and if it lay in my power to keep hearts from breaking I think I'd be very glad to do it, and then Loftie *is* nice, Bee. "

Beatrice sighed. For the first time there was a gulf between her and Catherine. As an intelligent and intellectual companion, as an affectionate friend, Catherine was perfect; but in matters pertaining to love—that great mystery which comes into most lives—her unawakened heart was as a blank.

"You ask a great deal, " said Beatrice, rising to her feet with irritation. "For some reason, I don't know what, I am of value to you and yours. I am not in your rank of life, still you want me. Your mother is troubled, and in some inexplicable way I, an ignorant and uninformed country girl, can relieve her. This is all very fine for you, but what about me? I sacrifice myself forever to give temporary relief. Catherine, you must tell me the truth. Why do you want me? Is it because of my money? "

"Have you money? " asked Catherine. Her big, innocent, honest eyes looked full at her friend, their expression showed bewilderment. When she looked at her in this way Beatrice suddenly burst into a fit of laughter. Then she put her arms round Catherine and kissed her two or three times.

"Kate, you are the sweetest girl I ever met in all my life. You are good, you are innocent. Kitty, I would do much for you. "

"And Loftus is very kind, " repeated Catherine; "and he's handsome, too. He often told me that girls fell in love with him. "

Beatrice patted Catherine's cheek.

"Little puss! " she said, "he ought not to breathe such words in your innocent ears. So it is not for my money your mother and Loftus want me so badly, Kitty. "

"I never heard either of them breathe the subject of your money. Have you any? "

"Yes, some. "

"That would be nice, for somehow lately we seem to be dreadfully poor. "

"If I were turned into a grand and patrician Bertram, and made into your sister, sweet little Kitty, you shouldn't be poor. I'd see to that. I'd dress you and pet you, and lade you with gifts. "

"Beatrice, how bright your eyes are. "

"Yes, I am excited when I think of the possible benefit I may be to you. "

"I only want you to be my sister, and to make my mother and Loftus happy. My mother has a hidden trouble about which I must not speak; and for some reason which I cannot in the least understand, if you marry Loftus that trouble will disappear. "

"And you want it to disappear? "

"I would give all I possess to make my mother happy. "

"Good, dear, little Kitty! You don't incline then to the belief that your brother wants me for the guineas' worth! "

"Beatrice, I don't think Loftus is really sordid and he loves you. Oh, how earnestly he told me that he loved you. And my mother, she often, often talks of you, and I know she cares for you, Bee. "

"Come into the house, " said Beatrice, suddenly. "Now that you have come you must spend the evening with me. We can send a messenger to the Manor to tell them, and after tea you and I will go on the water. We'll have a happy evening together, Kate, and we won't talk any more about Loftus, no, not another word. If I do a thing I do it generously, but I will not discuss the *pros* and *cons* even with, you any more. "

CHAPTER XXII.

SPARE THE POOR CHILD'S BLUSHES.

It was Miss Peters who first spread the news. She heard it whispered at the fishmonger's, spoken of aloud at the butcher's, and confirmed at the baker's. She could doubt this combined testimony no longer, and hurried home to put on her best bonnet with the wallflowers in it, and go forth on a visiting tour.

Miss Peters was in the seventh heaven of delight. To have news, and such news, to convey, would make her a welcome inmate that afternoon of every house in Northbury. She was intensely anxious to go out and convey her news without being accompanied by her large sister, Mrs. Butler. In Mrs. Butler's presence Miss Peters was only a shadow, and she had no wish to be a shadow on this occasion.

She had heard the gossip, not Martha—why, therefore, should she tell Martha for the sole satisfaction of having it repeated by Martha in her own tiresome way to each neighbor she met, while she, poor Miss Peters, who had really got the information first-hand—for the baker who served the two families with bread was so absolutely reliable—could only nod her head and roll her eyes in confirmation.

Miss Peters resolved, therefore, to tell her news to Mrs. Butler last of all; and her object now was to slip softly out of doors without being heard by her sister. She nearly accomplished this feat, but not quite. As she was going downstairs, with her best bonnet on, her lavender gloves drawn neatly over her hands, and her parasol, which was jointed in the middle and could fold up, tucked under her arm, she trod on a treacherous board which creaked loudly.

This was enough. Mrs. Butler popped her head out of the drawing-room door and confronted the little spinster.

"Where now, Maria? " she asked. "Dear, dear, and I've been wondering what was keeping you all this time. Where are you off to? Why, I declare you have on your visiting things? "

"I thought I'd just go round and see one or two friends, as the afternoon is fine, " answered Miss Maria, in a meek voice.

"The afternoon fine! " retorted Mrs. Butler. Have we any but fine afternoons in the month of August? I don't feel disposed to visit to-day. The lobster salad I ate last night disagreed with me. I shall stay at home. "

"Well, that's all right, Martha. I can take your compliments to any one, of course, and just mention that you are a little indisposed. "

"*You* take *my* compliments? No, thank you. You'll just have the goodness to take off your bonnet and come and sit in the drawing-room with me. I have had enough of my own company today, and I want you to pick up some stitches in my knitting. Come, you needn't ogle me any more. Go back and take off your bonnet and be quick about it. "

Very slowly Miss Peters turned and went up the stairs. She took off her neat little chip bonnet, adorned with the sprigs of wallflower, folded up her lavender gloves, and put back her heavily-fringed old-fashioned parasol in its case. Then she went down to the drawing-room; she sighed heavily as she did so. Poor thing; she had no money of her own, and was absolutely dependent on Mrs. Butler, who tyrannized over her as is the usual fashion in such cases.

The day was a glorious one, and from where Miss Peters sat she could get a splendid view of the bright and sparkling harbor. Little boats skimmed about on its surface, and Miss Peters longed to be in one of them—anywhere away from the tyrannical sister who would not allow her to go out and disburden herself of her news.

That news, bottled up within her breast, almost drove the little woman crazy. Suppose the baker told some one else? He had promised not; but who can depend on bakers? Suppose she was not the first to startle and electrify her fellow town's people after all? She felt so fretted and miserable that her sighs at last became audible.

"Well, Maria, you certainly are a lively companion! " exclaimed Mrs. Butler. "Fidget, fidget sigh, sigh, and not a word out of your lips! I'll thank you to hand me my knitting, and then you may read me a chapter from that book of sermons on the table. I often think it's in fine weather we should remember our souls most. "

This remark was so startling that Miss Maria's grievance was forgotten for a moment in her surprise.

"Why in fine weather? " she ventured to ask.

"Because, being prosperous and comfortable, they are like to sleep within us. Now, get the sermons and read. Turn to sermon five, page four, begin second paragraph; there's a telling bit there, and I think the cap will fit your head. "

Miss Maria was rising meekly to comply, when happening again to glance at the blue bosom of the water, she uttered a shriek, threw down Mrs. Butler's knitting, caught up the spy-glass, and sprang to the window.

"Good gracious! Maria, have you gone mad? " exclaimed her sister.

"It is—it is—" gasped Miss Peters. "There they are! It's beautiful; and it's true! "

"What's beautiful, and what's true? Really, Maria, you are enough to turn a person crazy. What *are* you talking about, and who *are* you looking at? Give me the glass. "

"Sister, " said Miss Peters, "they're in a boat together. Out there in the harbor. *Both* of them! In a boat! "

"If they weren't in a boat they'd be drowned to a certainty, " snapped Mrs. Butler. "And who are they? And why shouldn't they be in a boat together? "

"Look for yourself, sister—there they are! And beautiful they look—beautiful! "

Mrs. Butler seized the spy-glass and tried to adjust it.

"Where? " she asked. "What part of the harbor? "

"Over there, just under the old Fort. "

"My good gracious, Maria, you always do something to these glasses to make them go wrong. I can see nothing. Who, in the name of charity, are in the boat? "

"Martha, it's a secret. I heard it to-day. "

"Oh, you heard it to-day! And you kept it from your own only sister whose bread you eat! *Very* nice, and very grateful. I'm obliged to you Maria, I have cause to be. "

"It was the baker who told me, sister. "

"The baker? Hunt, the baker. And pray what had he to tell? "

"Well, you know, he delivers bread at the Meadowsweets. "

"I neither know nor care. "

"And at the Manor. He takes bread every day to the Manor, Martha. "

"H—m—only his seconds, I should say. Well, this is all very interesting, but I can't see what it has to say to two people being in a boat on the harbor. "

"Oh, Martha, you see the baker must know, and he told me for a positive fact. They're engaged. "

"What! Has Hunt made it up with Gracie Jones? It's time for him. He has been hanging after her long enough. "

"Oh, sister, I am not alluding to anything plebeian. "

"Well, my dear Maria, I'd be glad to know once for all to what you are alluding, for, to be frank with you, I think your brain is going fast. "

"It's Bee, " said Miss Maria. "It's our Bee. She's engaged. It's all settled. "

"Beatrice engaged? I don't believe a word of it. "

"It's true. Hunt said there wasn't a doubt of it, and he ought to know, for he takes bread—"

"You needn't go on about the bread. To whom is Beatrice Meadowsweet affianced? "

"To no less a person, Martha, than Captain Bertram, and there they are in a boat by themselves on the water. "

Mrs. Butler snatched up the spy-glass again, and after considerable difficulty, and some mutterings, focussed it so as to suit her sight. She was absolutely silent, as she gazed her fill at the unconscious occupants of the green boat.

After a long time she put down the glass, and turned to her sister.

"We'll go upstairs and put on our bonnets, Maria, I should like to go out. I want to call on the Bells. "

Mrs. Bell had lately tried to connect herself with the outside world by adopting a few of its harmless and inexpensive little fashions. She had a day at home. This universal mode of receiving one's friends was not generally adopted in Northbury, but Mrs. Bell, who had heard of it through the medium of a weekly fashion paper which a distant cousin in London was kind enough to supply her with, thought it would be both distinguished and economical to adopt the system of only receiving her friends on Thursdays.

She was laughed at a good deal, and considered rather upstartish for doing so; but nevertheless, on Thursdays the friends came, being sure of a good dish of gossip as well as sugared and creamed tea and home-made cakes in abundance.

On Thursdays Mrs. Bell put on every ring and ornament she possessed. Her one and only dark red tabinet—this was her wedding-gown let out and dyed—adorned her stout figure, and then she sat in her drawing-room, and awaited her company. Her daughters always sat with her, and they, too, on these occasions, made the utmost of their poor wardrobes.

Mrs. Bell was in particularly good spirits on this special afternoon, for rumors had as yet cast no shadows before, and the preceding evening she had been lucky enough to meet Mabel Bertram, and had almost extracted a promise from that young lady that she would come to her reception in the company of her gallant brother.

"Thank you, for Matty's sake, " Mrs. Bell had responded to Mabel. "Matty will be delighted to see you both, —delighted. "

Mabel had gone home a little bewildered and a little amused, and Mrs. Bell felt herself altogether in high feather.

When Mrs. Butler and Miss Peters appeared on the scene there had already arrived a fair sprinkling of guests. Mrs. Gorman Stanley who did most of her eating at her friends' houses, was enjoying her second cup of tea, and asking Alice for the third time to pass her the sponge-cakes. Mrs. Morris, considerably wrapped up on account of her bronchitis, was shivering by an open window, and Mrs. Jenkins and the two Misses Jenkins, and Mr. Jones the curate, were also in the room.

The eldest Miss Jenkins had managed, for the first time, to establish herself in the vicinity of Mr. Jones, when the maid—no one kept two maids at Northbury—threw open the door.

"Mrs. Butler, ma'am, and Miss Peters, ma'am. "

Whereupon the two ladies, portentous with their great news, came in.

As they walked down the street Mrs. Butler had warned her sister not to leak out a word.

"*I'll* tell, " she said, with simple gravity which impressed.

"But it was *my* news, " said poor Miss Peters.

"I prefer to tell, " said Mrs. Butler.

And Miss Peters was demolished.

Accordingly when they entered the room Mrs. Butler made straight for the sofa beside Mrs. Bell. She took her friend's hand, looked at her solemnly, and said:

"How are you? " in a lugubrious voice.

Mrs. Bell assured Mrs. Butler that she was in excellent health, and Matty was called forward to administer the tea and cake.

Mrs. Butler also favored Matty with a portentous glance.

"Has that girl got over the cough which she was so troubled with a year back? " she queried of the parent.

Mrs. Bell bridled at this. Never had her Matty looked stronger or more blooming, and after all the cough so solemnly inquired after, just for all the world, muttered the poor mother, as if it were a graveyard cough, had been but the remains of the whooping cough.

"Matty blooms, " replied Mrs. Bell. "Don't you, Matty, my love? I don't suppose, Mrs. Butler, you ever saw my girl looking better. "

"I'm glad of it, " said Mrs. Butler. "No more tea, I thank you, Matty. Well, then, as you are so pressing, just a tiny drop. You can put it on what's in my cup, if you like. Oh, yes, certainly more cream. I'm partial to cream, if it's good. It agrees with me. It doesn't agree with Maria, so I never give it her. Well, as I was saying, I'm glad you are in good health, Matty, for a girl who has a real fine constitution can stand up against shocks. "

"Shocks? " said Mrs. Bell. "I don't think we need talk of shocks at this time of day, unless indeed, they are joyful ones. Matty, my love, " here Mrs. Bell raised her voice to a high and penetrating key, "I wonder when our dear friends the Bertrams will be here. "

Matty blushed and giggled as only Matty could blush and giggle. Poor Miss Peters felt herself turning crimson. She ogled her eyes round at her sister, who rose solemnly and put down her cup and saucer.

The whole company had been impressed by Mrs. Bell's words. They ceased to talk, they seemed to know something was impending, and Mrs. Butler felt that her hour had come. She cleared her throat and looked around at her audience.

"H—m! ladies, I have called here with a little piece of news. I daresay you have not heard it yet, for it's fresh. It was told to me in confidence, but my source is a most reliable one. What's the matter, Maria? Oh, good gracious, I see you are taking cream. You know how ill cream always makes you. Will no one be kind enough to give Maria another cup of tea? Well, ladies, I've come with news. We're to have a wedding soon! "

Here Mrs. Bell, who had felt, as she afterwards expressed it, cold shivers going down her back, while Mrs. Butler was firing off her preamble, now bridled and even blushed. It was a little premature, certainly, but reports always did a trifle exceed the truth, and, as

Matty was so certain to be engaged immediately she could scarcely blame Mrs. Butler for alluding to it prematurely.

She bent forward therefore and touched her friend on the arm.

"Spare the poor child's blushes, " she whispered. "She's such a sensitive little thing. "

"Spare whose blushes, my good friend? The girl isn't in the room. Do you think I'd be so indelicate as to mention the sacred subject of the wedding before the bride-elect? No, no, Beatrice isn't by, unless she is hiding behind one of the window curtains. "

At the word Beatrice Mrs. Bell felt her spirit sink down to zero. She had an insane desire to take Mrs. Butler by main force, and drag her out of the room. Poor Matty's blushes changed to pallor, and her hand shook as she pessed Miss Peters her creamless tea. Mr. Jones also, who had been listening to the conversation in a half-hearted way suddenly felt himself turning very rigid and stiff, and the eyes which he fixed on Daisy Jenkins took a glassy stare as though he were looking through that young lady into futurity.

Mrs. Butler liked to tell her news with effect and she felt now that she had made a profound sensation.

"Good-bye, " she said, holding out her hand. "I thought I'd drop in and tell you, as being old friends, but I must go on at once to congratulate dear Mrs. Meadowsweet. There's no doubt at all; Bee is engaged, and we saw them just now in a boat at the other side of the harbor, all alone, and making love as hard as they could. It's a pretty match, and she's a fine girl. Good-bye, Mrs. Bell; come, Maria. "

"Yes, " said Mrs. Bell. "Yes. Not that I believe a word of the story— you didn't tell us the name of the—the future bridegroom—not that I believe a word. "

"Oh, yes, you do believe. Didn't I mention the bridegroom's name? Well, somehow I thought that went without saying. He's Captain Bertram, of course. Good-bye, Matty. Come, Maria. "

The two ladies disappeared, and the Bells and their other guests were left to face each other, and discuss the news.

CHAPTER XXIII.

THAT FICKLE MATTY.

"Well, doctor, and where are you off to now? " The speaker was the doctor's wife. "I do think it's unreasonable of people, " continued this good lady, "to send for you just when you are sitting down to your comfortable breakfast, and you so particular as you are about your coffee. "

"Who is it, Mary Anne? Who's the messenger from? " turning to the maid-servant, who stood in a waiting attitude half-in, half-out of the door.

"Oh, it's only the Bells. You needn't hurry off to the Bells, Tom. "

"As well they as another, " retorted Dr. Morris "Tell the messenger I'll be round directly, Mary Anne. Now, what's the matter, old lady? Why should you fidget yourself, and have such a spiteful tone when the Bells are mentioned? "

"Oh, I'm sick of them, and their airs and affectations, " growled Mrs. Morris, who suddenly put on her thickest and most bronchial tones. "What with their afternoon tea, and their grand at-homes, and the ridiculous way they've been going on about that little Matty lately, I really lose all patience with them. What's the consequence of all this kind of thing? Mrs. Bell chokes up her small drawing-room so full of visitors who only come to laugh at her, that one can't breathe comfortably there without the window open, and a fine fresh bronchitis I've got in consequence. You feel me, doctor. I'm all shivering and burning, I'm going to be very ill, there isn't a doubt of it. "

"Your pulse hasn't quickened, " said the doctor, "it's as steady as my own. "

"Oh, well, if you don't choose to believe in the sufferings of your wife, exhibited before your very eyes, go to your Bells, and comfort them. "

"Now, Jessie, don't talk nonsense, old lady. You know I'm the first to believe you bad if you are. But what's this about Beatrice Meadowsweet? Is she really engaged to young Bertram? "

"It's the gossip, Tom. But maybe it isn't the case. I'll call to see Mrs. Meadowsweet this morning, and find out. "

"I would if I were you. Beatrice is a fine girl, and mustn't throw herself away. "

"Throw herself away! Why, it's a splendid match for her. A most aristocratic young man! One of the upper ten, and no mistake. "

"That's all you women think about. Well, I'm off to the Bells now. "

The doctor presently reached that rather humble little dwelling where the Bell family enjoyed domestic felicity.

He was ushered in by the maid, who wore an important and mysterious face. Mrs. Bell quickly joined him, and she looked more important and mysterious still.

"Matty isn't well, " she said, sinking her voice to a stage whisper. "Matty has been badly treated; she has had a blight. "

"Dear, dear! " said Doctor Morris.

He was a fat, comfortable-looking man, his hands in particular were very fat, and when he warred to show special sympathy he was fond of rubbing them.

"Dear, dear! " he repeated. "A blight! That's more a phrase to apply to the potato than to a blooming young girl. "

"All the same, doctor, it's true. Matty has been blighted. She had set her young affections where they were craved and sought, and, so to speak, begged for. She gave them, *not willingly*, doctor, but after all the language that melting eyes, and more melting words, could employ. *The* word wasn't spoken, but all else was done. She gave her heart, doctor, not unasked, and now it's sent back to her, and she's blighted, that's the only word for it. "

"I should think so, " said the doctor, who was far too professional to smile. "A heart returned like that is always a little difficult to dispose of. Might I ask who—but perhaps you'd rather not tell me? "

"No, Doctor Morris, I'd rather tell you; I've sent for you to tell you, and it isn't so much that I blame him, poor young man, for it was all managed between his mother and Beatrice, all, from the very first, and it's my firm belief that he had neither part nor parcel in it. I did what I could, as in duty bound, to give him his chances, but those designers were too many for me. "

"You don't mean, " said the doctor—he really did not concern himself much about Northbury gossip, and no rumors of Matty's flirtations had reached him—"You don't mean Captain Bertram? Why, I have just heard he is engaged to Beatrice. You can't mean Captain Bertram? Impossible. "

"I do mean Captain Bertram, doctor. No more and no less. And I'll thank you not again to mention the name of that siren, Beatrice, in my presence. Now if you'll come upstairs, I'll show you the poor blighted child. "

Mrs. Bell had insisted on Matty's staying in bed. After the first awful shock of Mrs. Butler's news had subsided, she had made up her mind that the only r'le left to her daughter was that of the dying martyr. All the town should know that Beatrice had robbed her friend, and that this young and innocent friend was now at death's door.

Alice and Sophy were both in the room with their sister, and they were expatiating very loudly on what they considered "ma's cruelty. "

"You know perfectly, Matty, that he never cared for you, " remarked the candid Sophy. "It was all ma's folly from first to last. "

"First to last, " echoed Alice.

"And you're not really ill, " pursued Sophy. "You slept very sound all last night. "

"And snored, " continued Alice.

"Only ma will make a fuss, one way or other, " proceeded Sophy. "Now you're to be the forsaken one, and what ma would like would be for your funeral bell to toll the day Bee has her wedding chimes. "

"And we all love Bee, " said Alice.

"And we'd like to go to her wedding, " said Sophy. "Wouldn't you, Matty? Say, now, if you were going to have a new white muslin for it? "

It was at this juncture that the doctor and Mrs. Bell entered the room.

For a blighted invalid Matty did not look pale, and the doctor, who quickly discovered that there was no broken heart in the case, ordered his *régime* with a certain dry sense of humor, anything but comforting to the poor little victim.

"Miss Matty requires rest, " he said. "Absolute rest. And freedom from all undue excitement. I should recommend for the next few days, complete confinement to her bed with a simple diet; *no* tea nor coffee, nor any stimulants. Keep her quiet, Mrs. Bell, for while the illness lasts—I give it no name—under which she is laboring, she will have no desire, except to keep herself solitary. "

"And you think that will effect a cure, doctor? " asked Mrs. Bell, whose eyes had forced up a little moisture. "The child is frail, oughtn't she to be nourished? "

"In the way I prescribed, my dear madam. Milk diet, without stimulants. I'll see you again in a couple of days, Miss Matty. "

"And you say she's not to get up, doctor? "

"On no account, until I call again. "

The doctor departed, and Matty submitted to the remarkably dull life laid out for her.

In the course of the afternoon Mrs. Bell went out. To each friend she met she made the same remarks:

"Matty is very ill. I'm dreadfully anxious about her. Dr. Morris is in close attendance. She's to be kept strictly to her bed, and the greatest care has to be exercised to maintain her feeble strength. It's a heavy trial to have one's child so ill—and from such a cause. "

"Dear, dear, " the sympathizing neighbor would answer. "What can be the matter, and Matty always looked so fresh and hearty? Do you think she has gone and taken anything, Mrs. Bell? Some people prophesy that we are to have an epidemic of small-pox. It can't be that, surely? Taken so sudden too, for she was about yesterday. "

"Small-pox! " retorted Mrs. Bell, with withering scorn. "As if a child of mine who had her vaccination beautifully would have small-pox! No, no, it's heart-blight, neighbor, it's heart-blight, and I doubt if my girl will ever get over it. "

"Eh, ah—you don't say so, " the neighbor would instantly retort. Now the listener was full of intense curiosity, and longing to learn everything. Matty Bell ill with a heart affair! No wonder her mother looked troubled. Ah, men were deceivers ever! And who had dared to trifle with her young affections?

Then Mrs. Bell would sigh deeply, and lower her voice, and point in the direction of the Manor. It wasn't for her to name names, but a certain young man had gone far, very far. Why, they could bring an action against him, only they'd scorn to make public their poor child's feelings. Well, well, he might lead another bride, a certain designer, to the altar, but there would be no luck nor happiness for either of them, that Mrs. Bell would say.

It was in this manner that the good lady spread the report which she desired through the gossiping little town. Rapidly did the little piece of gossip swell and magnify. It even travelled into the country, and so huge did its dimensions grow there, that it not only killed Matty, but buried her, and placed a beautiful tablet in white marble over her grave, erected by the repentant Captain Bertram and the remorseful Beatrice Meadowsweet.

Meantime the dying martyr had a very dull time in her bed. She was not the kind of girl to love very deeply—her mother had done her utmost to make the poor child fall in love with Captain Bertram, but when all was said he had only managed to tickle her vanity. Now she considered that he had put her to shame and derision, and she began to dislike him very much. Her sisters fostered this dislike with the tales they brought in from the outside world.

"You're the laughing-stock of the town, " Alice would say. "Everybody is talking about you, and having a laugh at you. You needn't suppose that you are pitied, for you are not. "

"Oh, " groaned Matty. "How I wish, how I do wish, I had never met that horrid, odious man. "

"He's not horrid nor odious at all, " retorted the practical Sophy. "He looks lovely when he walks about with Beatrice. I saw them yesterday in the Green, and Beatrice came up at once and asked about you. What do you think ma did, Matty? She turned her back on Bee and sailed away. Poor Bee quite colored up, and didn't know what to make of it. "

"They say Beatrice is to have a lovely wedding, " said Alice. "And Mr. Ingram is going to have the whole church decorated with flowers. And a bishop is coming down from London to marry them. And Mr. Ingram is going to give Beatrice away himself, for he says she's like a daughter to him. And there's to be another great party at the Rectory the day of her wedding, Matty, and lots of fire-works in the evening. "

"Oh, dear, " sighed Matty, "I think Captain Bertram is a very base man. "

"You'd better give up that idea, " said Alice, "for no one else agrees with you. You know perfectly he never paid you attentions. It was all ma who would think so. And you know, Matty, you can't deny it—you did try to squeeze his hand the first day he danced with you. "

"I didn't, " said Matty, flushing all over with indignation. "I think you both are cruel. I've had a very heavy trial, and you neither of you sympathize a bit. And I'm sure, " continued Matty, in a plaintive voice, "not the least part of it is being stuck in bed now. "

"I wonder you stay, " said Sophy. "You're in perfect health. "

"No, I'm not. Dr. Morris is very anxious about me. "

"He isn't. No one is anxious about you. There isn't a thing the matter, except that you and ma like that you should pose as the dying martyr. Well, good-bye. Sophy and I are going to have some fun this evening. "

"Fun, where? Do tell me. "

"At the Jenkinses. Their brother Gus has come home; you know how you and Gus used to flirt long ago, Matty. Well, he's back for a fortnight. He has a long red beard, and his face is all over freckles, but he's full of fun, and he laughs like anything. We saw him and he asked for you. It's a pity you can't come. "

"Why can't I come? I don't see why I can't come as well as you. "

"Oh, well, we thought you were the dying martyr. Mrs. Jenkins asked us all in to tea, and we are to have tennis afterwards, and then high supper, in honor of Gus. We said you couldn't come, but that we would be there. Alice, it's time for us to dress now. We'll wear our muslins with the pink spots, and those sweet new pink sashes that we got in exchange for the old teapot from Mrs. Middlemass last week. Come along, Alice. We'll show ourselves to you when we are dressed, Matty. "

The girls skipped lightly away, and Matty fidgeted and tossed in her small hot bed.

The house was intensely quiet. Mrs. Bell was away, having taken advantage of a proffered lift from a neighbor to drive into the country to purchase some plums. Matty thought how intolerably dull her evening would be. She reflected on the pleasures of the Jenkinses' tea-party; she thought it would be nice, more than nice, to shake hands again with Mr. Gus. Why shouldn't she go? What was to prevent her? Only her mother's whim. Only the doctor's orders. But both doctor and mother were now far away. She would go, she would defy them both.

Slipping out of bed she flew across the room and drew the bolt of the door. Then she began to dress in quick and nervous haste. She put on her daintiest shoes, and open-work stockings. She arranged her limp hair with care, and finally she donned the gorgeous shot-silk.

The few days in bed had taken away some of her burnt appearance, and slightly moderated her high color. She looked really almost nice as she skipped to the door, and showed herself to her astonished sisters.

"I'm coming, too, " she said.

"Then you are cured, " said Alice. "I'm glad of it, I'm sure. What did I say, Sophy, when I was coming in. "

"You said if anyone could mend up Matty it would be Gus, " retorted Sophy.

That fickle Matty blushed. It was a way she had.

CHAPTER XXIV.

EVENTS MOVE APACE.

Mrs. Bell was very successful in her purchase of plums. In her way she was a notable housewife, and she returned home about eight o'clock that evening with a large basket of greengages, which were all to be boiled down for preserving the following day.

As soon as she entered the house the maid came to meet her.

"You take these carefully down and put them in the larder, Hannah, " said her mistress. "Be careful you don't knock any of them, or the bloom will go off. Why what's the matter, girl? Is Miss Matty worse? "

"Lor, no, ma'am. Miss Matty is up, and out a-pleasuring, ma'am. But if you please, there's a visitor in the drawing-room who would like to have a word with you the minute you come in. "

"A visitor? "

Mrs Bell felt her heart beat. The Northbury people did not stand on ceremony with each other, nor wait in each other's drawing-rooms, for the return of an absent hostess. A wild idea came across Mrs. Bell's brain. Could Captain Bertram have quarrelled with Beatrice, and come back to Matty, his first and only true love.

"A visitor? Male or female? " she inquired of the girl.

"A lady, ma'am. Dressed most elegant. "

"Dear, dear, dear! Then I suppose I must see her, and I so dead beat! She didn't give her name, did she, Hannah? "

"No, ma'am. But she have been a-setting in the drawing-room for over an hour. "

"And Miss Matty, you say, is out! "

"Oh, yes, ma'am; a-pleasuring in her shot silk, and the open-worked stockings you ironed up a fortnight back. "

"Well, I feel bothered altogether, but I must go and see this visitor. "

Accordingly Mrs. Bell entered her drawing-room, where she was instantly confronted by a tall girl who greeted her with warmth, flashed her brilliant eyes into her face, subjugated her in a moment, and then made a bold request.

"My name is Josephine Hart. About a month ago I took rooms at the Testers. I find Mrs. Bertram has forbidden them to receive me again. I don't know where to go, as I am not acquainted with Northbury, but I can pay for good rooms. Can you recommend any? "

"My dear child, now let me think. The place is packed just at present—simply packed. Dear, dear! I have heard of you, Miss Hart. And so Mrs. Bertram doesn't like you? "

"No, she hates me. "

"Well, I'm sure. You don't look like a young lady to be hated. "

"No one else hates me, Mrs. Bell, but she does, because she has a reason. I have come back to Northbury on purpose to make her uncomfortable, and I must stay. "

"So you shall, my dear. I applaud a girl with spirit. And so you hate Mrs. Bertram? And you have a spite against her with reason. Well, I may as well own that I don't love her, having good cause not to do so. She has been the means of breaking my young daughter's heart. My child is even now lying on her bed of—" but here Mrs. Bell remembered what Hannah had said about the shot silk, and the open-worked stockings. "I wish I could help you, my dear young lady, " she said.

"I was hoping you would help me. Might I not come and live with you here? I would pay you well. "

Mrs. Bell started and blushed. Caste was a very marked feature in Northbury society, and between the people who let lodgings for money, and those who lived genteelly on their means was a great and awful gulf. No people were poorer in their way than the Bells, and no one would have more dearly liked to add to her little store of this world's pelf than would poor Mrs. Bell. She could scarcely afford to take a fashionable girl in for nothing, and yet—dared she accept payment? Bell, if he knew, would never forgive her, and, as to the town, it would simply cut her dead.

The tall girl who was watching Mrs. Bell's face seemed, however, to be able to read her through. She spoke in a moment in a very gentle and pleading voice:

"I understand your position; you are a lady, and you don't like to accept money. "

"I couldn't do it, my dear. I couldn't really; Bell, he'd take on awful. It isn't the custom in Northbury, Miss—Miss Hart. "

"And I couldn't come to you without paying. Now, suppose you and I managed it between us and nobody knew. "

"Oh, Miss Hart, I'd be terrified. These things always leak out, they do really. "

"Not if they are properly managed. You might leave that part to me. And you need not name any sum. I shall see that all your expenses are covered. Have you a private cupboard in your bedroom? Unlock it every Monday. That's all you need do. You can give out to all your friends that you have received me as a visitor, because you were kind to me, and I wanted to come back to Northbury so badly. "

After considerable more parley on both sides, the matter was arranged, and who more cheerful than Mrs. Bell as she tripped upstairs to prepare Matty's room for her guest. She was quite obliged to Matty now for having left her bed, for the thought of that little secret hoard, which Monday by Monday she might collect, and no one be the wiser, had filled her heart with rejoicing. So she helped Hannah to spread Josephine's bed with her finest linen sheets, and altogether she made the little chamber cosy and pleasant for its new inmate. All signs of poor Matty's illness were removed, and that young lady's possessions were hastily carried into her sisters' joint bedroom. Here they would be anything but wanted or appreciated but what cared Mrs. Bell for that?

Mrs. Meadowsweet, meanwhile, was having a somewhat exciting time. Beatrice was engaged. That event had taken place which the widow had only thought about as a distant and possible contingency. Captain Bertram had himself come to his future mother-in-law, and said a few words with such grace and real feeling that the old lady's warm heart was touched. She laid her hands within those of the handsome lad, and blessed him, and kissed him.

She was not a woman who could see far beneath the surface, and she thought Loftus Bertram worthy even of Beatrice. Beatrice herself said very little on the subject.

"Yes, I will marry him, " she said once to her mother. "I have made up my mind, and I will do it. They want the wedding to be soon. Let it be soon. Where's the use of lingering over these things. "

"You speak somehow, Trixie, I mean Bee, my girl, as if you didn't— didn't quite like it, " said the mother, then a trace of anxiety coming into her smooth, contented voice: "You shan't have him, I mean he shan't have you, unless you want him with your whole heart, Bee, my darling. "

"Mother, " said Beatrice, kneeling down by her, and putting her arms round her neck, "it is not given to all girls to want a thing with their whole heart. I have always been happy, always filled, always content. Therefore I go away without any special sense of rejoicing. But oh, not unhappily—oh, far from that. "

"You're sure, Trixie—you are speaking the whole truth to your own mother? Your words are sober to belong to a young girl who is soon to be a bride. Somehow I wasn't like that when your father came for me. "

"No two girls are alike, mother. I speak the sober truth, the plain, honest truth, when I tell you that I am happy. Still, my happiness is not unmixed when I think of leaving you. "

"Hoots-toots, child, I'll do well enough. Jane will look after me, and that nice little friend of yours, Catherine, will come and cheer me up now and then. I shall have lots to do, too, this autumn, for I'm going to have all the chintzes recalendered, and the carpets taken up and darned in the weak places, and there are some sheets to be cut down the middle and sewn up again. I won't have breathing-time, let alone half-hours for fretting. So the thought of the old mother needn't trouble you, my dearie dear. And the captain has promised to bring you back as soon as ever he can get fresh leave, so I can look forward to that, if I have a minute of time to look forward at all. "

Beatrice smiled and kissed her mother.

"I don't think any one ever had a dearer mother than you are, " she said, "or a more unselfish one. "

"Oh, now, my pet, " replied the crafty old lady, "you know you'd change me for Mrs. Bertram any day; she's so stylish, Bee, and so — so genteel, darling. You know I never did aim at being genteel. I always acknowledged that I was a step below your father and you. "

"Hush! You were a step below no one. You stand on a pinnacle which no other mother can reach, as far as I am concerned. Compare you with Mrs. Bertram indeed! "

Here Beatrice tried to look scornful. The expression was so foreign to her face that her mother absolutely laughed and chuckled. Of course, she had meant Bee to say the kind of thing she had said; it was balm to the old lady to hear such words from her beautiful child.

Up at the Manor now everything went smoothly. Mrs. Bertram was in perfect health, and perfect spirits. The bustle of a coming wedding excited and pleased the girls. There was that fuss about the place which generally precedes an event of rejoicing. Such fuss was delicious to Catherine and Mabel. Captain Bertram not only looked perfectly happy, but all his best qualities appeared now on the surface. New springs of feeling, depths hitherto untouched, had been awakened by Beatrice. She had a power over this young man; she could arouse all the latent nobility which he possessed. He thought he was very much in love with her; he certainly did care for her, but more as his guardian-angel than with the passionate love he might offer to a wife. He made all sorts of good resolves when he was with Beatrice, and these resolves grew into his face, and made it look pleasant, and touched it with a light never before seen there, and strengthened it with a touch which banished for a time the evil lines of irresolution and weakness.

Captain Bertram had made up his mind—he had been rarely blessed—he was unworthy, but a treasure of good price had been vouchsafed to him. He would live worthy of her. He would cast away the useless life of the past; he would cease to be extravagant—

his debts should be wiped off and never incurred again. He would be honorable, true—a gentleman in every sense of the word—the girl who was lowly born, but whose heart was so patrician, and whose spirit was so loyal, should guide him in all things.

Captain Bertram had only one uncomfortable corner in his heart just then. He had one little secret chamber which he kept locked, and into which, even in spirit, he never cared to enter. Men, when they are turning over new leaves, often keep this little reserve-room of the past uncleaned, unpurified. All else shall be swept and garnished, but this room, carefully locked, can reveal no secrets. From its door the ghost of past evil-doing can surely not escape to confront and destroy. So Captain Bertram thought. He must forget Josephine; the wrong he had done her, the vows he had made to her, could never be washed out or forgiven, but in all else he would be perfect in the future.

Before he returned to Northbury for the express purpose of wooing and winning Beatrice Meadowsweet, he had written to Josephine. In his letter he had promised to marry her; he had promised to confide all about her to his mother. He said he should be at home for a month, and during that month he would watch his opportunity and break the news of his engagement to Josephine to his parent. He had asked Josephine to give him a month to do this in, and he had begged of her to leave Northbury for the time, assuring her that her presence at his mother's gates would be highly detrimental to their mutual interests.

Josephine had departed, and Bertram, after the fashion of men of his class, had almost forgotten her existence in his pursuit of a new quest.

Now he was engaged, and his wedding-bells would soon ring. If the thought of Josephine Hart did flash now and then before his mental vision, he could only hope devoutly that she would learn nothing of his betrothal to Beatrice until after their marriage. "She may appear then, and I may have to tell Bee everything, " he soliloquized. "Well, well, Bee could not be hard on a fellow, and we will both do what we can for poor Josephine. No doubt I should not have made her a good husband—no doubt, no doubt! Poor child—poor, beautiful child. " But as he said the words under his breath, Captain Bertram felt his heart beat hard and fast. "My God—I love her madly—I must not think of her at all, " he murmured. "I must not; I dare not! " He was uncomfortable, and even depressed, after these musings; and he was determined to keep the door of that chamber within him where Josephine dwelt more firmly locked than ever in the future.

When all the people concerned are of one mind on a certain point it is surprising how easily they can bring their wishes to bear fruit. It was all important, both to Captain Bertram and his mother, that his marriage should follow his engagement with the least possible delay.

Having decided to marry him, Beatrice would allow her lover to lead her to the altar the first day he cared to do so. Mrs. Meadowsweet was, of course, like wax in the hands of her daughter.

Accordingly, Beatrice would only be an engaged maiden for three short weeks, and on the 10th of September, before Captain Bertram's leave expired, Northbury was to make merry over the gayest wedding it had ever been its lot to participate in.

Mr. Ingram, who was one of Beatrice's guardians, and from whose house the wedding was to take place, had insisted on all his parishioners being invited. Both rich and poor were to partake of the good things of life at the Rectory on that auspicious day, and Mrs. Bertram, whether she liked it or not, must sit down to her son's wedding-breakfast in the presence of Mrs. Gorman Stanley, Mrs. Morris, Mrs. Butler, Miss Peters, and the other despised Northbury folk.

"Your son is marrying into one of the Northbury families, " the rector had said, when the proud lady had frowned a little over this. "Beatrice must and shall have her friends round her when she gives herself to Bertram. Your son is making an excellent match from a money point of view and from all other points of view, and if there is a bitter with the sweet, he must learn to swallow it with a good grace. "

When the rector had mentioned "from a money point of view" Mrs. Bertram had forced herself to clear her brows, and smile amiably. After all, beside this great and important question of money what were these small worries but pinpricks.

The pin-prick, however, was capable of going somewhat deeper, when Catherine informed her mother that Beatrice particularly wished to have her friends, the Bells, and Daisy Jenkins as bride's-maids at her wedding.

"No, no, impossible, " burst from Mrs. Bertram's lips.

But in the end she had to yield this point also, for what will not a woman do who is hard beset and pressed into a corner to set herself free from so humiliating and torturing a position.

Thus everything was getting ready for the great event. The bride's trousseau was the wonder of all beholders. The subject of Beatrice's wedding was the only one on the *tapis*, and no one saw a little cloud in the sky, nor guessed at even the possibility of trouble ahead.

CHAPTER XXV.

WEDDING PRESENTS.

Notwithstanding her crushing disappointment Matty Bell did not sink into an early grave. That report which had got into the country with regard to her funeral and tombstone began to be very flatly contradicted. It was now whispered on the breeze that Matty was not only in a fair state of recovery but also that a substantial means of consolation had been opportunely found her.

Not only was Gus Jenkins very much to Matty's taste, but she proved, which, perhaps, was more to the point, to suit him exactly. This hero, who was doing a thriving trade in the oil business in London, delighted in laughing, merry, giggling girls, and surely where could he find another to equal Matty in that respect. Whenever he looked at her she laughed, whenever he spoke to her she blushed and giggled. He began to consider himself a wonder of wit and fascination. Really it was no trouble at all to entertain a nice, little, soft, round thing like Matty Bell. He pronounced the shot silk a splendid robe, and asked Matty pointedly what place of amusement she would like best to see in London, and in whose presence she would most happily enjoy it.

Matty could scarcely speak when this remarkable question was addressed to her, unless giggles, blushes, gasps, and "Oh, Gus, how killing you are! " could be taken as a sensible reply.

Under these circumstances Mrs. Bell felt that the less she said about Captain Bertram and that old affair of his with Matty the better. She always mentioned it now as "that old affair, " and whispered in strictest confidence to her friends that Gus, poor dear fellow, was so absurdly jealous of Captain Bertram that she dared not breathe the captain's name in his presence.

"It's awful to see the thunder-clap that comes on Gusty's brow, " the good lady would say. "And what I'm so terrified of is that if he and the captain meet they'll do each other a serious mischief. My poor child, she is the innocent cause, Well, well, she has been much sought after. "

When Beatrice asked the Bells to become her bride's-maids, Mrs. Bell thought the time had arrived to let bygones be bygones, and to accept the proffered honor.

"It was the captain's wish, I make no doubt, " she said to her husband; "he knew he hadn't a chance of winning the girl on whom his heart was set, but he thought, at least, he might have the pleasure of seeing her at his wedding, and, so to speak, looking his last on her. It's my belief, too, that he'll relieve his feelings by giving Matty a very beautiful present. She must hide it from Gusty, though; Gusty is so terrible in the jealous excess of his feelings. "

As Beatrice had insisted on giving her bride's-maids their dresses, no difficulty could be experienced on that head, and the Bells, notwithstanding that stormy period which had gone before, enjoyed themselves immensely during the brief season of Beatrice's engagement.

Mrs. Bell certainly was happy during this time. If Matty was not engaged to Bertram she soon would be to a better man. Gusty Jenkins, as she invariably called him, was, of course, the better man now in her eyes. The three girls were being supplied with new and lovely dresses, in which Mrs. Bell assured her husband they'd look like angels wafted down fresh from the skies—for the occasion. When she said this, Bell did not agree with her, but that was not of the slightest consequence.

Mrs. Bell also during these happy weeks was making a little secret hoard of money, which further considerably added to the good lady's felicity.

That young visitor of the Bell's, Miss Hart, proved herself a most unobtrusive and retiring person. She was strangely reserved, no doubt, and would reveal none of the secret which she had dimly alluded to on the night of her arrival to Mrs. Bell, but she was chatty and pleasant enough to the girls when quite alone with them. She put them up to many small wrinkles with regard to their toilette, and insisted on dressing Matty's hair in a way which made it look both thick and becoming. When the Bells were quite alone she was present at their meals where she quite subjugated the hearts of Bell and his son, Albert. But when visitors appeared at the hospitable board Miss Hart would not present herself. She had a curious reserve about her, which everyone noticed at the time, and commented on largely by-and-bye. If the all-absorbing topic of the day, Beatrice's wedding, was discussed, she invariably grew grave, her face would become a shade paler than its wont, and her bright, restless eyes would be lowered.

Except on one occasion, she never asked questions about the approaching wedding. On the contrary, she markedly avoided the subject. Once, however, she inquired the date of the wedding from Matty. On hearing it she turned very pale, and left the room. Matty remembered this fact by-and-bye.

Once, too, Sophy saw her standing in her bedroom with her two hands pressed tightly to her side, as though something had given her an intense pain there. She was close to the window, and must have been looking out, and Sophy observed that Captain Bertram and Beatrice were walking down the street together.

Notwithstanding all Mrs. Bell's coaxings, Miss Hart would never go out during the day-time, but when darkness fell, and it came early now, in the beginning of September, she would wrap her gray cloak about her, and go away for long, long walks all alone.

Mrs. Bell thought this proceeding anything but proper, but Josephine Hart minded very little what any one thought about her.

As the days wore on, her white face seemed to grow whiter, and her big bright eyes often looked pathetic as well as bright. She ate very little, too, and scarcely spoke at all; but it never occurred to her or any one else to suppose that she was ill.

The weather during all this period continued very fine. Never had so glorious a summer been remembered at Northbury, and the good folk said it was a lucky omen for the young bride, who was a favorite with rich and poor alike. Every one in Northbury made Beatrice a present, and she began to collect quite a curious collection of gifts. None of these presents were splendid, few of them possessed intrinsic value, but the young girl treasured them, one and all, very much; for they were to her symbols of the love which had shone about her path from her birth.

Mrs. Bertram could not understand the joy Beatrice felt over the crude gifts of the fishermen's wives, nor her ecstasy when a poor girl whom she had once befriended, brought her a dozen yards of narrow and very dirty crotchet edging. Beatrice almost kissed that edging, and her eyes filled with tears as she folded it up and put it away.

No such soft radiance came to them when her future mother-in-law presented her with a beautiful diamond cross, which was an old family heirloom, and must belong by right to Bertram's wife.

"This is of great value, " Mrs. Bertram said; "and it will suit you, my dear, you are the sort of girl who can wear diamonds, and look well in them. "

"But I like flowers best, " said Beatrice, under her breath.

She kissed Mrs. Bertram, and thanked her for her gift, which she locked away very carefully, as she knew it was of much value. But her heart was not stirred by it as it had been by the crotchet edging which Jenny Ray had made for her.

Mrs. Gorman Stanley gave Beatrice a large piece of Berlin wool-work; it was not handsome, nor had it cost the good lady much, for she had picked it up years ago at an auction. Mrs. Gorman Stanley was not a generous person, and as the Berlin wool-work had always troubled her on account of its magnificence, its uselessness, and the almost certainty that the moths would get in and devour it, she thought it a good opportunity of making an effective present, and getting rid of a household care.

Once that wool-work had been put together with love and pride. The impossible lilies and roses, the huge peonies, and gigantic hollyhocks which composed its pattern, had been formed, stitch by stitch, by unknown fingers, probably now crumbled to dust.

The wool-work might have told a story could it speak, but it had never imparted its secrets, pathetic or otherwise, to Mrs. Gorman Stanley, and Beatrice received the gorgeous gift with little emotion, and some shrinking away from its bad taste.

Mrs. Butler, after a great deal of consultation with her sister Maria, decided to give the bride-elect a huge white, carved ivory brooch. This brooch was her own favorite ornament; it was of gigantic dimensions, and consisted of an elaborate circle of flowers, supporting the word "Martha" in the centre.

"You'll wear it for me, love, " said Mrs. Butler, "you'll never put it on, but you'll give Martha Butler a thought. "

Beatrice assured her friend that this must certainly be the case. She was really grateful to Mrs. Butler, for she knew the old lady adored that brooch, and it had cost her much to deprive herself of it.

Miss Peters smuggled her little gift into Beatrice's hand as they were parting. It was a yard of Honiton lace, very old, and much darned. Bee had often seen this lace round Miss Peters' little wintry throat. She kissed it when she looked at it now, and placed it very near the crotchet edging in her regard.

But it would take a much longer space than this story can afford to recount all the presents that came to Beatrice Meadowsweet. From the Bertram connection the gifts were of money value, from the Northbury people they were rich with something better than money. Not one of Bee's friends forgot her at this time.

September came on apace, and at last there wanted but a week of the wedding day.

On a certain evening when the wind blew rather fresh from the sea, Captain Bertram asked Beatrice to walk with him. She complied. They took a long walk over the cliffs, and it was quite late and dark when they returned home.

They had to pass the Manor on their way back to the Gray House, where Bertram was to stay for supper.

As they walked along, talking gravely, for Beatrice did not often laugh when alone with her lover, a slender and tall figure passed them quickly in the darkness. Bertram, who was walking very close to Bee, stumbled against her, and uttered a smothered oath.

"What is the matter? " she asked in astonishment. "Have you hurt yourself? "

"No, I thought I recognized a face, but I must be mistaken. "

"That slim girl who passed us so quickly just now? I, too, fancy I have seen her before. Certainly she is a stranger here. "

"Don't talk about her, Beatrice. It was a casual likeness. People look so different—distorted by the darkness. To-night it is very dark. There is no moon. "

"Still, I can see, " said Beatrice, pausing and looking back. "I can see, and I fancy the stranger is standing still and looking at us. Back there, by the hedge. Perhaps she is in trouble. Shall I run and speak to her? "

"No, not for the world. Come home. Forget her. "

His tone was almost rough. They walked on rapidly. The high wind of a coming storm beat in their faces. Beatrice felt tired and dispirited, and Bertram's agitation and complete change of manner puzzled her.

Presently they reached the house.

"Here we are at last; you will be glad of your supper, " she said.

"No, thanks, I am not coming in. "

"Not coming in? You promised. Mother expects you. "

"Excuse me to-night, Beatrice. I have a headache. I shall go straight home. Good-night. I'll come down early in the morning. "

He took her hand, dropped it hastily, and almost before the door was opened, had turned away. Beatrice did not go in at once. She heard his quick, retreating steps. Presently they quickened into a run.

CHAPTER XXVI.

WE WILL RETURN TO OUR SECLUSION.

"I am mad, " said Bertram to himself. "Mad, as ever was the proverbial March hare. That girl who passed us in the darkness was Josephine Hart. Yes, that girl was Nina, and I must, I will, see her again. "

His heart was beating tumultuously; he felt the great passion of his love tingling through all his veins. Money was nothing to him in this hour, debts were forgotten, disgrace and dishonor were nowhere. Nina and love were all in all. He *would* see her, he would kiss her, he would hold her in his arms, he would, he must. The very elements helped him as he ran back to the place where he knew she had paused to watch him. Why had she come back! She knew her power only too well. Why had she come to exercise it? It was mad of her, wicked of her, it meant his ruin, and yet he was glad, yet he rejoiced.

The moments seemed endless until he could reach her. Beatrice was as absolutely forgotten by him at this moment as if she had never existed.

At last he gained the spot where Josephine had brushed past him in the darkness. He knew it, he knew the sudden curve of the road, the bend in the path where it began to dip downwards. He stood still, and strained his eyes to look through the darkness. No one was there. Beatrice had seen the slender figure leaning against the hedge, but all now was emptiness and solitude. Not a soul was in sight. On this lonely road not a being but himself breathed.

He stood motionless, he listened hard. Once even he called aloud:

"I am here, Nina! Here, Nina! waiting for you here! "

But no one responded. He was alone; the vision, the delicious, heart-stirring vision, had vanished.

Captain Bertram wandered about, restless and miserable, for an hour or two. Then he went home and retired straight to his room.

That night he did not attempt to keep the secret chamber of his heart in which Josephine dwelt, locked and barred. No, he opened the doors wide, and bade her come out, and talked to her. Passionate and wild and loving words he used, and Beatrice was nothing to him. He did not go to bed that night. In the morning his face showed symptoms of the vigil he had passed through. His mother noticed the haggard lines round his eyes, and she gave vent to a sigh — scarcely audible, it is true, and quickly smothered.

Mrs. Bertram was happy, but still she lived on thorns. She felt that the fairy palace she had built over that sepulchre of the past might crumble at any moment. The lines of care on Bertram's brow gave her a sensation of fear. Was anything the matter? Was the courage of the bride-elect failing? At the eleventh hour could anything possibly injure the arrangements so nearly completed?

Catherine and Mabel were in good spirits. Their bride's-maids' dresses had arrived from town the previous night. They were of gauzy white over silk slips; the girls had never possessed such luxurious costumes before.

"You'd like to see us in them, wouldn't you, Loftie? " said Mabel. "Catherine looks splendid in hers, and those big hats with Marguerites are so becoming. Shall we put our dresses on, Loftie, for you to see before you run away to Beatrice? Shall we? "

Loftus raised his dark eyes, and looked full at his young sister. There were heavy shadows round his eyes; their depths looked gloomy and troubled.

"What did you say? " he asked, in a morose voice.

"What did I say? Well, really, Loftie, you are too bad. I do think you are the most selfish person I know. At one time I thought Bee was improving you, but you are worse than ever this morning. You never, never, take a bit of interest in things that don't immediately concern yourself. I thought our bride's-maids' dresses would have been sufficiently important to rouse a passing interest even in — now, what's the matter, Catherine? I *will* speak out. "

"Forgive me, Mab, I have a headache and feel stupid, " interrupted Loftus, rising to his feet. "I'm going out for a stroll; the air will do me good. "

He went up to the end of the table where his mother sat, kissed her almost tenderly, and left the room.

Catherine began to reprove Mabel.

"It is you who are selfish, " she said. "You know Loftie must have a great deal on his mind just now. "

"Oh, well, I don't care. Every little pleasure is somehow or other dashed to the ground. *I was* pleased when I thought Bee was to be my sister, and she was so sweet about the dresses, choosing just what we'd look best in. Loftus was nice, too, until this morning. Now I don't feel as if I cared about anything. "

Mabel never reflected on the possibility of her own words causing annoyance. She ate her breakfast without observing that both her mother and Catherine looked depressed. Presently, like the thoughtless child she was, she looked up with laughing eyes:

"Won't the Bells look funny in those grand robes. Do you know, Kate, I heard such a ridiculous thing yesterday. It was Mrs. Gorman Stanley who told me. She said Matty Bell was over head and ears in love with Loftie, and that Mrs. Bell had quite made up her mind that Loftie was to marry Mattie. She told such a funny story of the way Mrs. Butler broke the news of Beatrice's engagement to the Bells. Now, what's up? Have I said anything wrong again? "

"You have, Mabel, " said her mother. "You have been guilty of repeating common and vulgar gossip. You ought never to have listened to it. I had hoped that a daughter of mine, a Bertram, too, would have inspired too much respect to have any such rubbish spoken of in her presence. "

"Oh, really, mother, I don't think people much care whether we are Bertrams or not. "

"Hush, my dear, that is sufficient. I always feared the effect of the low society of this place on you both, and in especial on you, Mabel. My fears have been justified by the results. As soon as Loftus's wedding is over we will return to our seclusion, my dears. "

CHAPTER XXVII.

THE LIGHTS WERE DIM.

Early on that very morning Miss Hart tapped at Mrs. Bell's door. That good lady was not fully dressed, but she appeared in a voluminous morning robe to answer her young visitor's summons.

"I am going away, Mrs. Bell, " said Miss Hart.

"Oh, my dear! " Mrs. Bell's full-moon face turned absolutely pale. "Going away, my love! " she said. She thought of her private hoard, not nearly large enough, and her voice became absolutely pathetic. "Going away, Miss Hart? I'm truly grieved to hear it. And haven't I made you comfortable enough, my poor dear? "

"Oh, you misunderstand me, Mrs. Bell. I am going away, but only for a little—just for a day or two. I don't know exactly when I shall be back, but probably in a day or two. I am going by the early train, and I tapped at your door to say good-bye. "

Then Mrs. Bell in her delight and joy kissed Miss Hart, who soon afterwards left the house.

She walked to the station, the hour was early, and there was no special person about. She took a first-class ticket to a small town about thirty miles away, and immediately afterwards her train came up.

During the greater part of her journey Miss Hart had the compartment to herself. By-and-bye fellow-passengers got in, who almost started back at the sight of the pale face of the girl, who sat with her veil thrown back, looking straight out of the open window.

There was a strange expression on her face; her brows were slightly drawn together, and the curves of her lips had a, weary and pathetic droop. She had taken off her gloves, and now and then she clasped her slender white hands together with a nervous, passionate tension. Then the look in her eyes became almost ugly, and her fellow passengers were uncomfortable as they watched her.

At the little country town of West Brockley, Miss Hart alighted. She had brought all her luggage in a small handbag, and now she walked to her destination. It was in the outskirts of the little town, and amongst a row of poor houses. She stopped at one of these, and entered by the open door. A woman met her in the passage.

"Is Mr. Hart within? "

"I don't know, madam, I'll inquire. "

"No, don't do that. I'll go to him myself. He's at the top of the house, of course, as usual? "

"Why, as usual, madam? Mr. Hart has never been my lodger before. "

"I know his ways. He invariably seeks the top. "

"From no prejudice, madam. He seems a very quiet gentleman. "

"Exactly. Treasure him, he is a valuable lodger. Now let me pass, please. I am going to seek him. "

"Perhaps I had better tell him first, young lady. "

"I am his grandchild. It is all right. Let me pass. "

She brushed the woman aside, and flew lightly up the stairs. She knocked at the door of the top attic, but followed her knock into the room before any one had made response from within.

Old Hart was, as usual, messing over some cooking. He stopped it when he saw Josephine, and an iron spoon which he held in his hand clattered noisily to the floor.

"Now, Nina, what is the matter? "

"I am going to spend the day with you, Granddad, and probably the night as well. You can give me a bed in a corner of this delightful sitting-room. Is that breakfast? I wish you would serve it up; I am starving. "

"It's a very good breakfast, little Nina. Fried rabbit, done after a new method. Bacon and eggs to follow, with a sauce of port wine. Olives and sour claret for dessert. I know your taste, witch. "

"I love olives, " said Nina. "Sit at the table, Grand-dad, and let us begin. By the way, when did you shave last? "

"Ha—ha, who have I to shave for now, my pretty Nina? Nobody cares for the old man, nobody looks at him with eyes of admiration. Why should he waste his money and his time over the barbarous rite of shaving? Nature has her way with the old man now, sweet witch. "

"Nature doesn't improve you, Grand-dad. You require the refining touches of art. Your beard is unkempt, your hair too long. You shall visit the barber after we have concluded our meal. It is distressing to mankind in general to behold a spectacle like you. You owe a duty to the world at large. You must visit the barber. "

"Chut—chut! What a witch it is! Why didn't it stay at home, and not worry the old man? "

"Serve up the breakfast, Grand-dad, and believe in the salutary nature of your granddaughter's visitations. "

The two sat down to their meal, and both ate for a time in unbroken silence. After his third glass of sour claret, the old man spoke:

"How are you, Nina? You don't look up to much? "

"Would you be up to much if a fever consumed you day and night? Feel my hand, Grand-dad. "

The old man gripped the slender fingers, then flung them away.

"Good God! they burn! " he said. "Don't touch me, witch. You may have contracted something catching. "

"No, nothing that the old man can catch. Now, let us be pleasant, and enjoy the day together. "

"We can't. I am going to move to-day. "

"You must stay here to-day; you can move tomorrow. "

"Witch, how you order me. I won't be ordered. I shall move to-day. "

"You have no idea of moving, either to-day or to-morrow. Don't talk nonsense. You have had your breakfast. I will wash the things up. Go and visit the barber. "

The old man muttered and mumbled. Finally he tied a large crimson scarf in a loose knot round his throat, shoved a soft felt hat on his head, and donning a greasy and very old brown velvet cloak, he prepared to go out.

"It's a rare nuisance, " he said; "I meant to try some Chinese cooking for dinner; something with a subtle aroma, delicate, and hard to obtain. You boil the leeks for so many hours, and catch the essence in a distiller. Bah! you care nothing for eating, witch. "

"I like some of your dishes very well, Granddad, but I prefer cleanliness to luxury. Now, go out and get shaved. "

"It will cost me sixpence. "

"Sixpence well spent. Don't talk any more; go! "

He blew her a kiss, half of derision, half of pride, and shambled downstairs. A crowd of little boys followed him up the street; some pulled his cloak, some mocked him openly. He neither felt the pulls nor heard the words. He was absorbed in the thought of that delicious Chinese dinner which he could not now partake of to-day.

As soon as he was gone, Nina, too, ran downstairs. She went to a chemist's, and boldly asked for a small quantity of a certain drug.

"Have you a prescription? " the man inquired.

"No, but I understand the right proportions to take. Why do you hesitate? I am not asking for poison. "

The man stared hard at the bright, queer face of his customer.

"The drug is not poison, " he slowly repeated, "but taken in too large quantities it can inflict an injury. I will give it to you, but you must enter your name and address in this book. "

Josephine laughed lightly, entered old Hart's address in the book, paid for her medicine, and departed. As soon as she got home she took out of a cupboard a decanter which contained a small portion of a very bright and clear wine. She mixed a little of the powder with the wine. It dissolved instantly, and did not disturb the rare amber of the liquid. The rest of the powder Nina threw into the fire, burning both paper and string.

When Hart came back, shaven and neat, his hair shortened, his long snow-white beard trimmed, he looked what he was—a strikingly handsome man. His grand-daughter possessed his regular features, but, although her eyes were as bright as his, they were not dark. She had black eyelashes and black brows, but the eyes themselves were peculiarly light.

Nina was in an excellent humor now. She helped her grandfather with his cooking, and by-and-by, as the day wore on, she tempted him to come for a stroll with her. She spoke very little of her present life, nor did he question her. He had a certain fondness for his grandchild, but it never rose to the extent of a genuine interest in her concerns. Of late she had been to him a valuable chattel—a trump-card, by which he could extract the good things of life out of another. With Nina he was powerful, without her he was a helpless and penniless old man. But he did not love Nina because of this. He was proud of her for what she brought him, proud of her because if he was lowly born she was not. But he loved her, after the slight fashion with which alone he could bestow love, because, notwithstanding that good birth, she also belonged to him—she was bone of his bone, flesh of his flesh. The ties of blood were strong with him, and because of these ties he loved her after his fashion.

The two came home presently and partook of supper together. Nina bought some figs and peaches, and they had quite a dainty meal. Nina herself prepared the board, and she put the decanter with the amber wine close to the old man. He ate and drank. He said the wine was good, and he helped himself twice to the sparkling contents of the decanter. "I feel in spirits to-night, Nina, " he said, looking at his grandchild.

"Have a little more wine, Grand-dad, " she said, in retort.

In spite of all her efforts, her voice had an anxious ring in it as she spoke. He looked at her keenly. He was as suspicious as man could be. He half-stretched out his hand to seize the decanter, then with a sly smile he replaced the stopper in the neck of the bottle.

"No, no, witch, " he said. "This wine is rare and precious. It raises the spirit and warms the heart. I have not much more wine from so rare a vintage, and I'll keep what's in the bottle for another night, when you, pretty Nina, are far away, and the spirits of the old man fail him. "

"Do, " she said. "Keep the precious wine, you don't need it to-night. "

Then she handed him his pipe, and after a time he became drowsy and went to bed.

Hart's bedroom was a small attic inside the larger one. He shut the door, looked round for the key, for he generally locked himself in, could not find it, and then, being very drowsy, undressed and went to bed.

Nina was to sleep on the sofa in the sitting-room. She lay down, took a novel out of her pocket, and tried to read. Her heart was beating hard, and that burning fever of unrest and longing which was consuming her very life, kept coursing madly through her veins.

"The fever is my wine, " she muttered. "At first it supplies false strength, false cheer, false hope. Afterwards—afterwards—" a queer look came into her strange face—"I too, shall rest and sleep. "

Profound stillness reigned in the next room. Nina softly rose, and going to the sideboard took out the decanter of wine, opened a window, and emptied it into the area below. She washed the decanter afterwards and then put it back into the sideboard.

There was not a sound in the inner room. Candle in hand, she opened the door and went in. She put the candle on the mantelpiece, and then going to the bed, bent over it and looked at the sleeper.

"Poor Grand-dad! " said the girl. She stooped and kissed the old man's forehead. "You have been good to me after your lights—it was not your fault that those lights were dim. Had you been an educated man, Grand-dad, you'd have educated me; and had you been a good man, you'd have taught me goodness; and a kind man, you'd have guarded your poor Nina. Was it your fault that you were ignorant—

and wanting in goodness—and lacking in kindness? You did your best—, after your lights. "

Then she stooped and kissed him again. He was heavy from the drug she had put into the wine, and did not stir. She slipped her hand softly under his pillow.

"Poor old man, I am taking away your trump-card, " she said. She drew a thick letter, yellow with age, from under the pillow, put it into her pocket, and taking up the candle left the room.

CHAPTER XXVIII.

RIVALS.

A couple of days after this Beatrice Meadowsweet received a note from Mrs. Bell, asking her to call to see her. The note came early in the morning, and immediately after breakfast Beatrice went to the Bells' house.

Mrs. Bell took her into the drawing-room and shut the door behind them both.

"Beatrice, " she said, "I owed you a grudge, but that is past. You stepped in, where you had no right to step, and for a time, I won't deny it, my heart was very sore. I haven't sent for you to-day, though, to rip up past troubles. I'm inclined to think that all's for the best. It has pleased the Almighty to provide you with a wild mate — and my girl with a steady one. Last night as the clock struck nine, Gusty Jenkins popped the question for Matty, and all being agreeable, the young man torn with love, and rock-like as regards character, Gusty and Matty are now an affianced pair. Therefore, Beatrice, I say let by-gones be by-gones, and may you have what luck can await you in the future with that wild young man. "

"I don't see why you should take away Captain Bertram's character, " said Beatrice, with some spirit. "You liked him very much once. "

"I'm not saying anything against him, my dear. I mean not anything more than the truth can bear out. There was a time when I thought well of Captain Bertram. I'm the last to deny there was such a time, but handsome is that handsome does, and when a young man had not the courage to obey his heart's promptings, and when rumors will travel on the breezes of extravagant, not to say naughty ways, I say, Beatrice, a woman can't become blind as a bat when these things stare her in the face. "

No one in Northbury ever remembered seeing Beatrice in a passion. She was acknowledged to be sweet-tempered, and slow to be provoked. On this occasion, however, she was very nearly making the proverbial exception to her general rule. Beatrice was very nearly angry. A flush of color crimsoned her cheeks and brow, and an indignant light flashed from her eyes. In time, however, she was able to murmur to herself: "This is only Mrs. Bell's talk, and how could I be so silly as to mind Mrs. Bell? " So after a pause she said with effort, "I must congratulate Matty on her engagement; I am glad Matty is happy. "

"Ah, my dear, and well she may be! Glad should I be to know that other girls had half so bright a future before them. Rich, handsome, and young, that's what Gusty is! Devoted! he's like one of the old knights for devotion. I have had my qualms about the jealousy of his nature, but otherwise Gusty is, *song pear and song reproach*. "

At this moment the door was opened, some childish giggles and mirth were heard in the passage, and Matty rushed in, followed by the redoubtable Gusty. "Oh, Gus, you'll kill me! " she exclaimed; "you are too funny. Why, ma, is that you? And—and—Bee? How do you do, Bee? "

Matty came over and kissed her friend awkwardly.

"I am very glad to hear of your happiness, Matty, " said Beatrice; "and I congratulate you, too, Augustus, " she added, turning to the bashful swain.

"Oh, you want us to leave this room to yourselves, you two naughty things! " said the mother, shaking her head in fat ecstasy over her two turtle-doves. "Come, Bee; by-the-way, there's a young girl upstairs, a Miss Hart, a friend of mine, who is very anxious to see you. "

Mrs. Bell and Beatrice left the drawing-room, and Augustus Jenkins turned to his fiancée "By Jove, " he said, "that girl *is* a bouncer! "

"What girl? " said Matty, in a quick jealous voice. She had flung herself in a languid attitude on the sofa, now she sat bolt upright.

"Killing, I call her, " proceeded Gus; "simply killing. Such an eye, such a curl of the lip! By Jove—she'd bowl any fellow over. "

Matty flushed deeply, and turned her head away to look out of the window.

"What's up, now, little duck? " said the lover. "Oh, she's jealous, is she? By George, that's a good un! You were in luck, missy, to come in my way first, or I don't know what mightn't have happened; and she's got lots of the tin, too, I've been told! So she's Captain Bertram's fancy. Well, he's a good judge and no mistake. "

"I don't know that she's his fancy at all, Gusty. Ma always said that I—I—"

"Oh, by Jove! Matty, don't you try to come it over me like that. What a thunder-cloud? So she's frightfully jealous, is she, poor little duck? I say, though, you'd better keep me out of that girl's way; engaged or not, she'd mash any fellow. Now, what's up? Is that you, Alice? What a noisy one you are, to be sure! "

Alice had rushed into the room followed by Sophy, who was followed again by Daisy Jenkins.

"The bride's-maid dresses have come! " screamed Alice. "Let's all go and try them on, Matty! "

When Mrs. Bell took Beatrice out of the room, she said a few more words about Miss Hart. Finally she took Beatrice upstairs, and ushered her into her young visitor's bedroom.

Amongst the other luxuries which Josephine's money had secured for her in the Bells' house was an old-fashioned sofa, which was drawn across the windows. On this sofa Josephine often lay for hours. She was lying on it now, in a white morning dress. Mrs. Bell introduced the girls to each other, and then left them.

"I have seen you before, " said Beatrice, the moment they were alone; "once before I have seen your face. You were looking out of a window. Stay, " she added, suddenly, "I think I have seen you twice before. Are you not the girl who brushed past Captain Bertram and me the other night in the dark? Yes, I am sure you are the girl. "

"You are right, " said Josephine; "I am the girl. " She spoke in an eager voice, two burning spots rose to her pale cheeks; her eyes always bright now almost glittered. "I am the girl, " she repeated. She half rose from her sofa, but sat down on it again, and panted heavily, as though her breath failed her.

"You are ill, " said Beatrice, with compunction; "you look very ill. Have you been long here? Mrs. Bell says that you are a friend of hers, a visitor. "

"Yes, I am a friend and visitor. Mrs. Bell is very good to me. "

"But you are ill. You ought to see a doctor. "

"I ought not—I will not. "

"Can I help you? It was kind of you to send for me. Can I do anything for you? "

"Wait until I get back my breath. I will speak in a minute. Sit quiet. Let me be still. It is agitation enough to have you in the room. "

Her eyes glittered again. She pressed her white transparent hands to her throbbing heart.

Beatrice sat motionless. She had a queer feeling at her own heart, a kind of premonition that a blow was about to be struck at her. Several minutes passed. Then the girl on the sofa spoke.

"The struggle of seeing you is past. I see—I endure. Your name is Beatrice Meadowsweet—? "

"Yes, I am Beatrice Meadowsweet. "

"You are engaged to Captain Bertram? "

"Yes. "

"You are to be married on the 10th of this month. "

"Yes. "

"This is the 5th. You are to be married in five days! "

"I am, Miss Hart. Do you want to congratulate me? "

"I—yes—I congratulate you. You—are attached—to Loftus? "

"To Captain Bertram? Do you know him? "

"No matter. You—you love him? "

"Why should I speak of my feelings? To marry a man is a proof of love, is it not? Do you know my future husband? "

"I—once I knew him. "

"He has never spoken to me about you. Did you know him well? "

"No matter. I knew him—no matter how much. He loves you, does he not? "

"I believe he faithfully loves me. "

"Yes, I saw you together. There is no doubt. I heard the tone in his voice. You can't mistake that tone, can you? "

"I don't know. I have not much experience. "

"You ought to have, for you are so beautiful. Yes, he loves you. It is all over. "

"What is all over? "

"Nothing. Did I say anything wild of that sort? Don't believe the nonsense I speak. I am ill, and my brain sometimes wanders. There is a great fire consuming me, and I am tired of being burned alive. Sometimes in my pain I talk wildly. Nothing is over, for nothing really began. You will be good to Captain Bertram, won't you? How you look at me! You have very true eyes, very true. Now I will tell you the truth. Once I knew him, and he was kind to me—a *little* kind—you know the sort of thing. I thought it meant more. He has forgotten me, of course, and you'll be good to him, for he—he's not perfect—although he suited—yes, he suited me very well. How my heart beats! Don't talk to me for a minute. "

She lay back panting on the sofa. Beatrice got up and walked to the window. There was a long view of the High Street from this window. The street was straight and narrow, with few curves.

At that moment Beatrice saw Captain Bertram. He was a long way off, but he was walking down the street in the direction of the Bells' house. In about three minutes he would pass the house.

As Beatrice stood by the window she thought. A memory came over her. A memory of a man's steps—they were leaving her—they were hurrying—they were quickening to a run. In a flash she made up her mind.

She came back to the sofa where Nina sat.

"Can I do anything for you? Tell me quickly, for I earnestly desire to help you. "

"You are good, " said Nina. "You have a true voice, as well as a true face. Yes, I sent for you. I do want you to be kind to me. I want you to take a present from me to Captain Bertram. "

"A present? What? "

"This little packet. It is sealed and addressed. Inside there is a story. That story would make Captain Bertram unhappy. I know the story; he does not know it. On your wedding-day, after you are married, give him this packet. When you put it in his hands, say these words, 'Nina sent you this, Loftus, and you are to burn it. ' You must promise to see him burn the packet. What is the matter? Aren't you going to take it? "

"Yes, I will take it. Give it to me; I will put it in my pocket. Now, wait a moment. I want to run downstairs. I will come back again. "

She softly closed the door of Nina's room, rushed downstairs, and out into the street.

Captain Bertram was passing the Bells' door when Beatrice ran up to him.

"Loftus, I want you, " she said.

He turned in astonishment. He had been walking down the street, lost in a miserable dream. Beatrice, in her sharp, clear tone awoke him. He started, a wave of color passed over his dark face.

"Is anything wrong? " he asked, almost in alarm. "Bee, you are excited! "

"I am, fearfully. Come in, come upstairs! "

"Into the Bells' house! I don't want to visit the Bells. Beatrice, you look strange, and oh, how lovely! "

"Don't talk of my looks. Come in, come upstairs. No, you are not to see the Bells, nor are any of them about. Come—come at once. "

She ran quickly up the stairs. He followed her, wondering, perplexed and irritated.

"Beatrice, what is the matter? " he said, once.

"Not much—or, rather, yes, everything. Inside that room, Captain Bertram, is one you know. Go and see her—or rather, come and see her, with me. You know her, and once, you were, after your fashion, —a *little* kind. "

Beatrice threw open the door.

"Nina, " she said, "Captain Bertram is here, "—then she paused, — her next words came with a visible effort—"And his heart shall choose the girl he loves. "

Beatrice walked straight across the room to the window. She heard a cry from Nina, and something between a groan and an exclamation of joy from Bertram.

She did not look round.

CHAPTER XXIX.

THE FEELINGS OF A CRUSHED MOTH.

"I don't think it's right for Maria to be in the room, " said Mrs. Butler. "I'll listen to all you've got to say in a moment, Mrs. Gorman Stanley, but—Maria, will you have the goodness to leave us. "

"I'd rather stay, " pleaded poor Miss Maria. "I always was deeply interested in my darling Bee, and it's dreadful to think of her being discussed and gossiped over, and me not present. You know, Martha, you have a sharp tongue. "

"This from you, Maria? You, who eat my bread. Well! Mrs. Gorman Stanley, you are witness to this ingratitude. "

"Oh, my dear good creatures, don't quarrel, " said Mrs. Gorman Stanley.

She was a very phlegmatic woman, and hated scenes.

"If I were you, Mrs. Butler, I'd let poor Miss Peters stay, " she added. "I'm sure she's quite old enough. "

"Mrs. Gorman Stanley, my sister is never old enough to listen to improper subjects. Faithless, she is, ungrateful, perverse, but her innocence at least I will respect. Maria, leave the room. "

Poor Miss Maria slipped away. As she did so, she looked exactly like a crushed brown moth. In the passage she stopped, glanced furtively around her, and then, shocking to relate, put her ear to the key-hole. She felt both sore and angry; they were saying horrid things of Beatrice, and Miss Peters loved Beatrice.

Soon she went away, and burying her face in her little handkerchief, sobbed bitterly.

Inside the drawing-room, Mrs. Butler and Mrs. Gorman Stanley were holding awful conclave.

"You don't say, my dear, that she took the young man up to Miss Hart's *private* room? And who *is* Miss Hart? And what's all this fuss about? No, I'm glad Maria isn't here! I always tried to do my duty by Maria, and a scandal of this kind she must not listen to. What does it all mean, Mrs. Gorman Stanley? Is Beatrice Meadowsweet to be married on Tuesday, or is she not? "

"My dear friend, I can't tell you. There are all sorts of rumors about. I was at Perry's buying a yard of muslin, when Mrs. Morris came in. She had her mouth pursed up, and her voice perfectly guttural from bronchitis, so I knew she was keeping something in, and I made a point of going up to her. I said, 'you have got some news, Mrs. Morris, and you may as well out with it. ' Then she told me. "

"What? Mrs. Gorman Stanley, I trust you don't feel the draught from that window. I'll shut it if you like. But what—what did she say? "

"Well, she said some queer things. Nobody can quite make out whether Bee is to be married or not on Tuesday. Some say that Captain Bertram is married already, and that his wife is living in seclusion at the Bells'. "

"At the Bells'? I'll go over at once and poke that mystery out. Maria! *Maria*! She's sure to to be eaves-dropping somewhere near. Maria, come here quickly, I want you. "

"What is it, Martha? "

The little crushed moth put in a face, which disclosed very red eyes, at the door.

"What is it, Martha? Do you want me? "

"Ah, I thought you couldn't be far off. You'll oblige me, Maria, by running upstairs, and fetching down my bonnet and mantle. My *old* gloves will do, and I'll have my fur boa, for the days are turning wonderfully chilly. Yes, Mrs. Gorman Stanley, " continued Mrs. Butler, when Miss Peters had disappeared, "I'll soon get at the bottom of *that* bit of gossip. Are the Bells likely people to keep a close secret to themselves; you tell me that, Mrs. Gorman Stanley? Aren't they all blab, blab, blab? Ah, here comes Maria—and dressed to go out, too, upon my word? Well, miss, I suppose I must humor you! You'll have the decency, however, to remember to turn away your head if we matrons wish to whisper a bit among ourselves. Good-bye, Mrs. Gorman Stanley. I'll look in if I have any news for you this evening. "

"Do, " said Mrs. Gorman Stanley. "I'm all a-gog to hear. It's no joke to order a handsome dress for a chit of a girl's wedding, and then not wear it after all. I meant to get new curtains for my back parlor, heavy snuff-colored moreen, going a great bargain, but I had to buy the dress instead. Well, you'll let me know the news. Good-bye. "

As they were walking down the street to the Bells' house Mrs. Butler turned sharply to her little companion:

"Maria, " she said, "you are a perfect fool. "

"Well, really, Martha, I—I——"

"For goodness' sake, don't begin to snivel. I hadn't finished my speech. I'm a fool, too. We are both in the same box. "

"Oh, no, Martha, you always were——"

"Folly. You needn't roll your eyes at me. Don't flatter. I said we were both fools. I repeat it. We have been hoaxed. "

"Hoaxed? " said Miss Maria, with a high staccato note of inquiry.

"Yes. Hoaxed. Hoaxed out of our wedding presents by a girl who is not going to have a wedding at all. I miss my brooch. My throat feels naked without it. Last week I had a hoarseness. I attribute it to the loss of the brooch. "

"I don't miss my lace, " said Miss Maria. "I am glad she has it. I am very glad she has it, wedding or no wedding, bless her sweet heart. "

"Maria, your sentiments are sickly. Don't give me any more of them. Here we are at the door now. You'll remember, Maria, my hint, and act as a modest woman, if occasion requires. "

Here Mrs. Butler souded a loud rat-tat on the Bells' hall door. The little maid opened it rather in a fright. She poked her head out. This was a style usually adopted by the Northbury servants.

"Is your mistress in, Hannah? "

"I don't know, Mrs. Butler, ma'am. I'll inquire, ma'am. Will you walk in, please, ma'am. "

"I will, Hannah, and so will Miss Peters. Show us into the drawing-room, and tell your mistress we are here. If she should happen to be out we will wait her return. You will be particular to remember that, Hannah. We'll wait her return. "

"Oh, if you please, Mrs. Butler, will you—excuse me, ma'am, but *will* you come into the parlor, please, ma'am? "

"Into the parlor? Why into the parlor, pray? "

"It's Miss Matty, ma'am. "

"Oh! has Miss Matty become mistress of this house? And does she forbid her mother's visitors admission to the drawing-room! Hoots, toots—I'll soon put a stop to that sort of thing. Come on, Maria. "

"But really, Martha—do stop a moment, Martha—I'm sure Hannah ought to know best. "

"Oh, indeed, yes, Miss Peters—thank you, Miss Peters—missis did give orders most positive. These were her exact words: 'Hannah, ' she said, 'the parlor is for callers. You remember that, Hannah, and the drawing-room is for—'"

"Yes, " said Mrs. Butler, sweeping round, and confronting poor little frightened Hannah. "Who is the drawing-room for? "

"For Miss Matty, please, Mrs. Butler, ma'am. For Miss Matty and Mr. Gusty Jenkins. They're a—they're a-lovering in the drawing-room, ma'am. "

"Then they are engaged! That rumor also reached me. Come on, Maria. We'll go and congratulate them. "

No poor little ignorant maid-of-all-work could keep Mrs. Butler back now. She swept down the passage, followed by the shrinking, but curious Miss Peters. She threw open the drawing-room door herself, and intruded upon the abashed young people with a stately flourish.

"How are you, Matty? " she said. "Oh, pray don't let us disturb you. Is that you, Augustus? I'm pleased to see you, young man. I used to dandle you when you were an infant—good gracious, what red hair you had, and—it hasn't changed, not at all! Now, Matty, my dear, what are you blushing about? You have caught your young man at last, and much luck may you both have. If—' if at first you don't succeed, try, try, try again. ' You *have* tried again, Matty, and I congratulate you. You may kiss me, Matty, if you like. Maria, you may kiss Matty Bell. She's engaged to Gusty. Well, Gusty, you *are* a sly one. Never once have you been near my house since your return. Better employed, you will say. Ha, ha, *I* know young men. Marry in haste and repent at leisure. But come over now and sit near me by this window. I shouldn't object to a dish of gossip with you, not at all. Do you remember that day when you had your first tooth out? How you screamed? I held your hands, and your mother your head. You were an arrant coward, Gusty, and I'm frank enough to remind you of the fact. "

Just then, to Augustus Jenkins' infinite relief, Mrs. Bell entered the room; he was spared any further reminiscences of his youth, and he and Matty were thankful to escape into the garden.

After the necessary congratulations had been gone through, and Mrs. Bell had bridled, and looked important, and Mrs. Butler had slapped her friend on the shoulder, and given her elbow a sly poke, and in short gone through the pleasantries which she thought becoming to the occasion, the ladies turned to the more serious business in hand.

Mrs. Butler, who prided herself on being candid, who was the terror of her friends on account of this said candor, asked a plain question in her usual style.

"Maria, go to the window and look out. Now, Mrs. Bell, you answer me yes or no to this. Has Captain Bertram a wife concealed in this house, or has he not? In short, is my throat naked for no rhyme or reason! "

Mrs. Bell, who could not quite see what Mrs. Butler's throat had to say to a clandestine wife of Captain Bertram's, stared at her friend with her usual round and stolid eyes.

"I think your brain must be wandering, Martha Butler, " she said. "I don't know anything about your throat, except that it is very indelicate to wear it exposed, and as to Captain Bertram having a wife here, do you want to insult me after all these years, Martha? "

"I want to do nothing of the kind, Tilly Bell. I only want to get at the naked truth. "

"It was your naked throat a minute ago. "

"Well, they hang together, my throat and the truth. Has that young man got a wife in this house, or has he not? "

"He has not, Mrs. Butler, and you forfeit my friendship from this minute. "

"Oh, I forfeit it, do I? (Come, Maria, we'll be going.) Very well, Mrs. Bell, I have forfeited your friendship, very well. And there's no young woman who oughtn't to be here, concealed on these premises. (Maria, stay looking out at the window for a minute.) There's no strange young woman here, oh, of course not. Poor Bell, honest man, only *fancies* he has a visitor in the house. "

Here Mrs. Bell turned ghastly pale. Mrs. Butler saw that she had unexpectedly driven a nail home, and with fiendish glee pursued her advantage.

"A visitor! oh, yes, *all the lodgings were full,* packed! and it was so convenient to take in a visitor a—*friend.* Hunt the baker has been speaking about it. I didn't listen—I make it a point *never* to listen to gossip—but Maria—Maria, you can come here now. Have the goodness, Maria, to tell Mrs. Bell exactly what Hunt said, when you went in to buy the brown loaf for me last Friday. "

"Oh, sister—I—I really don't remember. "

"Don't remember! Piddle dumpling! You remembered well enough when you came back all agog with the news. I reproved you for listening to idle gossip, and you read a sermon of Blair's on evil speaking aloud to me that night. You shall read sermon ten to-night. It's on lying. Well, Mrs. Bell, *I* can repeat what my poor sister has forgotten. It was only to the effect that you and Bell must have had a windfall left you, and *he* never knew a visitor treated so well as you treated yours. The dainty cakes you had to get her, and the fuss over her, and every blessed thing paid down for with silver of the realm. Well, well, sometimes it is *convenient* to have a visitor. But now I must leave. Maria, we'll be going. You have got to get to your sermon on lying as soon as possible. Good-bye, Mrs. Bell. Perhaps you'll be able to tell some one else why the whole town is talking about Miss Hart—whoever Miss Hart is—and about Beatrice, and the wedding being put off—and Captain Bertram going off into high hysterics in—(Maria, you can go back to the window)—in a certain young lady's private room. Now I'm off. Come, Maria. "

CHAPTER XXX.

GUARDIANS ARE NOT ALWAYS TO BE ENVIED.

It would have been difficult to find a more easy-going, kind, happy-tempered man than Mr. Ingram. He had never married—this was not because he had not loved. Stories were whispered about him, and these stories had truth for their foundation—that when he was young he had been engaged to a girl of high birth, great beauty of person, and rare nobility of mind. Evelyn St. Just had died in her youth, and Mr. Ingram for her sake had never brought a wife home to the pleasant old Rectory. His sorrow had softened, but in no degree soured the good man. There had been nothing in it to sour any one—no shade of bitterness, no thread of unfaithfulness. The Rector firmly believed in a future state of bliss and reunion, and he regarded his happiness as only deferred. As far as his flock knew, the sorrow which had come to him in his youth only gave him a peculiar sympathy for peculiar troubles. To all in sorrow the Rector was the best of friends, but if the case was one where hearts were touched, if that love which binds a man to a woman was in any way the cause of the distress, then the Rector was indeed aroused to give of his best to comfort and assist.

On the evening after her strange interview with Josephine Hart, Beatrice put on her hat, and coming down to her mother where she sat as usual in the pleasant drawing-room, told her that she was going to see Mr. Ingram.

"It is rather late to-night, surely, child? "

"No, mother, it is not too late. I want particularly to see Mr. Ingram to-night. "

"Are you well, Bee? Your voice sounds tired. "

"I am quite well, dear mother. Kiss me. I won't stay longer away than I can help. "

She left the house. It was getting dusk now, and the distance between the Gray House and the Rectory was not small. But no Northbury girl feared to be out alone, and Beatrice walked quickly, and before long reached her destination.

The Rector was in—Beatrice would find him in his study. The old housekeeper did not dream of conducting Miss Meadowsweet to this apartment. She smiled at her affectionately, told her she knew the way herself, and left her.

When Beatrice entered the study the Rector got up and took his favorite by both her hands.

"I am glad to see you, my child, " he said. "I was just feeling the slightest *soupçon* of loneliness, so you have come in opportunely. Sit down, Bee. I suppose Bertram will call for you presently. "

Beatrice did not make any response to this remark, but she drew a little cane chair forward and sat down.

"Except your mother, no one will miss you more than I shall when you leave us, Beatrice, " said the Rector. "You are quite right to go, my dear. Quite right. I see a useful and honorable career before you. But I may be allowed just once to say that I shall be lonely without my favorite. "

"Dear Rector, " said Beatrice. She came a little nearer, and almost timidly laid her hand on his knee. Then she looked in his face. "I am not going to leave you, " she said.

"God bless my soul! What do you mean, child? Is anything wrong? You don't look quite yourself. Has that young scoundrel—if I thought—" the Rector got up. His face was red, he clenched his hand in no clerical style.

Beatrice also rose to her feet.

"He is not a scoundrel, " she said. "Although if our engagement had gone on, and I had been married to Captain Bertram, he would have been one. "

"Then you are not engaged? You have broken it off. "

"I am not engaged. I have released Captain Bertram from his engagement to me. "

"Beatrice! I did not expect this from you. His mother is attached to you—so are his sisters, while he himself, poor lad —! Bee, it was better you should find out your heart in time, but I am surprised — I am grieved. You should have known it before — before things went as far as this, my dear girl. "

"Please, Mr. Ingram, listen to me. Sit down again, for I have a long story to tell. I have not changed my mind, nor am I guilty of any special fickleness. But circumstances have arisen which make it impossible for me to keep my engagement. Captain Bertram sees this as plainly as I do. He is very thankful to be released. "

"Then he is a scoundrel, I thought as much. "

"No, he isn't that. But he has been weak, poor fellow, and harassed, and tempted. And his mother has used all her influence. I know now what she wanted me for. Just for my money. But I've been saved in time. "

"God bless me, this is very strange and dreadful. You puzzle me awfully. "

"I will tell you the story, Rector, then you won't be puzzled. Do you remember once speaking to me about a girl you saw at the Manor lodge. She was living there for a little. Her name was Hart. "

"Yes, yes, a very handsome, queer girl. I spoke to Mrs. Bertram about her. She seemed to me to have taken an unjust prejudice against the poor lonely child. "

"Mr. Ingram, Miss Hart is engaged to Loftus Bertram, and he will marry her next Tuesday. "

"Beatrice, have you gone quite mad?

"No, I am as sane as any other girl who has got a shock, but who is resolved to do right. Captain Bertram shall marry Nina, because in heart they are married already, because they love each other, as I never could love him, nor he me, because they were betrothed to each other before he and I ever met, because Nina was dying for love of him, and only marrying him can save her. Oh, it was pitiable to see Nina, Mr. Ingram, and I am thankful — I shall be thankful to my dying day — that I saw her in time to save her. "

"Beatrice, this is very strange and inexplicable. Where did you see Miss Hart? I thought she had left Northbury. "

"She came back, because she could not stay away. She is at the Bells'. I saw her there to day, and I brought Loftus to her, and—Rector, they love each other. Oh, yes, yes—when I see how much they love each other. I am thankful I am not to be married with only the shadow of such a reality. "

"Then you never gave your heart to this young man? "

"Never! I thought I could help him. But my heart has not even stirred. "

"You did not seem unhappy. "

"I was not unhappy. It always gives me pleasure to help people. And Catherine seemed so bright, and Mrs. Bertram so delighted, and Loftus himself—there was much to win my regard in Loftus. I did not know it was only my money they wanted. "

"Poor child! And yet you are wrong. No one who looks at you, Beatrice, can only want you for your money. "

"Dear Rector, in this case my money was the charm. Well, my money shall still have power. You are my guardian as well as my trustee. I want you to help me. You can, you must. I will take no denial. Loftus and I have had a long, long talk this afternoon. I have found at last the very bottom of Bertram's heart. He came to me to save him, and I am determined to be his deliverer. One quarter of my fortune I give to Loftus Bertram, and he shall marry Nina, and his debts shall be paid, and his mother relieved from the dreadful strain of anxiety she is now undergoing, and Loftus and Nina shall be happy and good. Oh, yes, I know they will be good as well as happy. You will help me, Rector, you will, you must. "

"Beatrice, you are the most quixotic, extraordinary, unworldly, unpractical creature that ever breathed. What sort of guardian should I be if I listened to so mad a scheme? What right has Loftus Bertram to one farthing of your money, without you? "

"He can't have it with me, Rector. I would not marry him now at any price. "

"Then he must do without the money. "

"No, he must have the money. Steps must be taken to secure it to him at once, and he must keep his wedding-day with Nina instead of me. Nina shall have my trousseau; we are exactly of one height — You have got to change the name in the marriage license. If that is impossible there shall be a special license. I am rich, I can pay for it. Oh, the joy that sometimes money brings! "

"My dear ward, you are a little off your head to-night. How could you possibly expect your guardian to be such a faithless old man. "

"Faithless? Mr. Ingram, have you quite forgotten my father? "

"No, Beatrice, I remember him to-night. "

"Let his face rise before you. Picture his face — his unworldly face. "

"I see it, Beatrice. Yes, Meadowsweet was not cankered by the sordid cares of life. "

"Truly he was not? Go on thinking about him. He made money. How did he spend it? "

"My dear child, your father was a very good man. His charities were extraordinary and extensive. He gave away, hoping for nothing in return; he was too liberal, I often told him so. "

"You were his clergyman and you told him so. "

A flash of indignation came out of Beatrice Meadowsweet's eyes.

"I don't think, Mr. Ingram, that a Greater than you has ever said that to my father. "

"Well, child, perhaps not. You reprove me, perhaps justly. Few of us have your father's unworldly spirit. "

"Don't you think his only daughter may inherit a little of it? Mr. Ingram, what is money for? "

"Beatrice, you could argue any one into thinking with you. But I must exercise my own common-sense. "

"No, you must not. You must exercise your unworldly sense, and help me in this matter. "

"What! And help you to throw away a quarter of your fortune? "

"I shall have fifteen thousand pounds left, more than enough for the requirements of any girl. "

"I doubt if the wording of your father's will could give me the power for a moment. "

"I am sure it could. I am confident that in drawing his will he trusted you absolutely and me absolutely. He often spoke to me about money, and told me what a solemn trust riches were. He charged me like the man in the parable not to bury my talent in a napkin, but to put it out to usury. He said that he made you my guardian, because you were the most unworldly-minded man he knew, and he told me many times that although he could not give me absolute control of my money before I was twenty-one, yet that no reasonable wish of mine would be refused by you. "

"And you call this a reasonable wish? "

"I do. And so would my father if he were alive. Bring his face once again before you, Rector, and you will agree with me. "

The Rector sat down in his arm-chair, and shaded his eyes with one of his long white hands. He sat for a long time motionless, and without speaking. Beatrice stood by the mantelpiece; there was a small fire in the grate; now and then a flame leaped up, and cast its reflection on her face.

Suddenly the Rector started upright.

"What day is this? " he asked.

"Thursday—Thursday night. "

"And you are to be married on Tuesday? "

"No, I may never marry. Nina Hart and Loftus Bertram are to be married on Tuesday. "

"God bless me! Beatrice, you have put me into a nice fix. Guardians are not always to be envied. What's the hour, child? "

Beatrice glanced at the clock.

"It is half-past nine, " she said.

"You say that this—this Miss Hart is staying at the Bells'? "

"Yes. "

"I must go to her. I must see her to-night. "

"Remember she is weak and ill. You will be gentle with her. "

"Beatrice, am I as a rule rough with people? Come, I will see you home, and then call on Miss Hart. "

CHAPTER XXXI.

CIVIL WAR AT NORTHBURY.

It is often very difficult to trace Rumor to his foundation. His beginning is sometimes as small as a particle of sand; the first dawning of his existence as impalpable as the air.

From these small beginnings, however, rumor arises, strong as a giant, cruel as death. Perhaps no foe has more injured mankind than idle rumor.

He was abroad now in the little town of Northbury, and no one quite knew the exact place of his birth. A good many people traced his existence to Hunt, the baker, who sold many loaves of bread, and many sweet and tasty cakes by reason of his love of gossip—some people laid it to Miss Peters' door, some to Mrs. Gorman Stanley's, some again to Mrs. Morris's; but soon, in the excitement which the Giant Rumor caused, people had no time to talk of the place of his birth—he was there, he was among them, and he was the only subject now discussed.

A great many afternoon teas, and small social gatherings were given during the next few days in his honor. As to the Bells' house it became quite notorious. People paused as they passed the windows, and even the paving stones round the time-worn steps were fraught with interest.

At the club the men talked of nothing but the story which was abroad. They took the opportunity to make bets and wagers. Their tongues were not so cruel as those of the women, but still their tongues did wag, and there was more than one wife in the town who felt the effect of Beatrice Meadowsweet's engagement for many a long day, because the father of the family had jeopardized a considerable sum in a wager on the probable issue of events.

When Rumor in his full magnitude gets abroad he never spares the young, the beautiful, the innocent. Beatrice was loved by every one at Northbury, but the inhabitants of this good, old-fashioned little town would have been immaculate had they not said evil things of her now.

Sides were taken on the occasion, and the people of the town divided themselves pretty equally, and in an incredibly short time started a fierce sort of civil war. The "Beatricites, " and the "Hartites, " they were called, and the war of tongues between them became so fierce that long before Saturday night one party would not speak to another.

Mrs. Bell was at the head of the Hartites, and Mrs. Butler was the general of the Beatrice army.

Mrs. Bell spoke in the following terms of the girl who had hitherto been everybody's favorite:

"Ah, she's a deep one, is Beatrice Meadowsweet. You never know what those quiet ones are till they are tried. I spoke to her, I warned her, but she wouldn't listen. 'Beatrice, ' I said, that young man cares no more for you than he does for the blackberries on the hedges. Beatrice, that young man's affections are given elsewhere. ' Heed me, would she? No, not she. But follow him she would, follow him from place to place, out on the water in her boat, and at the Hector's garden party until it was disgraceful to see. It's my firm belief she popped the question herself, and we all know what followed. Poor Captain Bertram gave in for a time, thinking of her fortune, which is none so great, if rumors are correct, but love her, no, not he. Why, over and over and over he has said as much to my child, Matty. Matty was stiff to him, I'll say that; he was an audacious flirt, and he tried hard to bring Matty into a scrape too, but would she encourage him? No, though she was persecuted by his attentions, and now what's the result? Matty is honorably engaged to a man who is a Bayard for knightliness, and that poor Beatrice is jilted. Was she in hysterics in my house? Well, it isn't for me to say. Did she go down on her knees to Captain Bertram, and wring his hand, and kiss it and beg of him not to forsake her, with the tears streaming like rain down her cheeks, and implore of him to give up his true love, who was in a dead faint before their two eyes, and to be true to her who had given her heart to him, neighbor, did these things happen in this very house? You ask me that question, neighbor, and I say, answer it I won't, for I'm a woman, and I have known that unfortunate, misguided girl and her poor mother for years. Yes, neighbor, I cast a veil over what I might say. "

This was the sort of gossip spread by Mrs. Bell, who further praised up Miss Hart, saying much about her beauty and her charms, and giving such a ravishing account of Bertram's love for her, and her adoration for him, that the neighbors who were on this side of the civil war crowned Josephine Hart as their chosen queen on the spot.

Mrs. Butler, who led the van of the "Beatricites, " was less voluble than Mrs. Bell, but her words were weighted with a very deadly shaft of poison. After Mrs. Butler had extolled Beatrice as a perfect model of all womanly graces and virtue, she proceeded, with keen relish, to take Josephine Hart to pieces. When she began to dissect Miss Hart she invariably sent her innocent sister, Maria, out of the room. It is unnecessary to repeat what passed behind the doors which were so cruelly closed on eager and curious Miss Peters, but it is not too much to say that poor Josephine had not a rag of character left to her when the good woman's tongue ceased to wag.

Thus the town of Northbury was in a distressing state of uproar during the three or four days which preceded Captain Bertram's wedding. And perhaps the cruellest thing about this fierce civil war was that none of the combatants, not even the leaders, knew what was really about to take place, nor who was to be married to whom on Tuesday, nor whether there was to be any wedding at all. The bridal dresses came home, and some of the ladies wept when they looked at them. Beatrice still received wedding presents, and the bridal robe of ivory-white silk trimmed with quantities of Honiton lace was absolutely sent down from London, all complete and ready for Beatrice to wear. Half the ladies in Northbury rushed up to the station when the news was brought to them that the box had arrived, and the porter, Payne by name, who carried the box to Mrs. Meadowsweet's, was followed by quite a little mob.

Thus time went on apace, and Rumor did his work, each lady saying when she met another:

"Well, what's the news? What's the latest? What did you hear last? "

Each Hartite bowed coldly to each Beatricite, or else cut each other dead, and, in short, the usual symptoms which accompany civil war made themselves felt.

It is a fact frequently noted that when Rumor, with his double-edged tongue is abroad, the persons most concerned often know nothing of the storm which is raging around them. In the present instance, two people who were keenly interested in coming events were in this position. One of them was Mrs. Meadowsweet, the other, Mrs. Bertram. The time would come when Beatrice would confide in her mother, but that moment had not yet arrived. The old lady wondered why she had so many visitors, and why people looked at her in a curious, pitying sort of fashion. Why also they invariably spoke of Beatrice as "poor dear, " and inquired with tender solicitude for her health.

"Brides usedn't to be 'poor deared' in my day, " the old lady remarked rather testily to her handmaiden, Jane. "Any one would suppose Beatrice was going to have an illness instead of a wedding from the way folks talk of her. "

"Eh, well, ma'am, " Jane replied.

Jane's "eh, well, ma'am" was as full of suppressed meaning as a balloon is full of air. She heaved a prodigious sigh as she spoke, for of course she had heard the gossip, and had indeed come to blows with a Hartite that very morning.

"Eh, dear! " said Jane. "Rumor's a queer thing. "

She did not vouchsafe any more, and Mrs. Meadowsweet was too innocent and indolent and comfortable in her mind to question her.

The other person who knew nothing was Mrs. Bertram. Of all the people in the world Mrs. Bertram was perhaps the most interested in that wedding which was to take place on Tuesday. The wedding could scarcely mean more to the bride and bridegroom than it did to her—yet no news of any *contretemps*, of any little hitch in the all-important proceedings, had reached her ears. For the last week she had taken steps to keep Catherine and Mabel apart from all Northbury gossip. The servants at the Manor who, of course knew everything did not dare to breathe a syllable of their conjectures. The bravest Hartite and Beatricite would not have dared to intrude their budgets of wild conjecture on Mrs. Bertram's ears. Consequently she lived through these exciting days in comparative calm. Soon the great tension would be over. Soon her gravest alarms would be lulled to rest, Now and then she wondered that Beatrice was not oftener at the Manor. Now and then she exclaimed with some vexation at Mr. Ingram's extraordinary absence from home at such a time.

The Rector had gone to London, and a stranger took his pulpit on that all-important Sunday before the wedding.

Mrs. Bertram wondered a little over these two points, but they did not greatly disturb her; —Loftus was at home and Loftus looked strangely, wildly happy.

Mrs. Bertram had been alarmed, and rendered vaguely uneasy by her son's gloom a few days ago, but there was no shadow resting on the young man's face now. He laughed, he talked, his eyes wore an exultant expression in their fire and daring. He caressed his sisters, he hung over his mother's chair, and kissed her.

"Ah, Loftie, " she said once, "you are really and honestly in love. I have had my doubts that you did not really appreciate our dear and noble Beatrice. But your manner the last few days, your spirits, my son, your all-evident happiness, have abundantly sent these doubts to rest. You are in love with your future wife, and no wonder! "

"No wonder, " echoed Loftus.

He had the grace to blush.

"Yes, I am in love, " he said. "No one was ever more madly in love than I am. " Then after a pause he added: "And I think Beatrice, without exception, the noblest and best woman on earth. "

"That is right, my boy. Ah, Loftus, I am glad I could do one thing for you. I have got you a wife whose price is above rubies. "

Bertram laughed.

"You have made a feeble joke, mother, " he said in some confusion. "I should like to know to which you allude—Bee's money or her personal charms. "

"Both—both—you naughty boy Beatrice is all that could be desired in herself, but in what position should you and I be in the future without her money? "

"That is true, " he said. And there was compunction in his voice.

On Monday morning two letters arrived at Northbury from the Rector. One was to his housekeeper, the other to Beatrice.

To his housekeeper, Mrs. Matthews, he said:

"Go on with all the wedding preparations, and expect me home this evening at six o'clock. "

His letter to Beatrice was much longer.

"The time to reproach you, my dear ward, is past, " began the Rector. "And you must promise never in the future to reproach me. You are an impulsive girl, and I may have done wrong to yield to your entreaties. Your father's face, has, however, over and over flashed before my mental vision, and the look in his eyes has comforted me. In one sense you are a fool, Beatrice; in another, you are thrice blessed. Forgive this little preamble. I have arranged matters as you wish. I shall be home this evening. Come to me in my study at nine o'clock to-night, my dear ward, and act in the meantime exactly as your true, brave heart suggests. "

Beatrice read this letter in her own room. She was quite mortal enough to shed some tears over it, but when she sat opposite to her mother at breakfast, her face was quite as jubilant as any young bride's might be, who was so soon to leave home.

Mrs. Meadowsweet looked at her girl with great pride.

"You feature your father wonderfully, Bee, " she said. "It isn't only the Grecian nose, and the well-cut lips, and the full, straight kind of glance in your eyes, but it's more. It's my belief that your soul features Meadowsweet; he was ever and always the best of men. Crotchety from uprightness he was, but upright was no word for him. "

"Well, mother, I should like to resemble my father in that particular. "

"Yes, my love, yes. Meadowsweet was always heights above me, and so are you also, for that matter. "

"That is not true, mother, you must not say it. It pains me. "

Beatrice looked distressed. She went over to her old parent and kissed her. Then she hastily left the room.

After breakfast Captain Bertram called at the Gray House.

He and Beatrice had a long interview, then she went to the Bells', and sat with Miss Hart for about half-an-hour.

After dinner that day Bertram spoke to his mother: "Beatrice wants to come up and see you. Can you receive her about six o'clock? "

"At any time, my dear son. But is she not dreadfully busy? Would it not convenience her more if I went to her, Loftie? "

"No, mother, she would prefer to come here. She has" —here his face turned pale—"she has a good deal to say to you—important things to speak about. " His voice trembled. "You will see her alone. You will not hurry her. Beatrice is the best—the best girl in the world."

Bertram looked very pale when he said this.

"How strange you look, Loftus! " said his mother. "And your words are very queer. Is anything the matter? Are you concealing any thing from me? "

"Beatrice will tell you, " he said. And he hurried out of the room.

A few minutes before six o'clock Beatrice arrived. Mrs. Bertram had given directions that she was to be sent at once to her private room. Clara had these instructions, and was about to carry them out literally when Catherine and Mabel ran into the hall.

They greeted Beatrice with raptures, and Mabel said in an eager voice:

"We have not yet seen you in your bridal dress, Bee. You know it was an old promise that we should see you in it the day before the wedding. Don't stay long with mother, Bee. Catherine and I can walk back with you, and you can try on your dress while we are by. "

"My dress is all right, " said Beatrice. "I have tried it; it fits. I don't want to put it on to-night. I am tired. "

Her face was pale, her expression anxious.

Mabel hung back and looked disappointed.

"But you promised, " she began.

"Hush, Mabel, " said Catherine. She hid quick intuitions, and she saw at a glance that something was the matter.

"Bee would not break her promise if she could help it, " she said to her sister. "Don't you see that she looks very tired. Bee, shall I take you to mother? "

"Yes, Catherine, " replied Beatrice.

The two girls walked away together. As they mounted the stairs, Catherine stole another glance at her friend. Then almost timidly she put her hand through Beatrice's arm.

"To-morrow, Bee, " she said, with a loving hug, "you will be *my* real, real sister. "

Beatrice stopped, turned round, and looked at Catherine.

"Kitty, I can't deceive you. I—love you, but I am not going to be what—what you suppose. "

"Then there is something wrong! " exclaimed Catherine. "I feared it from my mother's face when I saw her an hour ago. Now I am sure. Bee, are you going to fail us at the last moment? Oh, Beatrice, you have made him so nice, and we have all been so happy, and mother has said more than once to me, 'Beatrice Meadowsweet has saved us, ' and now, just at the very last, just at the very end, are you going to be a coward—a deserter? "

"No, " said Beatrice. "I won't desert you. I won't fail you. It is given to me to save your brother Loftus, to really save him. Don't be frightened, Kitty. I have a hard task to go through. I have to say some things to your mother which will try her. Yes, I know they will try her much, but I am doing right, and you must help me, and be brave. Yes, you must be brave because you know I am doing right. "

"I will trust you, Beatrice, " said Catherine. Her dark eyes shone, over the pallor of her face there came a glow. She opened the door of her mother's room.

"Here is Beatrice, mother. And may I—may I—stay too? "

"No, Kate, you are unreasonable. What a long time you have kept Beatrice. She has been in the house for ten minutes. I heard you two gossiping in the corridor. Girls are unreasonable, and they don't understand that the impatience of the old is the worst impatience of all. Go, Kate. "

Catherine's eyes sought her friend's. They seemed to say mutely:

"Be good to her, Beatrice, she is my mother. "

Then she closed the door behind the two.

People who have secrets, who find themselves hemmed into corners, who live perpetually over graves of the dead past, are seldom quite free from fear. Mrs. Bertram had gone through tortures during the last couple of hours. When she was alone with Beatrice she seized her hands, and drew her down to sit on the sofa by her side. Her eyes asked a thousand questions, while her lips made use of some conventional commonplace.

Beatrice was after all an unsophisticated country girl. She had never been trained in *finesse*; painful things had not come to her in the past of her life, either to conceal or avoid. Now a terrible task was laid upon her, and she went straight to the point.

Mrs. Bertram said: "You look tired, my dear future daughter. "

Beatrice made no reply to this. She did not answer Mrs. Bertram's lips, but responding to the hunger in her eyes, said:

"I have got something to tell you. "

Then Mrs. Bertram dropped her mask.

"I feared something was wrong. I guessed it from Loftie's manner. Go on, speak. Tell me the worst. "

"I'm afraid I must give you pain. "

"What does a chit like you know of pain? Go on, break your evil tidings. Nay, I will break them for you. There is to be no wedding tomorrow. "

"You are wrong. There is. "

"Thank God. Then I don't care for anything else. You are a true girl, Beatrice, you have truth in your eyes. Thank God, you are faithful. My son will have won a faithful wife. "

"I trust he will—I think he will. But—"

"You need not be over modest, child. I know you. I see into your soul. We women of the world, we deep schemers, we who have dallied with the blackness of lies, can see farther than another into the deep, pure well of truth. I don't flatter you, Beatrice, but I know you are true. "

"I am true, true to your son, and to you. But Mrs. Bertram, don't interrupt me. In being true, I must give you pain. "

Again Mrs. Bertram's dark brows drew together until they almost met. Her heart beat fast.

"I am not very strong, " she said, in a sort of suffocating voice. "You are concealing something; tell it to me at once. "

"I will. Can you manage not to speak for a moment or two? "

"Go on, child. Can I manage? What have I not managed in the course of my dark life? Go on. Whatever you tell me will be a pin-prick, and I have had swords in my heart. "

"I am sorry, " began Beatrice.

"Don't—do you suppose I care for a girl's sorrow! The sorrow of an uncomprehending child? Speak. "

"I have found out, " said Beatrice, in a slow voice, "just through an accident, although I believe God was at the bottom of it, something which has saved me from committing a great wrong, which has saved your son from becoming an absolute scoundrel, which has saved us both from a life of misery. "

"What have you found out, Beatrice? "

Mrs. Bertram's face was perfectly white; her words came out in a low whisper.

"Beatrice, what have you discovered? "

"That Captain Bertram loves another, that another girl loves him, has almost been brought to death's door because she loves him so well. "

"Pooh, child, is that all? How you frightened me. "

"Why do you speak in that contemptuous tone. The 'all' means a great deal to Captain Bertram, and to me, and to the other girl. "

"Beatrice, you are a baby. What young man of my son's age has not had his likings, his flirtations, his heart affairs? If that is all —"

"It is all, it is enough. Your son has not got over his heart affair. "

"Has he not? I'll speak to him. I'll soon settle that"

"Nor have I got over it. "

"Beatrice, my dear girl, you really are something of a little goose. Jealous, are you? Beatrice, you ask an impossibility when you expect a young man never to have looked with eyes of affection on any one but yourself. "

"I will not marry the man who looks with eyes of affection at another. "

"How you bewilder me, and yet, how childish you are. Must I argue this question with you? Must I show you from my own larger experience how attached Loftus is to you? Dear fellow, his very face shows it. "

"I don't want you to teach me anything from your experience, Mrs. Bertram. Captain Bertram does not love me. I do not love him; he loves another. She has given him all her heart, all that she can give.

237

He shall marry her; —he shall marry her to-morrow. "

Mrs. Bertram rose very slowly.

"Beatrice, " she said. "Your meaning is at last plain to me. *Noblesse oblige*. Ah, yes, that old saying comes true all the world over. You have not the advantage of good birth. I thought—for a long time I thought that you were the exception that proved the rule. You were the lady made by nature's own hand. Your father could be a tradesman—a *draper*—and yet have a lady for his daughter. I thought this, Beatrice; I was deceived. There are no exceptions to that nobility which only birth can bestow. You belong to the common herd, the *canaille*. You cannot help yourself. A promise to one like you is nothing. You are tired of Loftus. This is an excuse to get out of a bargain of which you have repented. "

"It is not. "

Beatrice looked at Mrs. Bertram with eyes that blazed with anger. She walked across the room, and rang the bell. Her ring was imperious. She stood near the bell-pull until Clara, in some trepidation, obeyed the summons.

"Is Captain Bertram downstairs? " asked Beatrice.

"I'll inquire, Miss Meadowsweet. "

"I think he is. I think you'll find him in the study. Ask him to have the goodness to come to Mrs. Bertram's room. "

Clara withdrew. Beatrice began slowly to pace up and down the floor.

"I belong to the *canaille*, " she murmured. "And my father—*my* father is taunted because he earned his bread in trade. Mrs. Bertram, I am glad I don't belong to your set. "

Beatrice had never been so angry in all her life before. The anger of those who scarcely ever give way to the emotion has something almost fearful about it. Mrs. Bertram was a passionate woman, but she cowered before the words and manner of this young girl. She had taunted Beatrice. The country girl now was taunting her, and she shrank away in terror.

The door was opened, and Loftus Bertram came in. Beatrice went up to him at once.

"I have prepared the way for you, Loftus, " she said. "It is your turn now to speak. Tell your mother the truth. "

"Yes, my son. "

Mrs. Bertram looked up in his face. Her look was piteous; it disarmed Beatrice; her great anger fled. She went up to the poor woman, and stood close to her.

"Speak, Loftus, " she said. "Be quick, be brave, be true. Your mother cannot bear much. Don't keep her in suspense. "

"Go out of the room, Beatrice, " said Loftus. "I can tell her best alone. "

"No, I shall stay. It is right for me to stay. Now speak. Tell your mother who you really love. "

"Go on, Loftus, " said Mrs. Bertram, suddenly. "You love Beatrice Meadowsweet. She angered me, but she is a true and good girl at heart. You love her; she is almost your bride—say that you love her. "

"She is the best girl I ever met, mother. "

"There, Beatrice, does not that content you? " said Mrs. Bertram.

"Hush, " said Beatrice. "Listen. He has more to say. Go on, Loftus—speak, Captain Bertram. Is Josephine not worth any effort of courage? "

"Josephine! " Mrs. Bertram clasped her hands.

Bertram stepped forward.

"Mother, I don't love Beatrice as I ought to love my wife. I do love Josephine Hart, and she is to be my wife to-morrow morning. "

"Josephine Hart! " repeated Mrs. Bertram. She looked round at Beatrice, and a smile played all over her face—a fearful smile.

"My son says he loves Josephine Hart—Josephine—*and he will marry her!* "

She gave a laugh, which was worse than any cry, and fell insensible on the floor.

CHAPTER XXXII.

THE NIGHT BEFORE THE WEDDING.

Mrs. Meadowsweet wondered why Beatrice did not come home. It was the night before the wedding. Surely on that night the bride ought to come early to sleep under her mother's roof.

Mrs. Meadowsweet had a good deal to say to her girl. She had made up her mind to give her a nice little domestic lecture. She thought it her duty to reveal to her innocent Beatrice some of the pitfalls into which young married girls are so apt to fall.

"Jane, " she said to her handmaid, "Miss Beatrice is late. "

"Eh, so she is, " responded Jane. Jane was a woman of very few words. Her remarks generally took the form of an echo. Mrs. Meadowsweet thought her a very comfortable kind of body to confide in. Jane was taking away the supper things.

"We were married ourselves, Jane, and we know what it means, " continued Mrs. Meadowsweet.

Jane was a widow—her husband had been a drunkard, and she had gone through a terrible time with him.

She shook her head now with awful solemnity.

"We do that, " she said. "It's an awful responsibility, is marriage— it's not meant for the young. "

"I don't agree with you there, Jane. How could elderly people bring up their families? "

"It's not meant for the young, " repeated Jane. "It's a careful thing, and a troubling thing and a worreting thing is marriage, and it's not meant for the young. Shall I leave the peaches on the table, ma'am, and shall I make fresh cocoa for Miss Beatrice when she comes in? "

"Make the cocoa with all milk, Jane, it's more supporting. I always made it a rule to sustain Beatrice a good deal. She wears herself out—she's a great girl for wearing herself out, and it's my duty in life to repair her. I used to repair her poor father, and now I repair her. It seems to me that a woman's province in life is to repair—first the husband, and then the children. Jane, I was thinking of giving Beatrice a little lecture to-night on the duties that lie before her. "

"Good sakes, ma'am, I'd leave her alone. She'll find out her worrits fast enough. "

"I don't agree with you, Jane. It seems to me as if the whole of a married woman's bliss consists in this—be tidy in your dress, don't answer back, and give your husband a good dinner. That's what I did—I repaired Meadowsweet, and I never riled him, and we hadn't a word, no, not a word. "

"All aren't like your blessed husband, Mrs Meadowsweet. Well, ma'am, I'll go now and get the milk on for the cocoa. "

She left the room, and Mrs. Meadowsweet sat on by the fire.

Presently there came a ring to the front door bell. Mrs. Meadowsweet started up. Bee had some—no, it wasn't Bee—it was Mrs. Morris.

Her bronchitis was almost gone to-night; her voice was high, sharp and quick.

"Well, my poor friend, and how are you? " she said.

"I wish you wouldn't call me your poor friend, Jessie, " answered Mrs. Meadowsweet, with almost irritation. "I don't know what has come to the good folks here of late—'Poor dearing, ' and 'poor friending' till I'm sick of the sound of it. When I was married, people didn't look like boiled vinegar over it; neighbors were chirpy and cheery about a wedding in those days. "

Mrs. Morris made no reply at all to this tirade. She sat down solemnly, and looked around her.

"Is Beatrice in? " she asked.

"No, she's not; she went to the Manor some hours ago—I'm expecting my girl back every minute. I've several things to say to her when she does come in, so you won't take it amiss, Jessie, if I ask you not to stay. "

"No, my dear neighbor, I won't take anything amiss, from you at present, only, if I were you, I wouldn't worry Beatrice with advice to-night. Yon have time enough for that. Time and to spare for that, poor dear. "

"There you are with your 'poor dear, ' again, Jessie. Now whose ring is that at the bell? Oh, it's Bee, of course; come back at last, my girl has. Well, Jessie Morris, I wish you good-night. "

"Stay a minute, neighbor—that isn't Bee's voice. " The door was opened, and Miss Peters came in.

"How are you, Mrs. Meadowsweet, " she said, running up to the good lady and giving her a kiss, which resembled the peck of an eager bird, on her cheek. "I ran on first, and Martha is following. I came to know how you are, and how you're bearing up—and is Beatrice in? "

"I do declare, " said Mrs. Meadowsweet. She rose from her easy-chair. "You mean to be good-natured, neighbors, but really you're enough to deave one. How am I bearing up? Am I the woman to bring ill-luck to my child by crying at her wedding? No, she's not in—she's at the Bertrams. But there's her ring now at the hall-door. Good-night, neighbors both. You mean it kindly, but don't stay just now. I have a word or two to say to the girl in private to-night. "

"I think that's Martha's voice, " said Miss Peters. "Don't say that I told you anything, Mrs. Meadowsweet. "

The door was opened, and Mrs. Butler came in.

This good woman, who led the army of the Beatricites, had now attained to all the airs of a victorious general. Her bonnet-strings were thrown back, her face was flushed, and her throat, conspicuous by the absence of her large white brooch, was bared to view.

"Well, my friend, " she said. "Well, the time is near. "

She took Mrs. Meadowsweet's fat hand, squeezed it hard, and looked with awful solemnity into her eyes.

"Good gracious, " said the poor woman. "I never felt more exasperated in all my life. Any one would suppose that my girl was drowned in the harbor from the faces you one and all bring me. "

"Mrs. Meadowsweet, " said Mrs. Butler, "there is such a thing as having the body safe and well, and the character drowned. "

Mrs. Meadowsweet's cheeks flushed deeply.

"I'll thank you to explain yourself, Martha Butler, " she said. "Whose character is drowned? "

"No one's, " said Mrs. Butler. "Or at least, no one who belongs to us. "

Here she waved one of her arms in theatrical style.

"I have fought for that girl, " she said, "as my sister Maria can bear testimony, and my friend Mrs. Morris can vouch—-I have fought for her, and I may truly say I have brought her through a sea of slander—yes, through a sea of slander—victorious. Now, who's that? Who's coming to interrupt us? "

"It's only me, Mrs. Butler, " said Beatrice. She came quietly into the room. Her face was white, but its expression was serene, and almost happy.

"It's you, Bee, at last, " said her mother.

She went straight up to the girl, and taking one of her hands raised it to her lips.

"You have come, Bee, " she said in a purring cone of delight and content. "My girl has come at last, neighbors, and now I'll wish you, every one, a very good-night. I'm obliged for all sympathy, and if I don't understand these new-fashioned ways about weddings with their poor dears, and their poor friends, and drowning of somebody's character, and saving of somebody else's character, it's because I'm old-fashioned, and belong to an ancient school. Good-night, friends. Is that you, Jane? "

Jane appeared, bearing in a cup of cocoa for Beatrice.

"Jane, show these ladies out. "

They all went. They hated to go, but they went, for the mantle of innocence and ignorance in which Mrs. Meadowsweet was so securely wrapped gave her a certain dignity which they could not resist. Jane shut the door on them, and they stood still outside the house, and wrangled, and talked, and worked themselves into a perfect rage of excitement and curiosity and longing. "Well, well, all surmises would soon be at rest. Who would win, Beatrice or Josephine? Who would be to-morrow's bride. "

"Mother, " said Beatrice, when the ladies had left—she looked into her old mother's face. There was an expression in her eyes which made Mrs. Meadowsweet cry out:

"Bee, you have got a hunger at your heart. Oh, child, you want your mammy—I never saw that look in your eyes since long, long ago, when you were a little tot, and wanted your mammy more than anything else in all the wide world. "

"I want her now, " said Beatrice.

She put her arms about her mother, and wept on her shoulder.

CHAPTER XXXIII.

THE MORNING OF THE WEDDING.

Beatrice had seen Mr. Ingram. She had gone to him, but not to stay.

"You must go to Mrs. Bertram's, " she said; "she has a trouble on her mind. Get her to tell it to you. She will be better afterwards. She fears much. I guess a little of what she fears. She does not know that by to-morrow night all her anxieties will be over. "

"And the wedding is really to take place in the morning, Beatrice? "

"Really and truly. I will be present as bride's-maid, not as bride. "

Beatrice went home, and Mr. Ingram hastened to the Manor.

There was much confusion there. Mrs. Bertram was very ill; she would not see her daughters, she would allow no doctor to be summoned. Mabel was crying in the drawing-room. Catherine was pacing up and down the corridor outside her mother's room.

The Rector came. Bertram saw him for a few moments alone; then he went into Mrs. Bertram's room. He stayed with her for some hours; it was long past midnight when he left her. Catherine and Mabel had gone to bed, but Bertram met the Rector outside his mother's door.

"Come home with me, " said Mr. Ingram; "I have a message to give you. I have something to say. "

"How is my mother, sir? "

"She is better, —better than she has been for years—she will sleep now—she has carried a heavy burden, but confession has relieved it. She has sent you a message; come to my house, and I will give it to you. "

The Rector and Bertram went quickly back to the cozy Rectory study. Mr. Ingram began his story at once.

"Have you any early recollections? " he asked. "Cast your memory back. What are the first things you can recall? "

Bertram raised his eyebrows in astonishment.

"I was born in India, " he said; "I was sent home when I was little more than a baby. "

"You don't remember your Indian life, nor your—your—father? "

"Of course I remember my father, sir. I was over twenty when he died. "

"Ah, yes, your reputed father. You cannot possibly recall, you have no shadowy remembrance of another who bore the name? "

"Good God, Mr. Ingram! what do you mean? "

"Have you any memory? Answer me. "

"No, sir, not the faintest. Is this a dream? "

"My poor lad, I don't wonder that you are staggered. Your mother could not bring herself to tell you. She has borne much for your sake, Bertram; you must be tender to her, gentle. She committed sin, she has gone through terrible hours for you. She was wrong, of course; but her motive—you must respect her motive, Loftus Bertram. "

"I am in a dream, " said Bertram. "General Bertram not my father! Whose son am I then? What is my name? Who am I? Good God, sir, speak! Get me out of this horrible nightmare. "

"Bertram, I have a good deal to tell you. You have a very strange story to hear. You must listen as quietly as you can. You must take in the facts as well as you can. The story concerns you deeply—you and another. "

"Do you mean my mother? "

"No, I mean Josephine Hart. "

"Josephine? This story concerns Josephine. Rector, my brain is whirling. "

"Sit down, keep still, listen. "

Bertram restrained his impatience with an effort. He sank into a chair; in a moment he rose to his feet.

"I can't keep still, " he said. "This story concerns Nina. Does my mother know Nina? "

"I will tell you the whole story, Bertram; I will tell it briefly, and you must listen with patience. You must remember, as you hear, that the woman who played this sorry part is your mother, that she did the wrong out of mistaken love for you, that she has suffered bitterly for her sin. "

"Go on, sir; I am listening. "

"Remember that the story is about your mother. "

"I don't forget. "

The Rector poured out a glass of water from a jug which stood on the table, drank it off, and began to speak.

"Your mother, Bertram, was twice married. Her first husband—my poor boy, I am sorry for you—was a scoundrel, a thief, a blackleg. He died in prison. You are his son. Your father died in a Bombay prison; you were in England at the time. "

"Stop, sir, " said Bertram. "What was my—my—what was the name of the man to whom I owe my being? "

"Your mother has not told me. She says she will never reveal his name. She says that your stepfather gave you legally the name of Bertram. That, at least, need never be disturbed. "

"Then Catherine and Mabel are not my sisters. "

"They are your half-sisters; that is a small matter. "

"True. Everything in the world is a small matter in comparison with the awful fact that I am the son of a felon. "

"I am deeply pained for you, Bertram. Your mother knew how this would strike home. Hence her sin. "

"I forgot. I have to hear of that. Go on, Mr. Ingram. "

"At the time of your father's death she was, she tells me, a very beautiful young woman. She was alone and peculiarly defenceless; Major Bertram, he was a Major at the time, made her acquaintance in Calcutta. You will be startled, Bertram, at the way in which these two made friends. She was asked to take care of Major Bertram's baby daughter. "

"Then he, too, was married before. "

"Yes, he had a young wife, who died when the baby was born. Little Nina was six months old when Major Bertram, who had to accompany his regiment up the country, asked your mother to look after her. "

"Nina, did you say Nina, Mr. Ingram? "

"Yes. I need not conceal from you who that Nina was. "

Bertram covered his face with his hands.

"I can't bear this, " he said. "This story unmans me. "

"You must listen. I am making the narrative as brief as possible. Your mother tells me that when the baby was given to her to care for she meant to be very good to it. She was miserable at the time, for her sorrows with and about your father had almost maddened her. She was good to the child, and very glad of the money which the Major paid her for giving the little creature a home. She kept the baby for some months, nearly a year; and whenever he could Major Bertram called to see her. Soon the meaning of his visits dawned upon her. He had fallen in love with her. He was, in all respects, a desirable husband; he was of good family; his antecedents were honorable, his own life stainless. She thought of you, she was always thinking about you, you were at a poor little school in England. She thought what your lot might be, if you were really the son of this honorable man. She tells me that at this time her love for you was like a terrible passion within her. Beyond all things in the world she dreaded your learning your father's history—she shuddered as she fancied your baby lips asking her artless questions which she could never answer. Your father's name was, alas, notorious. Bearing that name, you must one day learn the history of your father's ruin, disgrace, dishonor. "

"Mr. Ingram, " said Bertram, "you are crushing me. How much more must you say about my — my father? "

"Nothing more. I had to say this much to explain your mother's motive. One day Major Bertram called to see her. He was going away. Before he left he asked her to marry him. She refused. He persisted. She told him her history. He said he knew it already. Then she put off her decision. He might speak to her again on his return to Calcutta. It was during Major Bertram's absence that the temptation which led to your mother's sin came to her.

"Little Josephine was now between a year and two years old. On her mother's side she was of low birth. Major Bertram had married beneath him. He had fallen desperately in love with the beautiful daughter of a strolling minstrel. He had married her, found out his mistake when too late, but still, being a chivalrous and honorable man, had done his duty by his ignorant young wife; had never allowed her to guess at his feelings; and after her death had been filled with compunction for not loving her more, and had done everything he could to secure the welfare of their child.

"One person, however, he forbade the premises; with one individual he would have nothing to do. That person was his wife's father. From the moment he laid his young wife in her grave, he ignored the very existence of Hart. Your mother tells me, Bertram, that Hart was in all particuars a disreputable person. He was nothing but a needy adventurer, and he only approached Major Bertram to sponge on him.

"During the Major's absence your mother thought long and seriously of his proposals for her; the more she thought of them, the more desirable did they seem. She thought of herself in the sheltered position of a good man's wife. Above all, she thought of you. This marriage might save you. Suppose Major Bertram, for love of her, consented to adopt you as his son, to give you his name, and to present you to the world as his own lawful child. She thought this might be done; and the only difficulty in the way was the little bright-eyed, fair-haired Nina.

"Your mother did not wish to return to England calling Hart's granddaughter her child. She said she had an insuperable objection and repugnance to the idea, and an aversion for the poor little creature began to grow up in her mind. "

Bertram, who had sat during the greater part of this recital with his hand shading his eyes, now started up with an impatient and distressed exclamation. The Rector looked at him, sighed heavily, and said in a voice of sympathy:

"My poor boy, this is a very hard story for you to listen to. "

"Go on, Mr. Ingram, " said Bertram. "Get it over quickly; that is all I have to ask you. "

"While these thoughts were troubling your mother, " continued the Rector, "she was one day surprised by a visit from Hart. He said he had come to see his grandchild; and he took little Nina in his arms and kissed her. Your mother says she scarcely knows how it was, but she and Hart began to talk about the child, and both simultaneously revealed to the other his and her real feelings.

"Hart hated Major Bertram, and would like to do him an injury. Your mother had no love for Nina. I nead not lengthily describe this interview. Suffice it to say that they made a plot between them. It was a bad plot. I am sorry to have to use this word to a son about any act of his mother's, but the truth must be told at all hazards. The plot was bad, bad at the time, bad subsequently.

"Your mother arranged to give Nina to her grandfather. She would pay him for delivering her from the child. After receiving his bribe Hart was to leave that part of India at once, When the Major returned your mother would tell him that the child was lost. That she feared her grandfather Hart had stolen her. She would help Major Bertram to make inquiries. These inquiries, she would arrange beforehand, should turn out useless, for Hart was one of those clever individuals, who, when necessary, could hide all trace of his existence.

"Your mother sold some jewellery to raise the necessary money for Hart. He came the next day and carried off the child. Major Bertram returned. He believed your mother's story, he was wild with grief at the loss of his child, and did everything in his power to recover her. In vain. Your mother and Hart were too clever for him.

"After a time he renewed his proposals to your mother. She made her conditions. You were to be acknowledged as his son.

"Soon after their marriage they returned to England, and Major Bertram retired from foreign service. His friends received them. The old story was never raked up. No suspicion attached to your mother. All the world believed you to be Major Bertram's son. No plot could have turned out better, and your mother rejoiced in her success.

"Her daughters were born, and she began to consider herself the happiest of living beings. The serpent, however, which she fondly thought killed, was once more to awake and torment her. She got a letter from Hart, who was then in Egypt. Nina was not dead, she was alive, and strong, and handsome. He would bring her back to her father and all the past would be known, if Mrs. Bertram did not buy his silence at a price.

"For some years after this letter she had to keep the old man quiet with money. Then suddenly, with no apparent reason, he ceased to trouble her. She believed that his silence was caused by Nina's death. She assured herself that the child must be dead, and once more her outward prosperity brought her happiness.

"Your father died, and his will was read. There was a codicil to his will which only his wife and the solicitors knew about. It was briefly to the effect that if by any chance the child of his first marriage was recovered, and her identity proved, she was to inherit one-half of his personal estate. He left her this large share of his property as compensation for the unavoidable neglect he had shown her all her life, and also in sorrow for having ever confided her to the care of another.

"That codicil tortured your mother's proud spirit. She felt that her husband had never really forgiven her for allowing his child to be stolen while under her care. Still she believed that the child now was dead.

"Her hour of terrible awakening came. Hart had returned to England. A couple of months ago he wrote to her here. Knowing that Nina's father was dead he had gone to Somerset House, paid a shilling and read a copy of the will. From that moment your mother knew no peace. Hart had all the necessary letters to prove Nina's identity. He had a copy of her baptismal certificate, and of the registration of her birth. Mrs. Bertram had now to bribe the old man heavily. She did so. She gave him and Nina a third of her income. Wretched, miserable, defiant, she yet hoped against hope. To-night, for the first time, she tasted despair. "

The Rector ceased to speak. Bertram began to pace the floor.

"I can't forgive my mother, " he said, at last. "I shall marry Josephine to-morrow morning and take her away, but I never want to see my mother again. "

"Then she will die. She is weak now, weak and crushed. If you refuse your forgiveness you will have her death to answer for. I don't exonerate your mother's sin, but I do plead for your mercy. She sinned to shield and save you. You must not turn from her. Are you immaculate yourself? "

"I am not, Mr. Ingram. I am in no sense of the word good. I have been extravagant, reckless, I have been untruthful. I have caused my mother many a pang, and she has invariably been an angel of goodness and kindness to me. But her cruelty to Nina cuts me like a sword, and I cannot forgive her. "

The Rector went over to the window, drew up the blinds, and looked out.

"Come here, " he said to the young man. "Do you see that faint light in the east? "

"Yes, sir, the day is breaking. "

"The day of your wedding, and of your new life. To-day you realize what true love means. You take the hand of the girl who is all the world to you, and you promise to love and reverence and defend her. To-day you put away the past life. You rise out of the ashes of the past, and put on manliness, and honor, and those virtues which good men prize, like an armor, Beatrice tells me you have promised her all this. "

"Beatrice—God bless Beatrice: " Bertram's eyes were misty. "I will be a good husband, and a true man, " he said with fervor. "I have been a wretch in the past, and with God's help I'll show Nina, and Beatrice too, what stuff they have made of me. I'll be a true man for their sakes. But my mother—Mr. Ingram, you have given me a cruel shock on my wedding morning. "

"Bertram, all that you have said to me now will end in failure, will wither up like the early dew if you cherish hard feelings towards your mother. Did she ever cherish them to you? What about that bill she had to meet? That bill would have ruined her. "

"Beatrice met the bill. "

"Had there been no Beatrice? "

Bertram turned his head away.

"I have been a scoundrel, " he said at last.

The Rector laid his hand on his arm.

"You have been something uncommonly like it, my dear fellow. And the spirit of revenge does not sit well on you. Come, your mother is waiting. Change her despair to peace. Say some of the good things you have said to me to her, and the blessing of God will descend on you, Bertram, and on the young girl whom you will call your wife to-day. Give me your hand. Come. "

Bertram went.

CHAPTER XXXIV.

THE BRIDE!

Miss Peters was lying in sound slumber, and Mrs. Butler, with a wet sponge in her hand, was standing over the little spinster's bed.

"Maria, " she said, in her sharp voice. And at the same moment the sponge descended with unerring aim on the sleeper's upturned face.

"Good heavens—fire—water! What is it? —I'm drowning—" gasped Miss Peters.

She raised her eyes, choked, for her mouth had been open, and some of the contents of the sponge had got in, and then surveyed her sister in trepidation.

"Oh, Martha, it's you. How you frightened me! "

"I only applied the sponge, " replied Mrs. Butler. "It's an old-fashioned remedy for inordinate drowsiness, and effectual. "

"But surely, surely—I feel as if I had only just dropped to sleep. "

"Maria, it's five o'clock. "

"Five! What do you mean, Martha? Am I to be accused of inordinate sleepiness at five in the morning? "

"On this morning you are. This is the wedding morning—get up, dress yourself. Put on your bridal finery, and join me in the parlor. "

Mrs. Butler left the room. Miss Peters rubbed her sleepy eyes again.

"The wedding morning! and my bridal finery! " she murmured. "One would think poor Sam had never been drowned. I don't think Martha has any heart. She knows how I suffered about Sam. He certainly never proposed for me, but he was attentive—yes, he was attentive, and I—I suffered. It's thirty years now since he was drowned. Martha oughtn't to forget. People have no memories in these days. "

The little lady began to put on her garments.

"It does seem extraordinarily early to have to get up, even though Bee is to be married at eleven o'clock to-day, " she murmured. "Certainly, Martha is a most masterful person. Well, I don't mind so much, as it is for Bee's sake. "

Miss Peters proceeded with her toilet, took tenderly out of its folds of camphor and white linen, a little antiquated brown silk dress, put it on, crossed over her shoulders a neat fichu of white lace, mounted her bonnet, composed of a piece of silk, which she had artfully removed from the skirt of her dress. This bonnet was trimmed with three enormous lemon-colored chrysanthemums, and was further embellished with a pink ruching, which surrounded the good lady's face.

Miss Peters almost trembled as she placed this exquisite head-dress over her scanty locks. The moment the bonnet was on, she became conscious of an immense amount of moral support. In that bonnet she could even defy Mrs. Butler.

"Nothing gives a lady such a nice feeling as being properly dressed, " she murmured. "I am glad I went to the expense of a bit of pink silk to make this ruching. It is wonderfully soft, and becoming, too. I hope Martha won't object to the chrysanthemums. I chose the largest Perry had in his shop on purpose, in order not to be accused of aping youth. Now, my parasol, my gloves, my handkerchief. Oh, and my fan. I'm sure to flush a little when I see that dear child being given away. Now I'm quite ready. It certainly is an extraordinarily early hour to be dressed for a wedding, which is not to take place till eleven o'clock. "

"Maria! " screamed Mrs. Butler's voice. "If you're not quick, you'll not have time to swallow your coffee. "

"Dear, dear! " exclaimed Miss Peters, "is Martha's head going? I have not been half-an-hour dressing; can she have mistaken the hour? "

The little spinster ran downstairs.

"Here I am, Martha. Really I —"

"Not a word, Maria. Sit down at once, and drink off your coffee. You can munch a bit of bread in your hand as we go along. "

"But, Martha, it is not six o'clock yet. "

"What of that? We have not a moment to lose. There'll be crowds at the church. I am given to understand it will be packed, and as I intend to have a front seat, I'm going now. "

Miss Peters began to count on her fingers.

"But Martha, it surely is not necessary. "

"Now, Maria, that's enough. You'd argue any one black in the face. I don't often have my way, but I'll have it on this occasion. I am going to call for Mrs. Gorman Stanley; and Mrs. Morris asked me to knock her up, and we'll all of us just be at the church in good time. "

"In good time, " gasped Miss Maria. "But the doors won't be opened. "

"Oh, won't they! You just wait and see. I haven't fought that girl's battles for nothing. We'll be able to get into the church, Maria, don't you fear. I have made friends as well as foes of late, and there are these who can get me into the church, so that I may stand up for Beatrice to the last. Now, have you swallowed your coffee? "

"I have. It has scalded my throat frightfully. I hate drinking hot liquid in such a hurry. "

"Maria, you are dreadfully fractious this morning. And, good gracious me! What have you got in your bonnet! Here let me hold up the candle and look. "

"Don't—don't drop the grease on my brown silk, Martha. "

"Brown fiddlestick! Hold your head steady. Well—I never! The vanity of some folk! The apings of some people. Oh, I haven't a word to say if you like to make a show of yourself. I respect my years. I live up to them. Some people, I won't name who—don't. "

"Had I better take off the bonnet, Martha? I thought these very *large* chrysanthemums—I chose them on purpose—"

257

"Hideous—you're a perfect fright! Look at me. Is there anything to laugh at in my velvet bonnet? Does it poke itself on the back of my head? And does it deck itself in pink and yellow? "

"It looks funereal, Martha, it's all black. "

"Funereal! It looks suitable. Come on, or we'll be late. "

The two ladies left the house. They walked quickly in the early morning light. Presently, they were joined by Mrs. Gorman Stanley. She was completely clothed in bridal garments of yellow. Her robe was yellow satin, her bonnet was to match, with blue forget-me-nots cozily nestling in its folds. Mrs. Morris joined the group in terra-cotta cashmere, with a cream lace bonnet. Round her face and mouth she had enveloped a black woollen shawl, but this was to be discarded presently.

As the ladies walked to the church they were joined by several more Beatricites, and when at last they found themselves under the shadow of the old tower, and in the shelter of the ancient porch, they were quite a goodly company.

"We'll just fill the front seats comfortably, " said Mrs. Butler. "When Mrs. Bell and her Hartites arrive they'll have to go behind. "

"But how are we to get in? " again questioned Miss Maria.

"Oh, I'll manage that. I have it all arranged. I spoke to Hunt yesterday. "

Hunt was not only the baker, he was the church verger. He had quite sympathized with Mrs. Butler's wishes, while selling her a two-penny loaf yesterday. But why did he not put in an appearance now?

"Martha, " again whispered Miss Maria, "Who are those people creeping round there by the south wall? "

"No one, " snapped Mrs. Butler. "You're fanciful this morning, Maria. It's those horrid lemon-colored chrysanthemums; they have turned your head. "

"I don't know about that, " retorted Miss Peters. "I am sure I saw Mrs. Bell's snuff-colored bonnet. "

Mrs. Butler sniffed. She would not retort again; but she was conscious of a little sense of uneasiness. It was difficult, even for a person as blind as she considered her sister Maria, to mistake that snuff-colored, drawn silk bonnet, ornamented with a huge bow in front of pale blue ribbon. That bonnet was celebrated. It had been worn by Mrs. Bell in season and out of season for many long years; it had been altered in shape; it had been turned. Sometimes the bow which filled up the gap in front was yellow, sometimes red, sometimes mauve. But every one in the town knew that for the wedding the bow on Mrs. Bell's bonnet was to be a delicate and bridal blue. This was to be her sole wedding adornment. To the length of purchasing that bow she had gone, and no further. Therefore now Mrs. Butler felt uncomfortable. If the Hartites secured the front seats in church she would have to own to defeat and humiliation. Was Hunt—could Hunt be faithless? He was known to be something of a toady, something of a Sergeant Eitherside, a Vicar of Bray sort of individual. To all appearance Hunt was a sworn Beatricite, but if by any chance he had heard something in favor of the Hartites, he was just the man to go over to them.

"There are about ten or twenty people with Mrs. Bell, " said Miss Maria. "I'm sure that's Mrs. Bell. Yes, that *is* her bonnet. "

She raised herself on tip-toe, clutching hold of Mrs. Morris's arm as she did so.

"It's freezing cold standing by this door, " said Mrs. Morris, shivering. "I'll have an awful attack after this. Poor Beatrice, she'll cause my death. "

"Keep the shawl well over your mouth, " said Mrs. Gorman Stanley. "Really, Mrs. Butler, it is extraordinary that no one comes to open the door. "

"Hunt is faithless, " proclaimed Mrs. Butler. "Maria, listen to me. Never as long as I live will I buy bread from Hunt again. I'll eat Coffin's bread in future. "

"Oh, Maria, it's so musty. "

"Fiddle dumpling. Hunt is certainly faithless. Maria, do you think you could squeeze yourself through an open window? "

"I don't, Martha, " replied Miss Peters; "and, what's more, I won't. I have got my best brown silk on. Where am I to get another silk? Ah, " with a sigh of infinite relief, "here is Hunt. "

The baker, who was red in the face, and had a somewhat nervous manner, now appeared. He came by a sidewalk which led directly from the vestry.

"I beg your pardon, ladies, " he apologized; "I overslept myself, and that's a fact. Now the floors are open—find your places, ladies. "

Hunt vanished, and Mrs. Butler led her party into the sacred edifice. The light was still faint in the old church, and at first the good lady could not see very plainly. When she did, however, she beheld a sight which petrified her. As she and her party hurried up one aisle, she perceived Mrs. Bell and her party rushing up the other. There was not a moment to lose. It is disgraceful to have to relate it, but there was almost a scuffle in the church. In short, the two generals met opposite the front pews. There was a scramble for seats. The Beatricites and the Hartites got mixed up in the most confusing manner, and finally Mrs. Butler and Mrs. Bell found themselves side by side and crushed very close together in a small space.

Some awful hours followed. Mrs. Butler deliberately placed her back to Mrs. Bell. Mrs. Bell talked at Mrs. Butler in a loud whisper to a neighbor at the other side. Poor Miss Peters fanned herself violently. Mrs. Morris's breathing became so oppressed that it was audible; and in short, all these good ladies who had got up hours before their rightful time were as uncomfortable and cross as they well could be. But the longest time passes at last. From six to seven went by, from seven to eight, from eight again to nine. The waiting was awful. By degrees, without quite knowing it, Mrs. Bell was forced to lean against Mrs. Butler for support. By half-past nine she ventured to say to her neighbor:

"This waiting is intolerable. "

"Vile, " snapped Mrs. Butler, in response.

By ten o'clock the opposing generals were sharing the same footstool. By a quarter-past ten they were both nodding.

It was about that hour that Hunt in his position as verger once more appeared. The church doors were opened to the community at large, the bells began to ring out a merry and bridal peal, and the inhabitants of the town, the rich and poor alike, filed into the church.

Mrs. Butler was right. Long before eleven o'clock the building was packed. Mrs. Bell was also right. She communicated this fact to Mrs. Butler, who nodded in response. Both ladies chuckled over their individual sagacity.

All the side aisles of the church began to fill. It was really an imposing spectacle. The weary inmates of the front pews felt they were reaping their rewards.

At a quarter to eleven some of the bridal guests appeared on the scene. Those who had been especially invited by the Bertram family were magnificently attired, and occupied one or two seats reserved for them.

Then the bride's-maids came. They stood in groups near the door, waiting to follow the bride to her place at the altar.

Mrs. Bell turned her flushed face; looked down the church, and nodded to her girls. She thought she had never seen anything so heavenly as the vision of her Matty in her bride's-maid's costume. Her heart swelled so with exultation, that she could not help confiding some of her feelings to Mrs. Butler.

"Pooh, you're a goose! " nodded back this good woman. But a slow smile stole over her face as she said the words.

The moments flew on. The organist took his place at the organ, the choir boys filed into their places.

At the end of the church the bride's-maids looked nervously around. Had any one listened very attentively they might have heard Matty Bell's titter.

A thrill went through the waiting crowds. The bridegroom had appeared; he was accompanied by a strange youth, a young officer from his regiment. He walked slowly up the church, and took his place before the altar.

Bertram looked so handsome at this moment, so pale, so dignified, that every woman in the church fell in love with him. Miss Peters sighed audibly, and even shed a tear for the memory of that Sam, who had never proposed for her, but had been attentive, and had died thirty years ago.

Matty Bell felt quite a little tumult in her heart. No, no, whatever her mother might say her Bayard was not like Beatrice's Bayard. She did not even want to look at her Gusty this moment.

Bertram stood before the altar and waited.

The bride!

There was a little buzz through the church. All the occupants of the pews rose; all heads were turned towards the door. In the excitement of the moment the Beatricites clasped the Hartites by the hands, Mrs. Bell's fat fingers rested on Mrs. Butler's shoulder.

The bride! She had come. Beatrice would marry Loftus Bertram. The Beatricites would conquer. Slander would die.

No, no. What was the matter? What was wrong? Was anything wrong?

A girl dressed in shimmering bridal clothes was walking up the church. A very slender and very pale girl. She was leaning on Mr. Ingram's arm; she was beautiful. There was an expression on her face which melted hearts, and made eyes brim over with tears. A bride was coming up the church—not Beatrice Meadowsweet—not the girl who was beloved by all the town.

Close behind the bride followed the principal bride's-maid. She was in a plain dress of white. Round her head she wore a wreath of white lilies, and in her hand she carried a bouquet of white flowers.

The other bride's-maids wore green silk sashes, and green with the marguerites which trimmed their broad hats.

"May God have mercy on us! " exclaimed Mrs. Butler.

She made this remark aloud; it was distinctly heard, and Beatrice, as she passed the good lady, turned and gave her a swift bright smile.

The bride joined the bridegroom before the altar, and the bishop, who was to perform the ceremony, began the marriage service:

"I, Loftus, take thee, Josephine—"

When these words were uttered Mrs. Bell turned and faced Mrs. Butler.

"Whose cause has won? " she murmured, "who was right? "

"Never you say a word against that blessed girl, Beatrice Meadowsweet, " replied Mrs. Butler. "Watch her face—it's the face of an angel. "

"So it is, " said Mrs. Bell. And the ladies clasped hands and buried their feud.

CHAPTER XXXV.

BEATRICITES—EVERY ONE.

Mrs. Bell and Mrs. Butler had a cup of tea together after the wedding. They partook of their tea in Mrs. Butler's house, and they gossiped over the events of the day for long hours.

Part of the strange story of Beatrice's engagement the rector had told his guests at the wedding-breakfast—a sufficient portion of this curious romance was related to show some of the real nobility of this young girl's character. People were to conjecture about the rest. They were never to know. They never did know.

The Hartites and the Beatricites ceased to exist at the breakfast, or rather the whole community became Beatricites on the spot.

Bertram took his bride away, and the town was very glad to think they might keep Beatrice Meadowsweet with them after all. Neither Mrs. Bertram nor Mrs. Meadowsweet were present at the wedding, but they met that evening, for Mrs. Meadowsweet drove up to the Manor; she was accompanied by Beatrice and they both asked to see Mrs. Bertram.

They were admitted into the great lady's bedroom.

"I am sorry you are so poorly, Mrs. Bertram, " said Mrs. Meadowsweet. "I thought, as Bee was coming up, I'd call with her. There's nothing for worry on the nerves like Eleazer Macjones's Life Pills, and here's a fresh box of them. I thought I'd bring them up, and tell you that for my part I'm highly pleased. "

"Pleased, " said Mrs. Bertram.

She raised her white face and looked at her visitor.

"Yes, of course I am. I keep my girl. The young man wasn't suited to her, nor she to him. I guessed there'd be no luck about that engagement, when I was so deaved with 'poor dears, ' and 'poor friends. ' That's not the right way to speak before any wedding. They were neither of them more than half-hearted towards one another, and it's well they found it out in time. Now when I married Meadowsweet—"

"Mother, " interrupted Beatrice, "I think Mrs. Bertram is tired. "

"Well, my pet, and you want the old lady to stop her chatter. You try the Life Pills, Mrs. Bertram, I'll wait in the next room for Bee. She has a word to say to you. "

When they were alone together Beatrice went and knelt by Mrs. Bertram's sofa.

"So you never loved my son. Beatrice? " said Mrs. Bertram, raising her heavy eyes, and looking at her.

"I did not, I consented to marry him because I was silly and thought I could do him good. I was saved just in time from making a grave mistake. Josephine loves him. "

"You think she will do him good? "

"The greatest, the best. They were meant for one another. They ought to lead happy lives together. "

"Beatrice, I have heard—I don't know how to thank you—I have heard what you have done with some—some of your money. I don't know how to thank you, child. You have saved Loftus and me. "

Beatrice bent forward and kissed Mrs. Bertram on her cheek.

"I am glad, " she said in a simple, quiet voice. "My father would be glad too. I am abundantly content. "

"Beatrice, you would have been just the wife for Loftus. "

"No, he was not the husband meant for me. Some day my true lover may come. If not, I have always been a happy girl, Mrs. Bertram, I am happy still. I feel full of delight to-night. Now I must go. Only, first of all, do something—something for the girl who has been made your daughter to-day. "

"Something for—for Josephine? "

"For Nina, whose great love will raise and save your son. Take this packet; put it into the fire. "

"What is it, Beatrice? I am weak. Are there any more shocks? "

"No. Josephine does not wish the story of her birth to be ever revealed. She is a Bertram now without any need of proving her title. Her object is to guard her husband's secret, and she does this, when she asks his mother to burn this packet which contains the full proofs of her identity as a Bertram. "

Mrs. Bertram shivered. She touched the packet. Then she gave it back to Beatrice.

"Put it into the fire yourself, " she said. "Beatrice, you have saved us all. "

This little scene happened on the evening of Bertram's wedding-day. Just at that same hour Mrs. Bell and Mrs. Butler were hob-nobbing over their tea.

"For my part, " said Mrs. Butler, "I no longer regret the absence of my brooch. I will own I fretted for it when there seemed likely to be no wedding to speak of. For why should the Northbury folks put themselves out about the marriage of two strangers. But now I am glad Beatrice has it, for though she is not a bride she is a beautiful character, and no mistake, and such should be encouraged. "

"That's my way of thinking, too, " said Mrs. Bell. "I'll thank you for another lump of sugar, Mrs. Butler. Yes, I have no fault to find with Beatrice Meadowsweet. If she failed, she failed in a graceful fashion, and, when all is said and done, her intentions were of the best. "

THE END.

Lightning Source UK Ltd.
Milton Keynes UK
UKHW040627030921
389968UK00001B/74